GW00726128

David Burnell was born and bred at Cambridge University, *taugh*
came across Operational Research. After studying this at Lancaster
he spent his professional career applying the subject to management
problems in the Health Service, coal mining and latterly the water
industry. On "retiring" he completed a PhD at Lancaster on the
deeper meaning of data from London's water meters.

He and his wife live in Berkshire and own a small holiday
cottage in North Cornwall. They have four grown-up children.

David is now hard at work on further "Cornish Conundrums".

"Cornwall and its richly storied coast has a new writer to celebrate
in David Burnell. His crafty plotting and engaging characters are
sure to please crime fiction fans." Peter Lovesey, winner of the
Crime Writers' Association Cartier Diamond Dagger.

"A well-written novel, cleverly structured, with a nicely-handled
subplot..." Rebecca Tope, crime novelist.

"...suspicious goings-on on the Cornish coast...David Burnell has
written about what he knows. Great fun and informative to read,
this book has mystery and local colour." Dr Karen Morton, Bosco
Books, Looe, Cornwall; lecturer, Plymouth University.

"Doom Watch is a really good read with plenty of mystery. The discovery of a torso in a pool in the rough Cornish terrain sets off an intriguing trail of events that keep the reader guessing. Whilst trying to unravel the threads and get to the truth the characters have also to grapple with their own problems. The phenomenon of the shifting sands of the Doom Bar provides an excellent backdrop to the plot." Les Williams, Convenor, Thames Valley Writers' Circle

"A quaint, sparsely populated Cornish beach town is rife with secrets, subterfuge, and fraud until a murder cracks the area's deceptively tranquil veneer . . . enjoyable murder mystery." Publishers Weekly.

Doom Watch was a Quarter Finalist in the 2014 Amazon Breakthrough Novel Award

DOOM WATCH

A Cornish Conundrum

David Burnell

SKEIN BOOKS

DOOM WATCH

SKEIN BOOKS
Caversham, Reading

First published July 2013
Edition 2: September 2013
Edition 3: September 2015
Edition 4: May 2016

© *Copyright David Burnell 2013*
The moral right of the author has been asserted

This book, although set in a real location, is entirely a work of fiction. No character is based on any real person, living or dead. Any resemblance is purely coincidental.

ISBN-13: 978 - 1490931135
ISBN-10: 1490931139

The front cover photo was taken at low tide. It shows the Doom Bar sandbank in the Camel estuary, shot from near the Lookout on Stepper Point. Picture taken and edited by Chris Scruby.

NORTH CORNWALL

SUMMER 2008

Being abroad was a problem – cultural mismatches and language barriers. True, there had been a briefing but it was incomplete, with so much left to chance. The challenge was a swap when the opportunity came.

But who knew what calamities would come with this? Were there no alternatives?

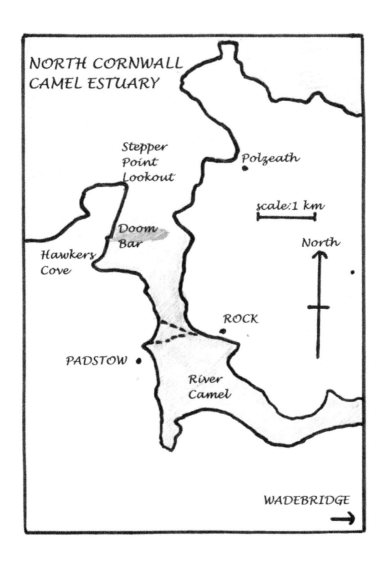

NORTH CORNWALL
CAMEL ESTUARY

Stepper
Point
Lookout

Polzeath

scale:1 km

North

Doom
Bar

Hawkers
Cove

ROCK

PADSTOW

River
Camel

WADEBRIDGE

vii

CHAPTER 1

'I've just seen what looks like a person in the water, out in mid-channel.' Toby Flanders was an enthusiastic volunteer at the Stepper Point Lookout. It was his first week of training.

'Keep your binoculars on him,' replied Bill Gilbert, senior man in the Lookout, as he fiddled with his radio. 'It would be easy to lose him in this mist and rain. First we need to be sure it's a human being - not just another piece of seaweed.' Toby had already marked his first week by prompting Bill to call out a lifeboat to rescue what had turned out to be a mass of drift-wood.

Toby turned back to the Lookout desk, relaxed his body once more to aid his concentration (as Bill had taught him) and peered through the mounted binoculars. These were pointing out across the Camel estuary.

'Lost him,' he muttered, 'where the hell's he gone?'

Bill sighed. 'Just keep moving the binoculars slowly around the spot where you last saw him. If it really is a person he might be in a trough. The waves are pretty ferocious out there.'

There was silence as Toby tried to follow his instructions.

'What made you think it was a human being, not just a clump of seaweed?'

'Well you don't normally see seaweed holding a body board. The stuff floats quite well on its own.'

'Oh yes? What colour was the board?'

'Bright green, if you must know. Is there some sort of colour code that sets out which swimmers we rescue first?'

1

'Toby, I just wanted to make sure it wasn't a plank. I was pretty embarrassed last time we called out the lifeboat. I want to be sure this is a genuine need.'

'Wait a minute, Bill. I think I've got him – or her. I can't make out the gender from here – they're in a wetsuit. Do you want to see for yourself?'

Feeling he wasn't being taken seriously Toby eased away from the binoculars and gestured to Bill to take over.

'It's OK lad, your eyesight's better than mine. If you can see it's a person in a wetsuit floating on a green body board then I'll accept it's not just seaweed. Our next problem is making this damn radio work. This storm's mucking up transmission. I'll keep trying, you just keep watching.'

Bill held the radio close to his face. The nearest emergency lifeboat was the inflatable used by lifeguards on Polzeath beach on the far side of the estuary. They'd be on duty: it was high season – the first Saturday in August. But could he reach them?

'Stepper Point to Polzeath Lifeguards. Are you receiving me? We have seen a swimmer in distress. Out in mid-channel, opposite Trebetherick Point. Request you go and assist.'

There was a pause. Then, faintly, the radio gave a reply. 'Polzeath Lifeguards to Stepper Point. Reception patchy but message received. As soon as colleague returns we will launch. But sea level visibility is poor. We will need your help to locate the swimmer.'

Bill felt relieved: something was happening. He turned to his companion. 'Keep him in view, Toby. You're the vital link now.'

'The chap's bobbing up and down like anything. It's as if he's waving his body board as a distress signal. He's lucky we've seen him. Why would anyone want to go swimming on a day like this?'

'Cornish weather, lad. It was sunny an hour ago. Plenty of folk were out then. And some like it rough.'

A few moments silence. Toby focused intently through his binoculars as Bill kept fiddling with his radio.

'Can you still see him?' asked the older man.

'Yes. He's thrashing about a lot less now. Does that mean the storm is easing?'

'Fat chance. More likely it means he's exhausted.'

Bill looked out the hut window. The dark storm meant it was almost impossible to see what was going on. Responsibility without power was not an easy calling. He clenched his fists in frustration. 'Hang on, mate,' he pleaded softly, 'there's help on the way. Not much longer to hold on.'

To his relief, he heard a sudden shout from Toby. 'Hey, I've got the lifeboat in view. And it's on the right track.'

Bill didn't understand why Polzeath Lifeguards hadn't told him they were launched. But the fierce storm was mucking up reception. Maybe they could still hear him even if he couldn't hear their response? He seized his radio once more.

'Stepper Point to Polzeath Lifeguards. We have spotted you. You are not far from the swimmer. Keep sailing up the main channel.'

'They're closing on him. Thirty yards now,' advised Toby, his eyes clamped tightly to his binoculars.

'Stepper Point to Polzeath Lifeguards. You are only thirty metres from the swimmer and closing fast.'

There was a tense silence in the hut. Nothing more either of them could do, now it was up to others.

'Oh, well done mate,' said Toby excitedly, responding to his view though the binoculars. He gave a huge sigh of relief. Then

3

he let go of the instruments, stood up and turned to Bill.

'They were alongside the swimmer and then a massive wave came along. One of the crew reached out and hauled him on board.'

Bill's face lit up with a grin. It was going to be all right. He put down the radio, strode across the hut and shook Toby's hand. 'Well done, lad. That's down to your alertness. He should be safe now.'

A further thought came to him. 'Which direction are they heading? If we can predict where they'll land I'll call up an ambulance to go directly to meet them.'

Toby peered through the binoculars once more. Then he moved them slowly around. 'That's annoying. I've lost the lifeboat. This storm makes it really gloomy out there. Visibility is lousy.'

Bill grimaced; but when all was said and done Toby was only a trainee. 'For future reference, Toby, it was a mistake for you to stop looking. We're meant to track boats as well as swimmers. Never mind. I'll try and contact the lifeboat once more on the radio.'

But before he could do so the radio burst into life. Faintly, and to their surprise, they could hear a voice addressing them.

'Polzeath Lifeguards to Stepper Point. We're launched now. Can you advise, please, on the direction to take if we're to find the swimmer?'

For a second Bill wondered if he was enacting a nightmare. The call disagreed entirely with what he'd just been told. Was this a bizarre joke from the Polzeath crew?

Then he realised it was the instructions he had just given over the radio to Toby's lifeboat that were the delusion. They hadn't been heeded or needed at all by the mystery boat doing the so-called rescue. They hadn't even been heard.

So, for the second time that week, Bill had to reverse an instruction to a local lifeboat. His many years experience of the sea allowed him to do so in a professional manner. But the Polzeath lifeboat crew did not sound too upset; they were mainly relieved that they could stop battling the storm and return immediately to shore.

When he was sure the Polzeath crew were safe, Bill turned once more to Toby. His doubts about the lad returned. It was, after all, only the trainee who had actually seen anything – or at least had claimed to do so.

'Are you really sure you saw a man being rescued? Imagination is a good quality in many fields lad, but please don't use it when you're on watch from the Lookout.'

CHAPTER 2

'Time to go home, gentlemen. You can come back for your cars tomorrow.'

The landlord of the Trewarmett Inn had been glad to host the stag party but now it was well past eleven. Experience had taught him there was a point when gentle persuasion to move on usually worked; and beyond which belligerence often followed. Trewarmett was only a small village and he needed to keep the peace.

The group had drunk plenty: beer, cider, and later on whisky. They had even sung songs. Tommy Burton, the best man and party convenor, was a competent guitarist and the landlord had been happy to let him use the Inn's battered guitar. The locals had joined in the sing-song and made it almost tuneful.

The party walked slightly unsteadily down the hill. Kevin Rogers, bridegroom-to-be, was in a bad way and was helped along by two of his heftier companions.

Tommy's guitar playing had meant he had drunk less than the rest. He was thinking clearly and still had some unfinished business.

It was a cold night with a clear sky and a full moon. Beyond the last streetlight their eyes grew used to the dark and the surrounding hillside emerged. High above, silhouetted against the stars, they could just see the outline of the tall Engine

House – the last remnant of the long-closed Prince of Wales slate quarry.

'That's where we're going,' declared Tommy. 'The path starts over here.'

If his companions had been sober they might have argued. But it was a stag party. Something outlandish needed to happen to the bridegroom. Kevin himself was too far gone to be aware of what that might be.

The party made their way up the hillside. The grass path wound steadily up through the gorse bushes, round a pile of abandoned slate and past a tall fence with the warning sign, 'Beware: Deep Water.'

At last they reached the Engine House. A hundred years ago this had housed a steam engine, used to pump out the water from the quarry and to propel each day's new slate down the hillside.

Now the building was empty. In daylight they would have had a fine view of the Cornish coast. In the dark they were limited to one or two lights from Trewarmett, half a mile away.

'We've all been to stag parties run by Kevin,' declared Tommy, 'and suffered his punishments. Now it's his turn.' There were cries of agreement: revenge was in order.

'I checked beforehand. This building's out of the way and we can easily get inside. The roof still has its slates. He'll stay dry - though not very warm. I doubt there'll be anyone here before late morning. We'll leave Kevin here to reflect on his past life and to sober up.'

'We're not going to leave him with his clothes on?' Max had helped Kevin up the hill. He was still smarting from his own stag do – having to walk home barefoot from a deserted beach.

'Hell, no. We don't want to make things too easy.'

7

The prospective bridegroom found himself stripped naked then tied by his wrists to the iron railings in front of the building. Tommy took several flash photographs.

'Those will help illustrate your best man's speech.'

'I'm not sure his new wife would approve.'

'Give him a strong incentive not to complain then.'

'We'll come back for you tomorrow afternoon,' Tommy told the bridegroom. You'll have a wonderful view of the coast at sunrise.'

There was poetic justice in the arrangement. Satisfied, the party turned to walk back down to the road.

'Hey - what about his clothes?' asked Max.

'No point in leaving 'em here. We'll put them in that pool as we go down.'

Kevin started to protest but could barely whimper. Tommy seized the groom's clothes, unthreaded the belt from the trousers and tied the whole lot, including shoes, into a bundle. Leading the way he set off down the path.

Soon they reached the fence around the quarry pool. 'With a bit of luck this'll make him more considerate at future stag parties.'

One heave and the bundle had gone. The splash, a few seconds later, told them that all the bridegroom's clothes were now under water.

It was nine o'clock the next morning, the last day of August, when a middle-aged dog-walker on her regular walk around the old quarry came across the unfortunate Kevin. The young man was half asleep but still firmly attached to the Engine House railing.

And it was the dog rather than the owner who did the

finding.

Kevin was cold, tired and thirsty but by now sober and feeling very sorry for himself. Being pawed by an enthusiastically barking terrier while unable to defend himself was the final straw. All his frustrations came out in an angry howl.

The owner, when she caught up and saw what had happened, was suitably apologetic. She soon had the terrier on a lead and then turned her attention to the victim. 'You're lucky they didn't use handcuffs.' Fortunately she had strong hands. With a struggle she managed to loosen the knots which held Kevin's wrists to the gate.

The released captive slowly exercised his numb legs. Embarrassment at being naked in front of a female stranger was the least of his problems. He beat his arms slowly across his chest. 'I'm bloody cold.'

His rescuer contemplated him for a moment. She also had been in the Trewarmett Inn the evening before, heard the young men singing and could guess what had followed. Young people, she thought. Still, we've all been young once.

She took off her thick coat and handed it over. 'You'd better have that. I won't freeze as long as I keep moving. It'll make you a bit less cold – and slightly more respectable. Do you know where your friends put your clothes?'

'It was my stag party; I feared something like this. So I took precautions. I was only wearing my oldest clothes, I can afford to lose them.' He paused. 'Trouble is my house keys were in my trouser pocket.'

'But they wouldn't take them far. They're probably somewhere around here.' She glanced at the surrounding bracken.

'I heard one of them say something about "putting them in the pool". There's one round the back.'

9

'We might as well have a look.'

Kevin was very cold and could move only with difficulty. The pair made their way slowly down the path and then across to the fence. A dark surface glistened far below. The pool was surrounded by bushes and thorns. But there were no signs of Kevin's clothes.

'I can't see anything from here. It looks very deep. Tell you what, I live just down the road. Why don't we go back there? A cooked breakfast will warm us up. My dog's had enough exercise. I'll lend you some clothes – you're roughly the same size as my brother. There are plenty of his old clothes around. Then we could come back with some gear and have a go at fishing your clothes out.'

'That would be great. Thank you. My name's Kevin, by the way - Kevin Rogers.'

'And I'm Gwyneth – Gwyneth Fry.'

Introductions made, the pair made their way down the grassy path to the road.

An hour later, a fully-clad Kevin accompanied Gwyneth back up the path to the quarry. The terrier remained locked up in the kitchen.

Kevin had a rucksack containing rope and a metal hook. If he could manage to recover his clothes and keys he could walk home and pretend nothing much had happened.

It was still only half past ten. How wonderful if all signs of his ordeal were removed before his friends came to gloat.

With some difficulty the pair climbed over the tall fence and down the embankment to the pool. There was no sign of a path: no doubt the pool's remoteness, tall fence and brambles kept visitors away.

Soon the big hook was fastened to one end of the rope, which Gwyneth threw into the pool. Kevin pulled the rope slowly back towards them.

But when it emerged the hook had caught nothing.

'Can't expect success straight away. We might be here for some time.' Gwyneth seized the hook and threw it out again.

Half an hour later Kevin was desperate to stop. His arms and legs ached like fury. He'd spent the whole previous night tied up. 'I can't stand much more.'

'Just one more go,' replied Gwyneth. 'I'll throw it as far as I can.' She coiled the rope and gave the hook an almighty heave. Kevin started to pull in the rope. But this time it did not come so easily.

'It's caught on something,' he shouted.

'Keep it as steady as you can. Let me pull as well.' Gwyneth stood behind Kevin, took a chunk of the rope into her hands and added her strength to the pull.

Slowly, ever so slowly, the rope came back towards them.

'How many clothes were you wearing?'

'Not many. Maybe it's jammed on the bottom.'

Whatever they had caught was coming reluctantly towards them. Finally, their catch started to emerge from the water.

But it was not what they'd hoped for. It was a large jute sack, tied with a series of loops. Their hook had caught firmly around one.

'Doesn't look like casual rubbish,' observed Kevin.

'It'd be worth looking inside. Keep pulling.'

The two continued to heave. With one last, strenuous heave the mystery sack reached the side of the pool.

'That's a very odd smell,' noted Kevin.

'You'd expect anything in that water to pong.'

'Not that much. Whatever is it?'

'Good job I brought my clasp knife,' commented Gwyneth. 'That's the only way we'll get those knots open.'

Kevin had been thinking it would be less trouble just to push the sack back into the pool. But he could see Gwyneth was excited.

'Never mind the rope. Let's cut through the sack. You hold the top and I'll cut.'

Kevin held the top while Gwyneth carefully ran her knife round, a foot lower down. As she finished the sack started to come apart.

And now they could glimpse what lay inside.

It was a very filthy sack. And it contained what looked horribly like a segment of rotting flesh.

CHAPTER 3

George Gilbert peered at the houses on the Padstow back street, hoping the number she was after did lie proportionately between two of the few numbers actually displayed; then knocked hard on the sturdy blue door.

The door swung open. A small but cheery, weather-beaten man stood there. He beamed when he saw who it was. 'My dear, welcome to Cornwall. Please come in. It's good to see you again.'

An encouraging start, thought George. Maybe her visit would work out after all. She seized her suitcase and followed him inside.

The man turned and saw the baggage she was carrying. 'Give me that. Dear me, I'm forgetting my manners. Not used to young ladies any more. On second thoughts, just pop it down there and come through to the kitchen. I'm sure you'd like a cup of tea after that long journey.'

George followed her host back through the cottage. There were traditional oak beams across the ceiling but she was not tall enough for them to affect her.

'This is a beautiful old cottage, Bill,' she observed as they reached the small kitchen, a recent addition at the rear. 'You've done well to modernise it.'

Bill Gilbert looked pleased. George guessed praise was a rare circumstance for him. He shuffled around the kitchen making them a pot of tea and augmenting this with a plate of chocolate biscuits. 'Let's go and sit in the lounge.'

She followed him back into the only other downstairs room, which was small but comfortably furnished. She seized one of the easy chairs. Bill put down the tea tray on the small table then lowered himself into the other.

'It's good you've been able to join us here for a couple of weeks,' he began, 'though I'm so sorry for the circumstances that caused us to meet in March.'

In truth the pair hardly knew each other; strictly speaking George was Bill's niece-in-law. They'd last met at the funeral of George's husband, Mark. Mark, Bill's nephew, had been killed in a plane crash earlier in the year. George was still coming to terms with her loss.

'It doesn't seem real,' she admitted. 'Even though that was five months ago. One minute Mark and I were both rushing about with our busy lives. I'd got some management consultancy to complete; he was off doing a marketing promotion in Turkey. The next thing I knew there was a visit from the police. The British Embassy in Teheran had been informed that my husband was one of the casualties in a plane crash at a remote airport on the western side of Iran. He shouldn't even have been in the bloody country.'

George paused, her eyes filling with tears. She tried not to think too much about the details of Mark's death any more, but she was still too close. By working to excess she had managed to insulate herself a little over the recent months. She'd feared meeting Mark's uncle would bring it all back again; and it looked as though she'd been right.

'M'dear, please forgive me,' her host responded. 'I didn't intend to give you more pain. We all miss him. Mark was very special.'

George managed to unfasten her handbag and retrieve a handkerchief. She snuffled for a few minutes and then forced herself to look up. She reached for her cup of tea and smiled wanly.

'I'm sorry Bill, I haven't cried for weeks. It's just that meeting one of Mark's relatives brings it all back. I'll be all right now, I think.'

'Give vent to your emotions, m'dear. Much better than trying to pretend you're immune. But maybe you still have to keep a stiff upper lip at home for Polly. Where is she now, by the way?'

Polly was George's daughter, the only child of their marriage.

'I left her with cousin Samantha. She lives close to us in London and she's a daughter of her own, just a year younger. I wasn't sure if it was right to leave her but Polly is fifteen years old. Life goes on: we knew we couldn't stand still. Mark would never have wanted us to do that. In a way the project you've dug out for me is good. It's forced the issue and made me look outwards.'

Bill looked on tenderly as she sipped her tea and nibbled her biscuit. He saw a dark, curly-haired woman in her late thirties, attractive rather than beautiful, but with plenty of energy. Even in the casual clothes she'd worn to drive down from London she looked presentable. He was reassured that he'd commended her to the committee.

He didn't really understand what she did but he had gathered that her firm was struggling so any business would help their survival.

And for Mark's sake, if nothing else, he wanted to do all he could to help.

'Let's not talk about work today. It's the day of rest. I'll let you get unpacked then maybe we can take a stroll round Padstow. Have you been here before?'

An hour later, dressed for the outdoors, George was ready for her tour of Padstow. Her host led her down the cobbled street, towards the picturesque harbour.

'I've been to Padstow once or twice,' she admitted. 'But I don't really know it. We did come to Cornwall quite a lot when Polly was small. Most of the holidays we spent around here were enjoying the beach at Polzeath. To be honest Polly wasn't interested in anything else. So I'm looking forward to digging beneath the surface once I start my project.'

She turned to face him. 'In fact I don't even know what you do?'

'I'm retired now, officially at least. I suppose Mark didn't have reason to tell you about me. I used to be in the Royal Navy.'

'I'm afraid I didn't know that. Mark didn't talk much about his family. He wasn't close to his parents; and as you know they both died young. But it's odd he didn't bring us to see you when we were on holiday here.'

'I can explain that. I've had my little house here for many years – it was my parents' before me - but I haven't been living here full-time until a couple of years ago. So I probably wasn't here when you were on holiday.

'After I left the Navy I worked in the Ministry of Defence. That's where a lot of military folk end up. I only retired from that at the start of last year.'

They had reached the harbour now. A selection of small shops, including ice cream and tea shops, were clustered around it. The crowds were modest. It was the last day of August, the end of the school holidays. George could see plenty of small boats - some smart and others rusty - moored in the inner harbour.

Bill led her round the jetty towards the sign proclaiming 'Ferry'.

George wasn't satisfied. 'Being "retired" only tells me what you don't do. What keeps you busy here nowadays?'

'Well, one thing is to help man the Stepper Point Lookout. That's on the headland two miles down the estuary. It monitors the entrance to the river Camel and oversees Polzeath beach. I'm one of a team of volunteer watchers, generally on duty on Saturdays.'

'I suppose your naval experience must help. You're not going to get frightened by storms. But isn't it lonely?'

'Oh, I'm never on my own. Normally there are two of us on duty; we have a monthly rota. And we have a notice outside, inviting Coast Path walkers to drop in. It's very important to hand on the vision to a younger generation. We have one or two young ones coming through. This past month there was a trainee I was showing the ropes to called Toby.'

'You make it sound like he was hard work.'

'He was keen enough. Probably too keen: television had led him to expect a rescue a day. Made up in his imagination what he couldn't see with the naked eye. On his second day he had me calling up the lifeboat to rescue what turned out to be a piece of seaweed. That was embarrassing. Then at the end of the week . . .'

'You make it sound like a soap. "Laughter in the Lookout." Hilarious. What happened next?'

For Bill it wasn't so funny. 'The end of the week. Well, that was a mystery or a muddle. Toby claimed he saw a swimmer struggling far out in the estuary. I cross-examined him carefully, but when he started detailing the body board the chap was hanging on to I had no choice but to take him seriously. "Better safe than sorry" is our motto.'

'So Toby did something useful; was the poor bloke rescued ok?'

'To be honest, I'm not sure. It was a bit of a fiasco. Toby was the one with the powerful binoculars. I didn't interfere: I find that's the only way for them to learn.'

Bill sighed. 'He said he'd seen the distressed swimmer being been picked up. But then he lost sight of the boat he'd been picked up by. It wasn't the official lifeboat. So unless he's a fantasist I've got to believe him but there's no independent evidence of what really happened. It's not normally like that.'

George liked to solve conundrums, but this was outside her range. She turned her attention to learning as much as possible about the small town, ready for the project she'd be starting next morning.

CHAPTER 4

Police Sergeant Peter Travers stamped his feet, glanced at his watch, turned and peered up the road. Surely the CID guys should be here by now? It was a couple of hours since he'd put in the call for assistance.

Travers hadn't liked the look of the sack and its contents: gruesome. He didn't want to move far from the scene before there were official reinforcements. Fortunately there was only one footpath up to the Engine House and he could guard that at the same time as waiting by the road.

At last a large black car appeared in the distance and then drew up beside him. The driver wound down his window and showed him his warrant. Detective Inspector Marcus Chadwick, Southwest Regional Crime Squad. The local policeman, acting like a supercharged traffic warden, waved him energetically up the slope to the grassy car park.

Chadwick clambered out and peered up the hillside towards the Engine House. Then he looked around for the local man to bring him up to date.

'Good afternoon, sir. Sergeant Peter Travers. I'm sorry we've had to drag you all the way from Exeter.' Travers didn't have much to do with detectives, his usual role was as the local community policeman. He thought a polite welcome couldn't do any harm.

Chadwick was a busy man with a gloomy demeanour. He already had a heavy case load in Exeter. He would have brought his regular sergeant but the man was off duty, apparently tramping Dartmoor. The local man would have to do.

'OK, so what've we got? The message I had was simply a call to look into a suspicious death. I wouldn't think you've many of those around here.'

'It's a body, sir – or at least part of one. Found in the pool behind that Engine House up there.'

'You'd best show me. Are Forensics here yet?'

'Still on their way. There was a lag in getting hold of them with it being a Sunday. But I got a local doctor to give us a preliminary assessment.'

Chadwick grunted. He'd seen a lot more bodies who'd come to an unpleasant end than any local doctor. He wanted to see for himself not hear a second-hand account. With no more ado the two men tackled the path up to the pool. A piece of sacking had been fastened over the fence and a rough path forced through the gorse bushes down to the sinister stretch of water.

Beside the pool the policemen could see a jute sack with its top now folded down; and exposed to their gaze was the upper part of a naked body with its head missing. The substantial breasts half sticking out from the sack made it obvious it had been female.

Chadwick assumed the man standing guard must be the local doctor. 'Detective Inspector Marcus Chadwick,' he introduced himself.

'Good afternoon. I'm Dr Brian Southgate. On a weekday I run the surgery up the road in Delabole. Peter Travers called me in once he got here and saw this. But it's too late for medical intervention.'

'You've not touched anything?'

'Well, I wouldn't in any case but I didn't need to. The victim was beyond help. The water in this pool is cold so there'd be no residual body heat even if she'd only been here for a couple of hours. But it's not a recent death. She's been in there for weeks rather than days.'

'Thank you for coming out, Doctor. It looks very unpleasant. And even if we find the head at the bottom of the sack it can hardly be an accident - or suicide. Even Houdini couldn't cut off his own head while he simultaneously drowned. Hm. Do you have any preliminary ideas on the cause of death?'

'Well there aren't any obvious wounds on the bits of the body so far exposed. I don't think we can say without a thorough post mortem. And even that might not be conclusive until there's a full body. For example, we can't possibly know if there's a bullet wound in the middle of the forehead.'

'The first challenge will be identifying the body,' asserted Travers. It was his first experience of the Crime Squad and he wanted to make his mark. 'That's presumably why the head's been sawn off.'

'It certainly limits the scope for photo-shots on the local television.' The Inspector mused for a moment. 'Any women around here been reported missing in the past few weeks?'

'I've not had time to check yet, sir. I haven't been back to the Police House since I got called out. But there's been no recent hue and cry over anyone that I can remember. Of course, it might not be anyone local at all.'

The Inspector seemed taken by this thought. 'It's certainly a remote spot. Someone could drive down here one night from, say, Bristol, dump the body and be away half an hour later without anyone being any the wiser. There are plenty of murders up there. If things had turned out differently it could be months - or even years - before the body was found. How was it found, by the way?'

'I haven't got the full story yet, sir. Something about dog walking and lost keys. I thought I ought to stay guarding the scene until you were here. I told the two who found it to wait to be interviewed. They're in one of the Trewarmett cottages – not far, but you can't see it from here. And they can't see us.'

The Inspector turned to Southgate. 'Would you mind holding the fort here Doctor, until our Forensics team arrive? It would be good to hear the finders' story as soon as possible – and to see if we can keep the body out of the limelight for a while. Travers and I'll go and talk to them now.'

Apart from informal chats with his friend Peter Travers - the two had grown up together in Camelford - Brian Southgate had never been asked to assist the police in any specific role. He was normally rather sceptical about their intrusiveness and wanted to keep his distance. But he had no doubt they were needed here.

As the two policemen wandered off he decided to take the chance of a closer look at the torso. In particular he wondered how the head had been removed from the body.

Fortunately the position of the sack meant it was possible to have a good look without disturbing the remains. He bent over and squinted closely. It seemed to have been quite a smooth cut. That suggested it had been done after death - maybe using a power saw?

As he peered further in he realised that the head was not the only piece of the body to have been removed. For both the victim's arms had been cut off just below the shoulder. No clue on marital status from rings on this body. Taking fingerprints would be as impossible as photographing the face. Someone was making it as hard as they could for anyone to find out who the victim had been.

He was just wondering whether the dismembering had extended as far as the legs - and guessing that he might be able to see that too, if he had thought to bring a torch - when a shout from the fence alerted him to the arrival of the Scene of Crime officers.

Southgate introduced himself to the head of the team, Jacob Anderson. As the team proceeded to wriggle into their plastic suits, outer shoes and gloves, Southgate explained that his police colleagues had gone to interview the people who had found the torso. 'They should be back within the hour.'

His position as the official guard of the corpse gave him status. He wondered afterwards whether they'd assumed he was the official police doctor. Whatever the reason, the SOCO team were in no hurry to dismiss him.

He decided to take the chance to stay on and see how they dealt with the case. How close were real-life procedures to the detective series he watched on television?

With some effort various pieces of equipment were humped up from the van parked down at the road. A simple tent was erected over the sack and a bright light installed, running off a portable generator.

Then one of the team hastened around, taking photographs of the sack and the pool from every conceivable angle. Some-one else took a few samples of the water from the pool, which they carefully transferred to labelled sample bottles. No-one could see any realistic source for fingerprints. There might once have been some on the fence, but they would certainly have been wiped away by the recent rain.

Southgate thought that, given the waterfall splashing down

into the far side of the pool, there was every chance that any interesting dissolved substance associated with the sack - drugs, for example, or poison - would have long washed away. The most critical thing to photograph, had it not been trampled down by the police team, was the pathway from the fence.

But it would not be politic to voice these opinions. He was hoping, before he was dismissed, to see more of the torso.

The standard procedures took a long time. He was standing outside the tent, wondering whether to slip away, when Anderson approached him.

'We've decided to take the torso out of the sack and lay it out on a stretcher. It'll be easiest to do that before we move it any further. Then we'll carry the body down to the van. But before we move anything could you give us an initial medical opinion?'

Southgate suspected his perceived status was being over-estimated. Nonetheless he was happy to oblige. But he needed to be cautious in any opinions expressed. It wouldn't be good to derail the investigation from the outset.

Shrugging his shoulders he followed Anderson inside the tent.

A clean piece of plastic had been laid out on the floor. Very carefully, with several of the team taking part, the body was extracted from the sack and laid, gently, on to the plastic sheet. As he had already observed there were no arms. And it turned out there were no legs either. Someone was very keen indeed to make identification difficult.

Southgate took a few minutes to examine the victim carefully.

'Well, there are no obvious signs of bullet or knife wounds. It's not clear what was the cause of death. Judging by the clean lines of cut on the body the woman must have been dead - or at least unconscious - before she was dismembered. But whether she died of natural causes or was murdered is hard to say – just from what we've got here.' He paused for thought.

'The post mortem might show whether the woman was still alive when she went into the water. But she's obviously been there for some weeks; that'll make any clues hard to decipher.'

'There are no signs of blood on the sack,' commented Anderson.

'True,' said Southgate, as if he had already noted the fact. 'So she was dead before they put her in there. And hence before being brought to this place.'

The doctor paused for thought.

'It looks as if all the limbs have been removed using some power tool – maybe something as simple as a household saw? But that'll have been disposed of in a different place altogether.'

The doctor continued to examine the remains. Anderson and his crew remained silent. If this was a movie he would spot something unusual they could start to work on. But an un-marked headless torso did not offer that much scope.

'How long do you reckon she's been in there?' asked Anderson.

'Well, you can see the skin is wrinkly and goose-pimpled. That happens in a couple of days. But below that the flesh has a fatty layer, almost soapy.

'Now I tested the water temperature. The pool isn't warm but it's not that cold. The corpse might reach that state after four or five weeks. The post mortem will narrow it down but I would say the body's been in here for no more than a couple of months.'

Southgate couldn't think of anything else useful to say. After all, he spent his life ministering to those hoping to stay alive rather than the recently dead.

For the moment his task was done. But he would make sure Peter Travers kept him informed on future progress.

CHAPTER 5

Monday September 1ˢᵗ. George Gilbert was up ready for action by eight, keen to meet new clients and learn what was required on her new project.

The evening before her uncle-in-law had refused to talk about what the work might involve. 'Better you start with a fresh sheet of paper and fill it straight from the horse's mouth,' he said, when she had tried to winkle details out of him. It was with difficulty she discarded an image of white paper being chomped by a racing filly.

'Well, at least you can tell me about the client?'

'Better not. You need to meet the people for yourself and make up your own mind rather than me giving you what's bound to be a biased view. I know most of them only too well. Of course, I'll be happy to fill in the details afterwards. But you only get one chance to take a first impression – as well as to give one.'

Now she was about to meet the "horse" and appraise it for herself.

After a cooked breakfast – more substantial than anything she would have eaten in London – George accompanied Bill once more down the quiet lane to Padstow harbour.

'We're off to meet a committee,' he told her as they strode down the road. Glancing around George saw that Padstow was not that crowded early in the day.

'Is this some long-standing group?'

'It's been running for a few months, started in June. I'm on it, but not significant; just an ordinary member – there to speak for the older generation.

'It was when someone said we needed an outsider to pull our various ideas together and boil them down to a workable programme that I remembered you. Mark told me once that you helped organisations with strategic planning. So after one frustrating session I suggested the idea. They could see they needed help and they were happy to have someone with loose connections here.'

'But as I told you yesterday I don't know much about Padstow.'

'Ideal. You'll come at our ideas with a completely fresh mind. Don't worry. The main task this morning is for the committee to present our ideas to you; your task is to listen hard. The fact that they want to impress should stop them lapsing into local short-hand. Don't worry, they're a friendly bunch – on the whole.'

George was intrigued by this homespun trailer. She thought of herself primarily as an industrial mathematician, seeking to apply calm, impersonal logic to practical problems.

In the real world logic was not enough. But it could expose illogical thought. And it might help narrow down the range of disagreements that inevitably arose when energetic people tried to do interesting but potentially competing things.

The committee met in the dining room of the Old Custom House, a hotel on the harbour forefront. 'They want us out of there well before lunch-time,' Bill explained. 'That enforces time discipline.' George was relieved to hear this. She'd feared locals might have parochial views and take hours to express them. It would help if boredom was not a problem.

Bill was keen to introduce George to key committee members as they milled round before the meeting.

'George, this is Major Fred Greenhow. He's the chairman of the committee. Fred, this is my niece, George Gilbert.'

George saw a smart-looking man in a brightly checked suit with a trim figure. She could imagine him in the army, though presumably he was now retired. 'Glad to have you here,' said the Major as he gave George a bone-crushing handshake. 'We need an outsider to keep us focused. And you're here for a fortnight?'

If I'm not crushed to death in the meantime, George thought, but did not say. The handshake was intended as a friendly gesture. But it suggested the Major was more at home with plans than with people.

'And this is Martha Singleton. She's our secretary.'

'Pleased to meet you,' said George, now in less of a rush to offer her hand. Martha was a purposeful-looking woman in a dark blue business suit, probably in her forties. 'A good secretary is vital to any committee.'

Once the elegant clock on the mantelpiece reached half past nine the Major called the meeting to order. He positioned himself at one side of the oval table with Martha beside him. George found herself next to Bill at the end nearest the door.

She retrieved her notepad from her brief case and drew an ellipse, ready to fill in names as these emerged. She marked in her own name and Bill's for starters.

'Good morning,' began the Major. 'This is the eighth meeting of the Padstow/Rock Active Modernisation Committee since we began work in June. It's good to welcome here today Ms Georgina Gilbert, who over the next fortnight is going to help us firm up our plans.'

George was so taken by the name of the committee that for a second she took no notice of how she had been introduced. When she realised, she wanted to correct the name given her; she had never been known (even to her parents) as Georgina. The Ms was wrong as well. She had been married until a few months ago. But by the time she had taken courage to speak the Major had moved on.

She made a mental note to remedy the error, politely but firmly, when she was given the opportunity.

George examined the rest of the committee as the formal business of fine-tuning the minutes of the last meeting were concluded.

There was a healthy range of people present; the youngest was in his thirties and the oldest in her seventies. She presumed one or two of the attendees must be from Rock, the village on the other side of the Camel to Padstow. She made a note to ask Bill how they had all been chosen.

'We agreed last time,' said the Major, as he glanced down the table to George, 'that this morning we would set out the ideas each of us has been working on, and let our facilitator hear them for herself, presented in our own way.'

'I will act as chairman,' he continued, 'to keep us to time. We have to be finished by half past eleven. I'll curtail any of you that go over ten minutes. I'll also make sure no key points from our preceding discussions are left out. Meanwhile Martha will record the highlights of what is said. Her goal is to produce the minutes by the end of today.'

Martha nodded, accepting the challenge.

'It would probably be best, Georgina, if you kept your initial comments and questions until we've each had a chance to speak. In fact, we're not expecting you to say much at all. We know it's all new to you. But it was Bill, I think, that suggested this freshness would give you – and us - the best chance of producing something distinctive. Is that ok?'

'Fine. Though please call me George - not Georgina. Otherwise I won't realise you're talking to me. But I'm hoping to come and talk to each of you over the next week once I've got the overview. I take it you'll summarise the overall aim of the group before you get into the detail?'

Two hours later George found herself with pages of notes and an increasing respect for the committee. They might be based in the middle of nowhere; but collectively they had found some interesting options.

The core goal was the need to take active steps to expand the area's significance in the tourist world. Cornwall had been a tourist attraction for over a century – ever since the railway reached it. Most parts of the county were happy to enjoy their legacy. But folk in Padstow, George was told, wanted new ways to stimulate growth - and to compete with competition overseas. This had led to the formation of the PRAM committee.

The challenge was to do this without frightening away more tourists than it attracted, and to choose the best ways of spending what, George guessed, would be limited funds.

Glancing down at her notes, George saw she had written:

Scope for an alternative "Eden Project" set in North Cornwall?
Need to improve links with Rock – maybe a vehicle ferry?
Wet weather attractions, for example a maritime museum?
Upgraded facilities e.g. smart swimming pool or new top-class hotel?
Make Padstow natural base for visitors to the rest of Cornwall?

Restore railway line to Bodmin so visitors can come by train?
Expanded use of boats?
How to manage the Doom Bar? (George had no idea what this was, but assumed Bill would explain afterwards.)

There might be reasons why these ideas would not work but George looked forward to discussing them in detail.

'So that's our main ideas,' concluded the Major. 'Do you have any immediate observations?'

'Thank you. They sound very interesting,' replied George after a pause, 'but I guess they would need to be arranged into some sort of programme; and that will involve setting priorities.

'Up to now you've not been competing with one another, and that's helped the ideas grow. But sooner or later you are going to have to rank them. If you could only do one, which would it be? Since they all have different kinds of benefit, over differing timescales, you might value some help in deciding that in a logical way.'

George looked around the table. 'I mean, you couldn't start these ideas all at once, even if you wanted to.

'And these initiatives would take funding. Have you done any work yet on who you might approach? Do many million-aires have holidays around here? You'd want to be sure that any developments remained under local control.'

There was silence in the room. The group had chosen to bring in an outsider to help them; but, when it came to the crunch, would they be willing to accept such help?

The Major was the first to respond. 'We invited your com-ments George so we need to think hard about what you've said. And of course to let you add new ones as you talk to us and understand what these ideas involve.'

He turned to the clock on the mantelpiece behind him. 'But I see its half past eleven. The hotel will want this room for lunch. That's been a good morning's discussion; thank you everybody. Could I suggest we meet here in a week's time to let George give us some considered feedback?'

CHAPTER 6

George had made no plans for what she would do immediately after the PRAM Committee, but there were several questions she needed answering if she was to make any sense of it all. She was relieved to see that her uncle had anticipated this. She found herself steered towards the Shipwright Inn, on the other side of Padstow harbour.

'We could have a light lunch while I fill you in as much as I can on what you heard. But tell me, what was your overall impression? Can you make any difference? Or is it all a lost cause?'

The town had woken up while they had been meeting. It wasn't massively crowded, but there were plenty of people about, though less children now most school holidays were over. The visitors were in no hurry but George had to take care not to bump into any of them as she hurried after Bill. She used the time to arrange her thoughts and work out what she could say – after all, he was a client too. Eventually they reached a quieter part of the jetty and she was able to reply.

'I found it far more fascinating than I'd expected. For an amateur group they're well organised – better than most small companies. And plausible. I don't know if their ideas can be made to work or would be more widely welcomed but none of them were totally daft.'

She paused to sidestep a youngster on a scooter who was careering towards them.

'There are several ways I can assist. First, by encouraging them to explain themselves to an outsider like myself, I can help them – you? – seem more professional. I could even draft the final report. I haven't seen their writing skills yet but I'm used to producing hard-hitting reports that might attract the right sort of attention; or I could edit the first draft if they'd prefer.'

A second lad on a scooter came towards them, moving even faster and causing her to take cover. He was probably chasing the first. Why weren't these lads at school?

'But before the report gets written there's a lot to do. There's a need to set priorities and justify these to the community. Otherwise the whole enterprise will become a bun fight between the various interest groups.

'There are technical ways of doing that; Multi-Criteria Decision Analysis is what the academics call it.' She could see Bill looked apprehensive. 'It's not as bad as it sounds. It means giving differing weights to different kinds of benefit, totalling them and then picking the overall winner. I could tell you more if you wanted – maybe later.'

By now they had reached the Shipwright. There were several tables outside, all occupied by tourists. George wondered where they were going to sit.

But Bill knew the trick. He led her inside and then up a spiral staircase in the corner of the main bar. Soon George found herself in a less crowded dining room, at a window seat. It gave an impressive view of the brightly-coloured harbour.

'There were lots of things this morning that I more or less understood. I'm happy to learn more about them but I can guess roughly what's involved and what might be possible.'

The two had each ordered a baguette. In the meantime they

35

were enjoying their drink: George had a half of a local cider and Bill a pint of Doom Bar bitter.

The analyst pointed at the name on Bill's glass. 'What made no sense was talk about the Doom Bar. That's obviously something local that I'm missing completely. Could you enlighten me?'

'You're right, my dear. We didn't explain it. Basically the Doom Bar is a treacherous sand bank that runs most of the way across the mouth of the Camel estuary. At low tide you can see traces from the Lookout at Stepper Point: the waves lap over it. It's been there for centuries.'

'What causes it?'

'There's a local legend. The story goes that there used to be a mermaid who lived in the mouth of the River Camel. One day a local fisherman who was out in the bay insulted her: said she was ugly.'

'He was probably drunk,' said George derisively. The only time Mark had been dismissive of her was once early in their relationship when he had had too much wine.

'Maybe. Though fishermen don't drink much when they're about to go to sea. They know they might need all their wits to deal with an emergency. Anyway, she made a great fuss and demanded an apology. But none came. So in retaliation the mermaid put a curse on the mouth of the Camel. And that's why, to this very day, there is the Doom Bar sand bank.'

George was silent for a moment, assessing how seriously she was supposed to take this. 'I'm sorry to disappoint you Bill but I don't find that completely convincing.'

Her uncle smiled. 'That's all right my dear, neither do I. In truth no-one really knows exactly how and why the sandbank is formed – and more to the point, why it moves about. It shifts over time, from one side of the estuary to the other. That makes it quite a threat to shipping in the River Camel.'

'When you say "threat" you mean it makes boats run aground?'

'Oh no, much worse than that. In bad storms boats could, and indeed still can, be completely wrecked. There have been something like six hundred wrecks on it in the past two hundred years. Most of them a long time ago, of course. The biggest is the Antoinette. She was a coal barge - sailed in 1895, got caught in a storm around Lundy Island, struggled back almost as far as Padstow but then got caught on the sand bank. She disappeared but recently parts of her turned up again. At low tide you can see some of the boat's remains, her ribs – that's the vertical posts on the sides - still sticking up out of the sand.'

'Wow. No wonder you need a manned Lookout at Stepper Point.'

'Not just for that; our Lookout deals with everything that happens in the bay. From swimmers in distress or surfers drifting out to sea through to boats about to capsize, even potential collisions. The Doom Bar is not the only focus of our efforts.'

Bill took a reflective swig of his bitter. 'But it needs taking into account in any expansion of boating activities. It's certainly a hindrance to progress. As an outsider, I think you've picked up something we had all overlooked. Well done. It warrants more attention than our PRAM committee has been giving it.'

It had been sold to him as a technical partnership. His colleague was the boss and he was the apprentice. In due season the promise was that he too would become an expert. He'd certainly done his fair share of drudgery and endured more than his share of danger. But the future now seemed less certain.

CHAPTER 7

Peter Travers was in a bad mood when he met up with Brian Southgate at the Bettle and Chisel Inn in Delabole that Monday evening. His mood had nothing to do with the weather: it was a fine, warm evening. The pair sat outside in the rear garden, keeping apart from the remaining drinkers.

'Does your Detective Inspector not work evenings?' asked Brian. 'I'd expected you'd be on the case night and day once you were working with the Crime Squad.'

'Huh. You'd think a naked, headless torso found in a remote pool would have some claim on police attention. But I guess I'm the guilty one. I did the damage yesterday. I suggested the body might have been dumped down here after some gang battle in Exeter or Bristol. And when I looked through my records and couldn't find any local woman who'd been reported missing in the past couple of months that seemed to clinch it. As soon as he heard that, Chadwick decided it would be a waste of resources to dredge the pool and cleared off back to Exeter.'

'You mean your Detective Inspector prefers to deal with glamorous crime in the big cities?'

'I doubt any of the crimes he deals with are glamorous. Mostly unsavoury gangs of thugs, beating one another up. But be fair, the body was dumped in the pool by someone. And it wasn't a rushed job. You saw the way that sack was tied up. All those ropes and knots - that'd take ages.'

The policeman took another sip of his cider and then continued.

'The Prince of Wales Quarry looks remote but it's actually not that secluded: half a mile from Trewarmett. Plenty of dog-walkers exercise their animals around there - even if the interest in industrial archaeology is low.'

'So it would be a huge risk to dump in daylight.' The doctor was used to logical inference. 'You'd need light to fasten all those knots. But you couldn't use a torch near the quarry – it'd risk attracting attention. So preparing the body for disposal couldn't be done on the spot at night.'

'That's right. And if it couldn't be done there by day or by night the murder must have been done somewhere else. Almost certainly a car ride away.'

'Ah,' said the doctor, 'I see. And once a car's being used, why should it be a local crime at all? It might as well have come from Bristol as from Boscastle. So Chadwick lumped it in with the rest of his portfolio.'

'It seems so. So unless someone local saw the sack being dumped, the Crime Squad view is that there's nothing else to work on here. And no need for a Detective Inspector to fritter his valuable time in the back of beyond.'

'Now I see why you're looking so gloomy, Peter. No doubt, as the man on the spot, you've been asked to interview all the local dog-owners and see if any of them saw anything suspicious a few months ago? A land rover parked by the roadside, say, with a memorable number plate; and two bulky men with distinctive tattoos heaving a sack up the path towards the pool. What a pity the Prince of Wales Quarry doesn't have CCTV cameras.'

'If it had the body would have been dumped somewhere

else.'

'And I'd have had my Sunday all to myself.'

In fact the doctor had nothing much else on that day, and had been happy to answer the call from his long-standing friend. It was frustrating, though, that it hadn't given the local policeman much chance to impress the Crime Squad.

A thought occurred to the doctor. 'If it was a gang from miles away they must have done some investigation? It might be an ideal spot but it's not easy to find. The pool is well hidden. Unless you walked up to the Engine House and saw the "Danger Deep Water" sign you'd never suspect the pool was there at all.'

'I agree: it's almost perfect. Far enough from the road that you wouldn't be spotted by a passing motorist when dumping the body.'

'And so seldom visited they might have expected the body would stay hidden for years.' The doctor mused for a moment. 'I wonder if there are other bodies in there as well?'

'One's more than enough.'

'Could they have found out about it from the internet or a tourist leaflet?'

'That's something I can check on.' The policeman made a note. 'But I've never seen the quarry promoted anywhere. There are lots more straightforward attractions round about.'

'The height of the fence would discourage most visitors. What made our couple decide to climb in there, anyway?'

Peter Travers would not normally dream of divulging the details of his police interview the afternoon before, with Kevin and Gwyneth, to a non-policeman. But his friend had been part of the team at the scene and he did want to talk it over with someone. Briefly he sketched out how the find had occurred.

'So we were lucky to find the body,' commented the doctor. 'It wasn't just a matter of climbing over and seeing it. They needed a reason to go fishing there - and a strong rope.'

'And they had to persist long enough for the body to be found and then hauled out.'

'Yes, it wasn't just dumped. It was well away from the edge. That body wasn't intended to be found in a hurry. Whoever committed the crime will feel really angry when they hear it's been found.'

'That might not be for some time,' responded the policeman. 'At the end of the interview Inspector Chadwick was pretty hard on the pair. First he observed they'd certainly been trespassing once they climbed over the fence. But this would be overlooked if they cooperated from now on. Then he spoke on how the police needed time to conduct a post-mortem and carry out various enquiries.'

'So if that was the carrot,' asked Southgate, 'what was the stick?'

'The Inspector warned them it wasn't in their interest for the media to learn the details. Once that happened anyone could find out who'd found the body – including any assailant. Chadwick hinted at possible reprisals. Then he observed that someone who had murdered once could easily do so again.

'By the time he'd finished they both looked terrified. They swore they would not say anything to anyone until the police told them they could. I guess that embargo applies to you as well.'

'I'm not accustomed to breaking patient confidentiality,' said Southgate impatiently: Travers should know that by now. 'Mind you, she wasn't much of a patient by the time I got to see her. So Chadwick reckons he can keep the lid on for a week or two, does he? That'll be alright as long as no-one else saw the police forensic tent yesterday – or the body being put into the police van.

'Forensics told me,' the doctor continued, 'that the body would go to Exeter for a post mortem. That might just give you – us - some clues about how she died. And her DNA might match up with someone on the police database. Otherwise she's going to be hard to identify.'

Southgate shook his head. 'It's not an easy crime to solve, I'm afraid, Peter. You need to be careful that failure to solve it isn't all put down to you.'

CHAPTER 8

George found the concept of a sand bank like the Doom Bar, which could changes its position in the estuary so radically over a few decades, intriguing. It would make any future development of Padstow as a port more challenging. Bill had told her there were two sand dredgers based at Padstow to keep the estuary clear. Keeping these running day after day and year after year must be a significant cost to the Harbour Commission.

But presumably even more dredging would be needed if the channel was to be made wider or deeper?

That evening Bill had gone out. Was he attending quiz night in one of the pubs around the harbour? George had not pressed to go with him, she was tired after a day of meeting new people.

But as she sat in Bill's cosy lounge with a mug of hot chocolate, her mathematical mind returned to the Doom Bar; and she started to wonder how its movements might be modelled.

The idea was ridiculous, of course. Whole departments studying coastal behaviour, with many erudite professors, could commission many doctoral theses on the ocean currents and sand movements involved. Even these models would be poor predictors of real-world behaviour. She wondered if any institution – maybe Plymouth University, it was only fifty miles away – had done such work.

But she also knew there were many sorts of models: complexity was not always a virtue. George's speciality was simple computer models, dealing with just the main factors but geared to management decisions. Just for fun she started to conjecture what facts would need to be included; and what historic data might be available.

This might not sound like fun but George was, after all, a Cambridge mathematician who liked solving logical problems. If she had been at home she might have listened to classical music. But in Padstow she was more dependent on her own wits.

What had caused the Doom Bar to shift its position so radically? What had changed? One possibility was variations in dredging: certainly she would need data on how much had gone on over the period.

The Padstow Harbour Commission seemed to take a pride in its records. The data should be around somewhere. The shift in the Doom Bar's position might be down to systematic dredging. For example persistently working to keep the eastern side of the estuary clear would nudge the Bar over to the west.

But what if the dredging had gone on for many decades? Bill had pointed out one of the dredgers on their walk through the town. It didn't look very modern – it could well be half a century old. If it had spent its working life on the Camel that would predate the recent movement of the Doom Bar.

So were there any alternative causes?

It was a pity Bill was not around. He might know the answer or could direct her to someone who did.

On the other hand her own experience told her it would be useful to develop ideas of her own - even if they were completely wrong. They'd give her a better basis for hearing the official view when she came across it and for asking questions. As an outsider she would be able to ask the daft questions that were perhaps not daft at all.

Swirling her chocolate she got up and fetched her notebook from her cagoule.

One possible cause was changes in the weather. Someone here must keep old weather data. Bill's Lookout might track it, or the Tourist Office might hold it for visitors. She would need an archive going back several decades, with wind direction and wind speed as well as sunshine hours, rainfall and temperature.

The Doom Bar must form where two opposing flows met. One of these was the Atlantic waves pounding in. Had there been any change in the depth of tides over the past half century? These Atlantic flows would confront the water coming down the River Camel.

Maybe that was another data source she needed to chase. How had the Camel flow rate varied over time? That must reflect rainfall over Bodmin Moor and the rate at which it discharged into the river system. Even if the rainfall had not changed, the time it took to reach the river might have altered.

Before she started building any sort of model it would be important to gather as much historical data on each of these factors as she could and then set them out beside one another.

Most important of all was a record of how the Doom Bar had moved over the decades. Did the switch happen slowly over many years or had it flipped? If so, were there two almost matching forces acting on it in a chaotic system? And did the change happen steadily over the year or at particular times – say the spring or autumn?

George wondered if it was an indulgence to be thinking of such things: she was almost out of her depth. This sort of modelling was not why she'd been brought down to Padstow.

But a high level model might help clarify the town's thinking on how much effort it should put into harbour-based developments, compared to other facilities along the shore.

George decided that, as she interviewed the "PRAM gang", she would keep an eye open for historical data.

But it might be impossible. She mustn't raise any expectations until she had the data needed to take the model further.

CHAPTER 9

On Tuesday, with no further instructions from Detective Inspector Chadwick, Peter Travers continued to seek eyewitnesses of the dumping of the torso at the Prince of Wales Quarry.

The trouble was he was not sure when the incident had occurred. The only clue so far was the state of the body. On the basis of comments from his friend Dr Southgate he was reduced to referring back to "the past two or three months", hoping this was a wide enough period to cover whatever had happened.

He would have to be very careful not to let slip any details. So far Chadwick had treated him with respect. But he was a man under pressure who could easily blow if things went wrong. He'd have no mercy if the local policeman were found to be the source of a media leak.

Travers started with Gwyneth Fry in Trewarmett. She must be able to tell him the names of the other dog-walkers around the quarry.

But she could only give him a couple. 'I can give you rough descriptions of the other three but we've never had any reason to exchange names. I know their dogs' names, but that's probably not much use? But the two I've given you may know the others.'

Gwyneth herself had no memory of any car being parked near to the entrance followed by someone struggling up the hillside with a load. 'There's a grassy car park, up a slight ramp, that I can just see from my spare bedroom window. You can see its height restriction bar. But apart from one of the dog-walkers who's a bit lazy and drives up from Tintagel I never see any cars parked there. It's not a tourist attraction.'

After reminding her of the need for complete secrecy about what she had helped to extract from the pool, Travers set out to find the remaining dog-walkers. As a local he knew enough of the inhabitants of Trewarmett and Treknow (the next village along) that he could make the required enquiries without stirring up trouble.

John Wimshurst was the nearest. He lived in a small cottage at the far end of Trewarmett. 'Yes, I take Rover up there just about every day,' he declared. 'Except when it's raining or windy. And we don't go if there's hail or snow. Or if the forecast's bad. On those days Rover makes do with the back garden. Usually we go there in the morning, straight after breakfast – the quarry that is, not the back garden.'

It sounded as if the poor dog would be lucky to get that far. 'And have you seen anything odd up at the quarry in the past two or three months?'

'Ah, you mean youngsters trading drugs? Well -'

'I was more thinking of something to do with a vehicle.'

Wimshurst paused for thought. Finally he shook his head. 'Do you know, I've never seen a vehicle parked at the quarry car park. They hardly get any visitors.'

'OK, I'll try and find someone who goes there later in the day. Could you tell me the names of any of your fellow dog-walkers?'

Three tedious hours later, Peter Travers had interviewed all known regular visitors to the quarry and drawn a complete blank.

'Sergeant Travers here, sir, speaking from Delabole. I've now interviewed every regular visitor to the Prince of Wales Quarry. None of them remember seeing anything significant.' Peter Travers had finally got through to Marcus Chadwick. According to the Exeter Police Station switchboard he was "extraordinarily stretched".

'Well, Travers, the news here's not much better. My sergeant attended the post mortem yesterday, I got the preliminary report late this morning.' There was the rustle of a document.

'Our victim was not a virgin. Her age was between thirty and thirty five. And she used to smoke - not excessively, but regularly.'

'Can they say if she'd had sex recently, sir?'

'They didn't say. Or couldn't. Remember, she'd been under water for several weeks. Long enough to wash fluids away, anyway.'

The Inspector continued, 'They're still doing chemical analysis of the blood and the contents of the stomach. So in terms of identity they've told us virtually nothing.'

'How about the date of death, sir?'

There was a pause as the Inspector glanced down the report. 'The torso had been in the pool for from four to six weeks – but when you try and pin 'em down they become more hazy. They say the deterioration of the skin depends on the temperature of the pool and darkness of the water, and so on and on. Oh yes - and the acidity of the water in the pool, which they're still analysing.'

'If she'd been poisoned that might show up in the analysis still to come, sir,' Travers thought a sliver of optimism couldn't do any harm. 'How long will it take to have her DNA identified?'

'The Forensics Lab is under huge pressure at the moment. I've told them it's urgent - but they say that's true for all the cases they're looking at. We should have it by Thursday. Then we might be able to know who the victim is.'

'Provided they're on the Police DNA database, sir.'

'I suspect this is part of some sort of gang warfare, maybe in Exeter or Bristol. That's why we're so busy here. It's like an action replay of World War Two except without bombers. All the gang cases in Exeter come under my overall control. So with a bit of luck we'll have traces on her from an earlier incident.'

Travers was not so sure but thought it unwise to argue. Their relationship was still at an early stage. 'Anything else you want me to check in the meantime, sir?'

'All I can think of right now is: who's responsible for the water in that pool? Presumably someone's supposed to check from time to time on the water quality? And the risks of flooding. After all, it's a public water source.'

'Another question might be, do they ever check the state of that fence around the pool?'

'That's an even longer shot. It seemed in good condition when we climbed over it on Sunday. If it could take my weight it was doing OK. But I guess that whoever it is must be found in North Cornwall: maybe the local Environment Agency?'

'Right sir, I'll do my best.'

It was clear, thought Travers, that Chadwick wanted to take the case seriously. But it was by no means the only case he was currently tasked with. And given their total ignorance on the identity of the torso there was no obvious place to start looking.

51

CHAPTER 10

O n Tuesday, George Gilbert started on her interviews of the Padstow/Rock Active Modernisation Committee. A schedule had arrived, along with the minutes of the meeting George had attended the day before.

George saw both as she tucked in to Bill's cooked breakfast – his customary fare. A good job she was only down here for a fortnight or her daughter might no longer recognise her.

The analyst approved of minutes drawn up while attendees could still recall what had happened. It was less strain on every-one's memory. And she saw the timetable gave her plenty of space between meetings. These gave her time to write them up or to meet other interested citizens in the town. She was glad they'd not tried to box her in.

Her first interview was with Hamish Robertson, whom she'd classified as a forceful Scottish businessman. Robertson now seemed to spend all of his time in the southwest. He had busi-ness interests across Cornwall but had been staying in the Metropole Hotel overnight.

Robertson was pushing for a local variant of the Eden Project. George had not visited Eden but she had taken the precaution of looking it up on the internet. It had a million visitors a year – an average, she computed, of three thousand a day.

'There's scope to modernise Cornwall,' the businessman began, when the two had taken a corner table in the hotel lounge and ordered a large pot of coffee. 'Och aye. And a chance for someone to make a packet in the process.'

George was glad that he spoke with some animation, as well as a highland lilt. Little was achieved in business without a glint in the eye. And there was some humour along with his ambition. She was glad she'd done her homework.

'So you think something like the Eden Project might work in this area?'

'Not exactly the same. The Eden Project's about active biodiversity. Personally I don't care that much about the environment. If my family wants to see tropical plants we'll take a holiday in the Caribbean. But I've got shares in this hotel. A lot of our guests go to the Eden Project during their holidays – especially when it's raining. And the roads to get there are slow: lots of traffic jams in the summer months.'

'So what's your alternative?'

'Well, there are several patches of land here that lead down towards the Camel - belonging to struggling farmers, who've been exploited by supermarkets. At the right price it should be possible to buy one of them out and make what I've been calling a "Game Park". I'd buy the farmhouse as part of the deal, ready to be redeveloped. Not too near the town, but easily accessible – and much closer than Eden.'

'Are you thinking people would travel to it by bike, along the Camel Trail?'

'Well, some might. It would make a useful halfway point from Padstow to Wadebridge. My daughters have cycled the Trail several times – and enjoyed it. Make no mistake, it's fun: safe entertainment, well away from roads. But they tell me there's no place to buy refreshments as you go along – not even a drink. I'd like to offer a smart, riverside restaurant – there are fabulous views for customers across the estuary. And also to sell ice-cream and snacks.'

'With, no doubt, a bar?'

'Of course - even a couple. But majoring on soft drinks. Though, as far as I know, you can't be charged for being drunk in charge of a bicycle.'

George did not disagree but remembered that the Camel Trail went over the Petherick Creek on a long girder bridge. You'd need to be sober to cross that without a hitch.

'So what's at the heart of this development? Is it primarily a source of food? Or have you other ideas?'

'Well, Padstow is in an Area of Outstanding Natural Beauty. So the Council won't allow anything that's noisy, like racing quad bikes.'

'That must limit the options. What did you have in mind?'

'I was thinking of a high level adventure playground. You could call it a silent battlefield. Especially if we could get hold of a patch of land for my Park that includes a stretch of woods - and maybe an abandoned slate quarry.'

'Sorry, you've lost me.'

'Well, have you ever played the game of Diplomacy?'

'Yes. I mostly resisted, but some of my friends got besotted. Personally I preferred relaxing with amateur dramatics. One of their games went on for months. It's a slow rerun of the First World War, isn't it, campaign by campaign?'

'That's right. And roughly speaking my idea is an outdoor version of the same game. The Park would be broken up into territories. Special fences would mark their boundaries.'

'With border posts?' suggested George, 'Manned by Park

staff?' Inventing this semi-fictional world was quite fun.

'Like Diplomacy, there would be a series of rounds, i.e. campaigns. On each round, each team would try and capture one of the other territories. That would involve making alliance with the forces, i.e. the teams, in adjacent territories. But, of course, double bluffing might happen: not all the alliances would hold. Or they might be beaten by a bigger alliance on the other side.'

'So would there be real fighting?'

'Not with real guns: much too dangerous. I suppose if all the combatants agreed they could go in for physical fighting.'

'It would be best,' he continued, 'if there were rules to determine who wins each skirmish with an element of chance. Setting the rules could be the first part of the exercise. For instance, you might want to count men as being worth more than women on the battlefield.'

'If you fancied a fight with women's right groups,' said George with a wry smile. It was clear the man was not a Guardian reader.

Even so George was warming to the idea: Robertson's enthusiasm was catching. 'But if it's an outdoor game physical skills would be needed somewhere?'

'Oh yes, they'd matter a great deal. For example, you would need to track opposing forces and estimate their strength. And meeting for diplomatic activity might require orienteering to find particular locations.'

George thought for a minute about other aspects. It was exhilarating to play God. 'How about a swimming pool?'

'Yes, I'd thought about that. Better than swimming in wild streams. But I'd want to make it part of the Game Park. Give it a physical look, make it a natural divide between two or more territories. So it would be outdoors and I guess unheated. That would separate the men from the boys.'

'And the women from the girls,' added George. A moment's doubt struck her. 'You do see this as a mixed-sex activity?'

'Of course.'

George went on to ask the businessman about his projected finances. He spoke at length, even producing sheets of figures. A strong discussion ensued.

'The trouble with my projection,' he admitted, 'is to know how many tourists would be interested. With good numbers it could be a win for the town and for the promoter. But with lower numbers it would be a financial disaster.'

George could see what he meant. He was being very optimistic, she thought, if he hoped to match the Eden Project.

'That's why I'm so keen on this plan to modernise Padstow,' the businessman concluded. 'It would make a lot of difference to go with the flow, rather than being an isolated development. In fact I wouldn't go ahead if there was nothing else going on. I'd turn my attention to another part of Cornwall.'

CHAPTER 11

George's next meeting followed on Tuesday afternoon. She had taken the opportunity, after talking to Hamish Robertson, to explore Padstow further. She had been intrigued by the small shops in the winding streets behind the harbour, selling all sorts of odd items – this was no standard high street. It was an attractive little town.

Nonetheless, the questions really were: could it become more than that, did it wish to do so, and if so, how was that to be done?

She met Mary Elston in a beamed cottage overlooking the town. The historian had not dominated the PRAM committee but though quiet she was clearly knowledgeable in her field.

A pot of tea was prepared 'to aid the flow of conversation'. George was quietly amused that the tea set itself looked antique. It could be the starting point for a museum on its own.

'So you believe Padstow has much more history than most of its visitors recognise; and for the town to achieve a higher profile this should be more strongly exploited?'

'Well, let me demonstrate. You said yesterday that you were a relative stranger. Can you tell me anything at all about our history?'

George racked her brains. Bill had made a few comments as he showed her round on Sunday but she hadn't taken much notice. She wished she'd known this question would be coming her way.

'There was a railway here, I believe. But it closed in the 1960s. And now there's the Camel Trail running along the old track up as far as Wadebridge.'

'And when did the railway reach here – and where from?'

'It must have been the nineteenth century. That's when railway growth happened in this country. And I suppose it linked up with the line at Bodmin – that's where the Camel Trail finishes, isn't it?'

'Half right. The railway reached Padstow in 1899. But what brought it here was a line from Waterloo that passed though Okehampton and down to the Cornish coast. It came through Camelford then down to Wadebridge and Padstow.'

'But what happened in Padstow before that?' the historian continued.

'I suppose all the communications must have happened through the port. So was it a fishing village?'

'Good guess. Padstow, tucked in to the Camel estuary, is the best natural harbour on the North Cornwall coast. But as well as the fishing the port allows the export of Cornish goods such as tin, copper and slate. As well as importing coal from South Wales.'

George nodded.

Her host continued. 'But it also had a thriving shipbuilding business – at least while ships were made of wood rather than iron.'

'OK. So it was a thriving town even before the railway came. But how might that be better presented? What do *you* want from PRAM?'

'Publicity is easiest with interesting characters. Did you know, for example, that in the sixteenth century Frobisher and Hawkins put to shore in Britain, after sailing round the world, right here in Padstow?'

'You mean, it used to be really important?'

'No. But they judged it safer to land here than to sail round the rocks at Lands End to reach Falmouth or Plymouth.'

Mary continued, 'And someone even more famous than those two didn't just land here but was Warden of Cornwall, just down the hill. Can you guess who?'

George hadn't expected to be answering questions. She couldn't remember much history – most of her time had been spent with higher mathematics. But she had to make some effort.

'Was this another seafaring Elizabethan?'

'It was. Though more associated with goods from South America: one a staple diet ever since, the other a health disaster.'

This was a nightmare. George shut her eyes. Why on earth was this called general knowledge when it was so scarce? Then it came to her. 'Oh, was it Sir Walter Raleigh? With his tobacco and potatoes? The man who invented the bicycle?'

She knew the last point was wrong but wondered how the historian would take a joke. Her hostess just gave an impatient sniff.

Mary continued to expound the history of the area. Padstow had been the place from where many Cornish folk emigrated on their way to the Americas. 'That was when tin mining had started to falter.'

When, finally, she paused, George judged it was time for her to start asking the questions.

'This is all very interesting, but how do you think this history might be given a higher profile? Some sort of museum like they have in St Ives?' George didn't often visit museums, but she and Mark had taken their daughter there once, when it was too wet to do anything else. Polly had found it "quite interesting".

'That's how Hamish Robertson inveigled me onto PRAM. There is a museum in Padstow, actually, over the Post Office, but it's small. I was hoping for some sort of living museum – maybe in one of those warehouses along the jetty, where the railway station was until 1967.'

'With wooden ships being built by locals, dressed up in eighteenth century clothes?'

'Maybe. Visitors could ask questions and learn the history - like they do in Morwellham Quay. And it could feature videos of the return of Frobisher and Hawkins.'

'You'd score a hit with American visitors if you could show that any of those emigrating from here made good in the United States – the ancestor of one of their Presidents, for example.'

'That would need a lot of work. But it's possible, I suppose.'

As she wandered back from the meeting, George concluded that Mary's ideas, though interesting, were marginal to the PRAM plan. If any major developments went ahead the living museum might be included as one of the items. But the idea was not a showstopper.

George resolved to visit the existing Padstow museum. It was foolish to start an enhanced version in a new location if what was already there was adequate. The alternative of enhancing the old would also need to be considered.

When she returned home, George was slightly irritated to find a note from her host. 'Sorry, got to be out this evening. Suggest you sample one of the local restaurants.' Bill had been generous in his hospitality but he wasn't doing so well as a companion.

So far, since she had come to Padstow, she hadn't had to use her car. But this was an opportunity to have a look at the area Hamish Robertson was eyeing for his Game Park. How easy was it to access?

Her map showed several minor roads branching off to the estuary from the main road to Wadebridge. She also noticed one or two beer-glass pub signs. Good: one of these would do for her evening meal.

George drove out of Padstow and as far as Trevance, where she turned left. The road was very narrow indeed. She went down a steep slope and up the other side and finally ended up at the hamlet of Lower Halwyn.

Robertson was right about one thing: there was a splendid view across the estuary. Even at eight in the evening there were still cyclists tackling the Camel Trail.

Now it was time to eat. George turned back towards the main road but missed the way she had come. The roads were too minor to warrant signposts. She was starting to despair when she came to some grass in front of a fine-looking pub: the Pickwick Arms.

Parking her car, she saw a fantastic view over the estuary. And a lot of people, sitting at the tables outside, enjoying it. The meal, too, was all that she could have hoped for.

George wondered, as she drove back to Padstow later, just how much research Hamish Robertson had carried out on his big idea. A lot of work would be needed to widen the roads to his Game Park.

Robertson was not the first to realise that the estuary gave good evening views. But that meant there was already serious competition to the restaurant he was hoping to provide.

CHAPTER 12

The Environment Agency office responsible for monitoring water quality around Trewarmett was in the nearby town of Wadebridge. Sergeant Peter Travers rang to make an appointment with local manager Dr Martin Sutcliffe for the next day.

On Wednesday morning the policeman parked in the town-centre and made his way to the address given. To his dismay he found himself facing a manicurist's salon by the name of Black Nails. Through the window he could see women having hands or feet processed while others waited in the foyer. The notice in the window announced that tattooing was also on offer.

Whatever the reason, the place gave off an overpowering smell. Travers was glad that he did not have to go through such processes.

After scratching his head for a moment the policeman spotted a brass sign beside a side door. It turned out that the Agency office was not at street level but located over Black Nails.

'I bet you lose a few customers down below,' he observed, once he'd gained access. It was intended as a joke. But an earnest-looking Martin Sutcliffe nodded unhappily. It was not the first time such a comment had been made.

'We've only got a small office. We don't expect many direct visits. There are just two of us based here. But my colleague is on leave this week and I'm out taking water quality samples most days. The sample processing and notification of results all happen in Exeter. I had to put visits aside this morning to be here so this had better be important. Tell me, how can I help?'

It looked an efficient office. Charts of water quality and rainfall trends covered two of the walls. A huge fridge, which presumably stored sample bottles before they were packed off to Exeter, occupied a corner. The further wall had a packed book-shelf and a filing cabinet.

Travers had pondered how much he should tell the official. Chadwick's warning about not alerting the media was still ringing in his ears. How could he pose key questions without letting slip some confidential information?

But Sutcliffe was some form of civil servant. Travers decided to explain the need for confidentiality and trust he wouldn't be let down.

'The police are investigating something serious, which for the moment we are keeping out of the media. So before I say any more I need your assurance that this conversation will remain private.'

Sutcliffe's eyes looked like they were about to pop out of his head: this was not how interactions in this office began. No opening gambit like this featured in his training. He glowered at the policeman.

'I'm not sure I understand you. Or more significantly that you understand me. This is an Environment Agency office. The Agency has to maintain water supply and guarantee water quality and to protect citizens against flooding. If you know something about any of these items that relates to a local water source you can't ask me to be quiet. On these topics my authority supersedes yours.'

Travers was flabbergasted. The question of authority had not crossed his mind. What would Chadwick do? Maybe Dr Sutcliffe was making a reasonable point. And he'd come here to seek cooperation, not to wage a turf war.

'All right, I accept you are the authority on water quality. And we need your help. That's why I've come.'

Though Dr Sutcliffe was a serious scientist, he had a sense of perspective. He didn't want a turf war either. 'We're used to keeping all sorts of secrets. We certainly don't tell the media what we're doing. I'm happy to continue this conversation on that basis.'

An acceptable basis for cooperation. Travers continued, 'The thing is, sir, we've found something unexpected in a freshwater source near Tintagel and we need help to make sense of it.'

'How unexpected?'

'I'll not say, sir, for the minute. What I was wondering about was how your sampling regime would operate for such a source?'

'You're sounding more like Inspector Lewis by the minute. Can you tell me where the place is? This office covers the North Cornwall coast from the Camel estuary up as far as Bude. But we don't sample every little stream and ditch. If the source is small I might never go anywhere near it.'

'Well, do you know the old quarry just outside Trewarmett, on the road down to Tintagel? The Engine House associated with it stands high up on the hillside.' He saw Sutcliffe nodding.

'The place I'm concerned about is the pool beneath the old quarry, behind the Engine House. It's not stagnant, you understand: there's a waterfall gushing into it from one side so the water must seep away somewhere else - through some underground stream.'

'I think I know where you mean. There's a tall, metal fence round it, with a big sign on it, warning about the dangers of deep water?'

'That's the one: you've obviously been there.'

'A month ago. It's a charming spot. That fence is intended to be hard to climb over. But there's a locked gate lower down that I get in by. I don't have to battle through the gorse and brambles.'

'So how do you get your water sample?'

'I've got a device on a long cord that I just throw in. We're supposed to take a water sample there every six months. So I'll guess you want to know when I was last there?'

Without waiting for the policeman to answer, the environmental scientist strode confidently across the room to the bookshelf on the other side. He glanced over its many volumes.

'Ah, here's the one. "Water Quality History: Sites around Tintagel".'

He brought the volume back to the desk, sat down and started to flick through it. The policeman remained silent. The man was cooperating. Whatever happened he mustn't precipitate another argument.

'Here we go,' said the scientist. '"Stream behind Prince of Wales Quarry, Trewarmett." The typical flow-rate of the waterfall is over ten thousand litres per day. For that rate we need to take a sample every six months. My latest visit, I see, was just over a month ago: July 31st. And the one before that, which my colleague did, was on March 4th.'

Promising: the end of July was inside the date-range of interest.

'And what did the sample show, please?'

Sutcliffe peered at the file. 'The water quality there at present is extremely good. Dissolved oxygen level is high and there's no trace of ecoli. A fine source of potable water for the houses further down the valley. There's no problem at all.'

Then he remembered who was asking. 'Or at least, there wasn't at the end of July. Is there something more that I should know?'

'Before I say any more, sir, could I ask you about your sampling regime? Suppose a sheep had got trapped in the pool and drowned. Would you be able to tell there was something wrong - of that sort - just from the water quality tests?'

'Yes, I should say so. An animal as big as a sheep, fully immersed in the pool, would pollute that stream very quickly. The water quality test would indicate there was something wrong almost at once – say within a day; and would persist for as long as the animal was in there.'

'But once the farmer had got the sheep out, would the water quality improve by itself? Or would special measures be needed to restore it?'

'The natural world is pretty self-correcting if you give it time. The waterfall flushes the pool thoroughly. A week after the sheep had gone there'd be almost no trace.'

'Just one more question if I may, sir. When you were last at the pool, on July 31st, did you see anything out of the ordinary? And besides your own, were there any vehicles in the car park?'

'What odd questions. It's a very quiet spot. One of the most peaceful places I know. But how the heck do you expect me to remember details of a visit I made over a month ago? I'm sure there was nothing illegal – I'd have remembered and taken action. Or even a couple cavorting in the bracken. I can't remember ever seeing another car there. Look, are you going to give me any more clues or do I need to visit the place again for myself?'

'I'm sorry sir, but we do have solid reasons for not saying any more at the moment. But I'd say it would be a good idea for you to sample the water there again; and to do so sooner rather than later.'

He could see Sutcliffe was not satisfied with his answer and was after more detail. But Travers had got what he wanted and was not inclined to say more.

The two parted on civil terms but without much warmth.

As he strode down the stairs and away from the office, Travers felt there was something else he should have queried. Black Nails, he saw, was still doing its thriving and odious business below. Was it something there which was nagging away at the back of his mind?

For the moment whatever it was would have to wait. But it had not been a futile visit. Assuming the water quality sample had been tested properly, he now had an early limit on when the torso could have been dumped.

Back in the Agency Martin Sutcliffe also had a nagging feeling of having missed something. But for the time being it, too, would have to wait.

CHAPTER 13

On Wednesday morning George set out to learn more about the maritime aspects of the PRAM plan. She might also pick up some data to help build her simple Doom Bar computer model.

Her first interview was to be with the harbour manager, Paddy Watmough. Bill had explained over breakfast that Paddy and his staff operated out of one of the huts on the jetty.

When George got there she was met instead by his deputy, Paul Walsh. Paul was a bearded, rather mean-looking man in his thirties. An alpha male, hostile to females. No doubt he considered running a harbour was a male activity.

'Mr Watmough has too many meetings this week to fit you in. It's a pity but I've worked alongside the estuary most of my life. I know as much as he does about the issues you'll be interested in.'

George was frustrated that her schedule had been so lightly set aside. Watmough had been speaking on Monday. He had been articulate and she'd looked forward to a wide-ranging discussion. How could Walsh know what she would be interested in? But she hid her irritation; there was no point in starting off on the wrong foot.

The analyst retrieved her notebook and flipped to her agenda.

'Various issues came up at the committee meeting on Monday. I'd like to go through these and check that I've understood them properly, then to ask some additional questions.'

'Fire away,' said Walsh confidently.

'One item was the ferry between here and Rock. It's only a passenger ferry. Is there any case for increasing the route capacity, or even switching to a vehicle ferry?'

Walsh threw back his head and roared with laughter. 'So that's the sort of mad idea they're talking about in PRAM. Idealistic and crackers. Come over here.'

He escorted George to the window overlooking the Camel. 'The first thing to take into account here is the effect of the tide. It makes a huge difference to everything that sails. Right now – see - it's close to high tide. There's water right across to Rock and up towards Wadebridge. You might think that you could sail anywhere. And at this moment you'd be right.'

'But if you're still here this afternoon,' he continued, '– you could be, I don't know how long your agenda is – we can look out again. By then there'll be a miserable, narrow stream of water between here and Rock. That's low tide. Then the ferry starts half a mile downstream. It can't even reach the harbour: passengers come ashore on the sands.'

Walsh seemed angry; George had no idea what had upset him. It couldn't possibly be her questions – she'd hardly started. Maybe it was her gender. 'So a bigger ferry with a deeper draft wouldn't be suitable. It couldn't operate at low tide. But there are other ways of boosting capacity. What about two ferries, interchanging from side to side?'

'I suppose that'd be possible. They could squeeze pass one another in mid-estuary, even at low tide. But they'd only be half full, so they'd charge passengers twice as much. There aren't many times – except in the height of summer - when there are more passengers wanting to cross than there are spaces on the ferry.'

'In terms of a car ferry . . .'

'That'd need a bigger draught. Even harder to reach the harbour. But they could hardly unload their cars onto the beach.'

George had feared from the casual way it was talked about in PRAM that it wouldn't be that straightforward. But she had an alternative up her sleeve. 'Well, how about a hovercraft? That skims over the water. So the tide wouldn't limit it.'

'It'd make a hell of a racket, though. It wouldn't be very popular. And how many drivers would pay the fare needed to make it viable? I mean, they can get over the Camel by driving a few miles upstream. There's nowhere on the other side you'd need to get to in a hurry, it's all villages. The pace of life here's not that frantic.'

It was as well Watmough was on the PRAM committee rather than Walsh. But maybe his gloomy comments were valid and his boss was over-optimistic. She looked forward to running the conflict past Bill and getting his verdict.

'OK, let's leave the ferry. You've explained the general impact of the tide on vessels. And I guess on the sand movements. Am I right that this means two sand-dredgers are needed to keep the channel open?'

'The dredging is a vital part of keeping the port going. We've had the two from not long after the Second World War. They concentrate on the main channel to the open sea; make sure it stays deep enough – and in roughly the same place.'

'Do they work all the time or simply around low tide?' This was a guess, but fortunately it was correct.

'That's right. The flow is too fast at high tide. It's only around low tide that they can see what they're doing.'

'And where do they put the sand that they scoop up?'

Despite his opening hostility Walsh could see that George was asking sensible questions. Maybe she wasn't so stupid.

'They store it on board. Then, when the tide's risen, they dump it near to the shore. We also have workers with tractors; they come at low tide to take it away to sell. Once it's dried it's of good quality: builders are keen to use it.'

'Do you track how much sand is dredged up by the boats and how much gets removed by the tractors?'

'My boss insists on keeping the statistics. "Performance measures" he calls them – as if anyone cares about performance but him. But if you want them you'll need to go into his back office.'

'Thank you, I might be glad to do that. You see, one thing that intrigues me is the Doom Bar, and how it keeps moving around the estuary. Do you know what causes that? It doesn't sound as if it can all be blamed on the dredging.'

'The Bar happens where the incoming tides from the Atlantic come up against the outgoing river flows and the sand being carried drops down. Once there's a small bar of sand that sets where the two forces will meet on the next tide. So more sand gets left in the same spot and in the end it forms a significant bar.'

'Yes, I can see how that would work. But what you've said doesn't explain why the position of the bar should move around over time. So what happened between 1970 and today to make the channel shift from one side of the estuary to the other?'

'Good question. Folk around here have argued over that for years. And not come to a settled answer.'

'But doesn't that mean it might change again?'

'Mm, I suppose so. But no doubt there would still be some

channel to the sea, one side or the other, we could keep on dredging.'

George privately thought this answer was weak. If they wanted to make more of the estuary surely they would need more certainty? Was her high level computer model needed after all?

'Would the harbour manager have data on how the position of the bar has changed over the years?'

'He certainly would. It's another "performance measure". If you're really interested in that, you'd need to spend a day in his back office, chasing through his dusty old files.'

'I'd like to set the changes against other factors. Wind speed, for example. And maybe the historical flow rates in the River Camel.'

'We don't keep data on all those. You'd need to talk to the Environment Agency over in Wadebridge.'

George could sense that broaching an area beyond his responsibilities had made her source less voluble. She would visit the Agency when she could. But it would be good to finish the interview on an area where Walsh was knowledgeable. She recalled one of the other issues mentioned at PRAM.

'Is the estuary a good place for bird watching?'

Walsh's face broke into a smile. 'Terrific. All the way up to Wadebridge. Especially on the creeks that flow into the estuary. I'm often out there with my binoculars.'

'Oh, you mean Little Petherick Creek?'

'That's marshy and got a lot of waders. There are even more on the next creek along: Curlews and Kingfishers and Shovellers and Mallards and a host of others. Are you interested in wildlife?'

George managed to give an indeterminate answer. She

wasn't very good at full-scale lying. Actually she'd never been bird watching in her life. But expanding the practice of bird-watching, and Padstow's reputation for it, might be of interest to the PRAM committee.

She was thankful, as she left, that she had managed to avoid being invited to bird-watch on the Camel with Walsh. He had thawed out as the interview progressed but not to the extent that she wanted to spend more time with him.

CHAPTER 14

Kevin Rogers' friends had been baffled and slightly deflated when they had returned to the vicinity of the Engine House on Sunday afternoon and found no trace of the prospective bridegroom. In fact, once the police interview was over, Kevin had gone to ground.

He had stayed at home on the Monday and only crept out, to drive to work in Launceston, mid-morning on Tuesday. It was Wednesday evening before the prospective groom felt confident enough to venture as far as the Cornishman pub in the centre of Tintagel.

It was his friends' favoured meeting place: there was little chance of his appearance there going unspotted. Once they found him, his friends were eager to make sense of the puzzle: what had happened after they had gone? But Kevin, mindful of his instructions from Detective Inspector Chadwick, was reluctant to say anything about.

His stag party had expected he would be proud to have escaped and eager to boast about the details. It wasn't exactly the Great Escape, but it was a worthwhile talking point by Tintagel standards.

But it seemed, oddly, that Kevin would prefer to say nothing at all.

The group tried direct provocation. He couldn't deny what had happened. One of them still had their camera to hand. The images were viewed of the naked man shivering in the Engine

House gateway. Caught by flashlight in the blackness of the night he looked discomforted and pathetic.

But somehow, within the group, not knowing the sequel seemed to reduce the pictures' impact.

Even the threat of passing on copies to his fiancée or the local press seemed insufficient to break Kevin's silence.

In the end, it was the best man, Tommy Burton, who suggested they had no choice but to make intelligent guesses about what had occurred, then judge from Kevin's body language whether their guesses were correct.

Tommy knew his friend was a limited actor; he was bound to react in some way. The group could sense whether the answer was 'yes' or 'no' by observation. It would make for a sort of quiz game.

With their competitive instincts aroused discussion became more focused. They knew the knots he'd been tied up with had been tight: he could not possibly have loosened them on his own. From whom might his help have come? There were not many casual visitors to the quarry. It was occasionally visited by industrial archaeologists but surely not on a Sunday morning?

It did not take long for the idea that Kevin had been discovered by a dog-walker to emerge.

Further guesswork suggested the dog-walker was a woman; and for a while it was taken that in the run-up to his wedding it was simply the embarrassment of being found naked by a strange female which had silenced the prospective groom.

But was there more? How many rescuers might have been involved?

Had the woman found the knots too tight? Some wild ideas were proposed. Might the fire brigade have been summoned? That might have been the case had Kevin been chained up, or if his rescuers had needed to gouge the iron railings away from the Engine House.

But Kevin's body language suggested that nothing like this had occurred.

Then someone conjectured that the police had been involved. For a few minutes Kevin had been starting to relax; now he tensed up again. So, they deduced, the police must be part of the story. But how might they be drawn in: was it down to him being drunk or completely naked?

Although he was poor at hiding his reaction to the truth once an idea had been floated Kevin still wasn't saying anything. They were starting to tire and the "game" might well have ended in a draw.

But at that point the local policeman, Peter Travers, off-duty and in search of relaxation after a day of interviews, came into view for a moment as he passed through to the other bar.

'Did you end up being interviewed by Peter Travers?' asked Tommy. Might as well ask, he thought.

The awkward squirm that followed showed this had indeed been the case. There was a pause while the next question was formulated. The party had learned that there was no point in an open question: that simply wouldn't be answered. It had to be one that only required the response 'yes' or 'no'.

'But you were being interviewed as a witness, not as a criminal?' Again the answer, judging by the squirm, was 'yes'.

'So what the hell had you witnessed?' asked one of the group, by-passing the need for a yes/no question. This was no longer a game. His neighbour, equally impatient, expanded the point further.

'What crime could have been committed, last Sunday morning, on that remote hillside? Judging by your reaction, it must have been serious. But why would anyone commit a crime at all if they knew you were watching?'

There was an awkward silence. Kevin was clearly wrestling with conflicting emotions.

'Look guys, I've been given strict orders to say nothing. It was very unpleasant and I'm trying hard to forget it. But I doubt if I ever will. I've hardly slept for the last three nights. I hadn't intended even to admit this much; but please, don't force me beyond what I've already said.'

The stag party had not intended to be overheard. But in their excitement voices had been raised. At the other side of the bar a dowdily dressed woman in a faded, brown jacket, with her back to the group, made a comment to her companion. Then she pulled out a notebook and scribbled down as many phrases as she could remember.

'Don't you ever stop working, Harriet?' muttered her companion. 'This was meant to be our time together.'

'I'm sorry, Janey, but journalism is about opportunism: making the most of being in the right place at the right time. You can't choose when that will happen. But when you are then you need to seize the moment. Look, I can see you're upset but at least keep pretending to talk to me. I don't want the lads to notice anything odd.'

Her long-suffering companion made inconsequential asides, mostly archly dismissing the lads' clothes sense, as Harriet looked at the phrases written in her notebook and tried to link them together.

There were some interesting words. The term fiancée had come into the banter and talk of an imminent marriage – and some threat from photographs. With a flash of inspiration she realised that, given the male composition of the group, this could be the residue of a stag party. There was certainly something here worth investigating. Was this her breakthrough moment?

Harriet had not taken much notice of the group when she first came in. They were all younger than her Janey and she'd not recognised any of them. The most-silent one, she gathered from the asides, was Kevin. And his leading questioner was Tommy. No doubt the landlord would be able to tell her their surnames and name one or two more. She would ask him before she left.

But she had recognised for herself the local policeman, Peter Travers, as he walked through. He had been part of the story too. She had never talked to the officer of the law directly but he was, she judged, an amiable sort; not too bright and probably no good at keeping a secret. A speculative visit might be fruitful.

It would certainly be worth having a look at the Engine House and the old quarry. This seemed to be the site of the mystery. She'd never been there though she'd often seen the square stone building on the hillside near Trewarmett – and wondered what was inside. Maybe she could still find traces of whatever crime had been witnessed?

She had given him some pills to help him recover. Not just over-the-counter pick-me-ups but prescription drugs – presumably from some local doctor. But what she had failed to say was that he was not to combine them with alcohol. A couple of pints of cider that Saturday evening – given all he'd gone through that day – seemed hardly excessive.

It wasn't that he had blacked out. But it was almost as if he had lived for a short time in a parallel universe. And what he couldn't be sure of – and now there was no-one left to ask – was what he had done in that shadow existence?

CHAPTER 15

George Gilbert wrinkled her nose and tried to concentrate on the numbers on her laptop but she was unsettled. The deadening weight of grief, which she had dared to hope would start to lift as she began a new project in a beautiful location, had descended once more.

Wednesday morning had started fine. She had only one PRAM interview scheduled for the day, down at the jetty. In the afternoon she had gone on to visit the Environment Agency in Wadebridge. On her return, fired up by her conversation with the local historian the afternoon before, she had set out to explore Padstow in greater depth.

It was a fairly safe objective. Although she and Mark had been there a few times on their holidays it was not one of their special places. It was too embarrassing to admit, but the reality was that she had never been on the ferry from Rock to Padstow in all the times their family had stayed at Polzeath. (Was that a common experience? If more people knew about it maybe there would be more custom. It was a relevant question in the context of ferry capacity.)

Polly had no interest in moving far from the surfing beach at Polzeath, and they had been happy to oblige. Mark was at least as keen on surfing as his daughter. She had been happy to sunbathe and read books. Both adults had been glad of a relaxing holiday. It was a contrast with their hectic working lives.

Consequently Padstow had always seemed a significant car

journey away, not their nearest local town.

On her wanderings George had found the town's museum, which Mary Elston had damned with faint praise the day before. She had climbed the stairs and been pleasantly surprised.

True, it was a traditional museum, more a collection of artefacts and documents to enlighten someone who knew what they were looking for than a fresh experience to grab the attention of youngsters. Nonetheless she had enjoyed her visit and spent a couple of hours there.

The trouble had begun when she found herself outside the town's church of St Petroc, towards the top of the hill surrounding the town. She recalled from her conversation with Mary Elston that St Petroc, coming to Cornwall from Ireland, was the founding father of the town. In the interests of completeness she'd better look inside. She found it was a traditional stone building, beautifully laid out.

What had upset her was her walk round the churchyard afterwards. For there she had found several gravestones which carried the names of members of the Gilbert family.

Grief was like that, she thought miserably. It caught up with you when you were least expecting it. Of course, none of the graves were for her beloved Mark; his remains had been cremated in North London. But she spotted a Mark Henry Gilbert, buried here two hundred years ago and that had upset her badly.

When she thought about it the sighting wasn't unexpected at all. Bill had said his parents used to own the cottage where he now lived and she was staying. So when they died they could well have been buried in this graveyard; and they were called Gilbert. And possibly their ancestors were here too?

Later, the experience had prompted her to ask Bill for his

memories of Mark over their evening meal. That had been a mistake too. For though Bill's memories were amusing and had been well told, and were largely new to her – he had several tales of Mark as a naughty child, causing havoc with his parents in the local playground or nearby beaches – they had made her heart ache for him even more.

'Do any of Mark's old friends still live around here?' she asked.

'Hardly any, I think. They were all bright sparks: wanted to spread their wings. Oh, just a minute, there is one. He went off to Bristol University, the same as Mark. He trained to be a doctor then came back to work around here. But I'm not quite sure where.'

So that had not been much use either.

After the meal Bill had suddenly announced, 'I've got to go out now.' She had not remembered before, but the phrase was exactly the one Mark had used – and now she thought about it, had used surprisingly often. He had never said where he was going either.

On the other hand, she had never asked. It was too late to do so now – much too late to ask anything at all.

Irritated, George pushed aside her laptop. She was too wound up for subtle analysis. It was time, anyway, for her nightly call to Polly.

She had just gone downstairs to the phone in the hall when it rang. Bill had told her not to bother answering the phone when he was out: it wouldn't be for her. Her calls would come in on her mobile. She had heard several calls downstairs on other nights and had easily ignored them. But standing right beside the phone was different; without thinking, acting on instinct, she picked it up.

A male voice spoke. 'No progress yet; but meet as agreed.' George was about to tell him who she was and to ask him his name when, without a further word, the caller rang off.

An odd call but there was nothing much she could do about it.

The analyst noted down the few words, put 'MESSAGE FOR BILL AT 8:30 PM' at the top of the sheet then left it on the kitchen table, anchored by the sugar bowl. Bill always had sugar on his cereals, he would be bound to see it next morning.

George returned to the hall, seized the phone and called her daughter. But even this regular nightly ritual did not bring her calm. For Polly sounded lonely; she had also been thinking about her dad. George knew she had to remain strong for her daughter so she couldn't even share much of the travails of her own day.

When the call ended, George opted for a hot bath and an early night. Bill probably wouldn't be late home but she had done enough talking for one day. She wished, more than ever, that she could learn more about what Mark had been doing; and not just how but why her beloved had died.

CHAPTER 16

Thursday morning found Harriet Horsman exploring the path up to the old Engine House, puzzling as to what exactly she was looking for, when she met Gwyneth Fry exercising her dog. The meeting was a stroke of pure luck. With a start Harriet recalled that dog-walking had featured in the previous evening's interrogation. The trick at this point, she told herself, was to act as if she already knew a lot more than she did.

As always with meetings on a country walk, friendly greetings were exchanged and the weather warily commended. No-one would back it to continue for long. But Gwyneth seemed in no hurry. Was it possible that she, too, had a story to tell? She was obviously a regular dog-walker round here. Hey - might she even have been the rescuer for Kevin?

'Is the place always as peaceful as this?' asked Harriet, glancing up the hillside towards the old Engine House on the skyline.

'I bring Rumpole here most mornings. It is usually.'

'But not always? Does it get used for parties? I suppose it would make a fine base for a mid-summer festival – or for a firework display. You're obviously local. Is it booked for that sort of thing?'

'Not officially, as far as I know.'

'Oh.' Harriet paused for a moment, confused.

Then enlightenment dawned. 'You mean it gets taken over by unofficial parties? But what sort of people would bother to come up here? We're miles from anywhere.'

'That's exactly what some people want.'

'What type of people?'

'Well, isn't it what you'd want if you were organising a stag party?'

'Oh I see, it's starting to make sense. I must have met the most recent example in the pub yesterday evening. I gather it hadn't ended well – especially for the bridegroom. I think his name was Kevin.'

Gwyneth wished now that this conversation had not started, but the other woman seemed to know a lot already. What else had Kevin let slip? She recalled she'd been told not to say anything about the torso - but not forbidden to talk about everything. Could she fob the woman off with some of the less controversial details?

'Yes. They left poor Kevin tied up all Saturday night on that railing you can see in the doorway – and completely naked.'

'I bet he was cold by dawn. And you found him when you were exercising your dog on Sunday morning? That must have been embarrassing for both of you. So what did you do? Call the police?'

'No, of course not. Well, not at first anyway.'

'My gosh, it got worse? This sounds like a living nightmare. The stag party from hell. Go on then, what happened next?'

But Gwyneth remembered that she had been commanded to hold her silence. How had she got talking to this woman? She seemed remarkably nosey. Gwyneth really didn't want to add to her knowledge.

'I'm not allowed to say more. I shouldn't have started talking about it. But I live on my own. I've thought about nothing else ever since. When something bizarre happens it's hard to hold it all in.'

Harriet looked at her in silence, hoping she would continue. But it looked as if the woman was not going to say any more.

The aspiring journalist ransacked her memory. Was there anything else she'd overheard from last night's conversation that might prompt more disclosure?

'I understand – well, I don't actually, but please don't say anymore. It's a free society but we all need to take notice of police orders. But I'm surprised Travers was that strict.'

'Oh, it wasn't Travers. He was just the local plod. Came back later, in fact, much more civilised and pleasant. He wanted to find out the names of the other dog walkers around here so he could interview them. It was the plain-clothes man from Exeter who laid down the law: some senior detective or other. It was what he said that terrified me.'

'And these guys are paid to protect us. Here was me thinking the days of police bullying were behind us. Don't worry, the police are not around today.' The conversation was clearly at an end.

'Mind you,' concluded Harriet, 'before I go, I think I'll just wander up and have a look at that Engine House – and whatever's behind it.'

Later that morning the putative journalist knocked at the door of the Police House in Delabole for a hastily arranged appointment with Peter Travers. A docile black Labrador, borrowed from the landlord of a local pub that she knew well, accompanied her.

The policeman guided her through to his working area, invited her to sit down and then offered her a cup of coffee. He'd never spoken to the woman before, though the dog looked vaguely familiar. His departure into the kitchen to make the drink gave her chance to glance at the various notices pinned to the board behind his desk. One, she saw, was a list of phone numbers for senior policemen in Exeter. She just had time to photograph this before the policeman returned.

'I understand you are interviewing all the dog walkers who exercise their dogs around the old Prince of Wales Quarry in Trewarmett,' she told him as she started on her coffee. 'Gwyneth Fry told me about it this morning. I met her at the quarry.'

'That's right. It's just a routine inquiry. We're trying to find out if anyone has seen anything odd there around the beginning of August.'

'That's a while ago. Not just at the weekend, then. What sort of odd thing?'

'Well, I'm interested in any vehicles that stopped in the car park below the quarry.'

'What a peculiar question. There are hardly ever vehicles parked there, are there?'

'It's a long shot; but my boss is certain a vehicle was involved. You didn't see anyone bringing what would look like rubbish onto the quarry site, by any chance?'

'No. The rubbish tip is on the other side of the road. And it's well signposted. No-one would get the two confused. Is this peculiar line of questioning your own or your boss's?'

'Chadwick? He doesn't get into the local detail. He's far too much to do in Exeter. No, they're just my ideas.'

'Well, to answer your question, I haven't seen anything remotely odd at that quarry, either at the start of August or any other time. And it was certainly peaceful enough this morning.'

A few minutes later Harriet and the Labrador were shown the door. Complete waste of time, thought Travers. There were no useful witnesses around here to anything that happened in that quarry.

But Harriet rated the incident rather differently. She now knew that the name of the senior policeman on the case was Chadwick from Exeter; and she also had his internal office telephone number from the list she had photographed. Detective Inspector Marcus Chadwick, no less. A senior detective implied a real crime.

She still hadn't discovered what had prompted the investigation or why it was being kept secret; but she had at least started on the trail.

CHAPTER 17

On Thursday morning George had her first taste of the passenger ferry over to Rock. She was pleased that, with the high state of the tide, the ferry started where the sign on the jetty said it should. And as the deputy harbour manager had predicted, there were far fewer people waiting to take it than there were seats on the vessel. There was no case for a second vessel, based on this tiny straw poll. Though maybe there were fewer travellers to Rock today because it was drizzling?

As the vessel meandered across, George started to appreciate the complications of navigating the Camel: it was far from a straight crossing. Sitting alone in the spray near the bows also gave her chance to reflect on her visit to the Environment Agency the afternoon before.

The Agency man had sounded fed up when she'd rung him. 'I've had to come in this morning specially to deal with one visitor,' he said. 'I suppose you might as well make my day and come this afternoon.'

It wasn't until she had got to the scientist's office in Wadebridge, met Dr Martin Sutcliffe and heard that his main job was to be out taking water samples that she could make any sense of his attitude.

'I really appreciate you seeing me at such short notice,' she began. It was always good to start on a positive note. Most egos could do with a massage.

'I hope you're not going to ask me lots of questions but tell me nothing to explain why they're being asked.'

'Is that what your visitor this morning did? That seems a bit unfair.'

'Huh. He was a policeman. He'd found something odd in a stream near Tintagel but daren't – or at least wouldn't - tell me what it was. Too much secrecy about these days.'

'Don't worry, my questions are on a much longer time frame. I'm doing some work for a group in Padstow and I'm trying to make sense of the Doom Bar and why it moves about so much over time. Does your Agency collect data on the flow volumes in the River Camel?'

The scientist was probably more comfortable with this type of question than he'd been with those from the policeman earlier. And it was clear he had done some thinking about the Doom Bar as well.

'Yes, that's a puzzle. I suspect the movement happens when the balance between the incoming tides and the downstream flows gets perturbed. So what do you want? I've got the average weekly flows for all the rivers around here going back half a century.'

The scientist had taken her over to see one of the many trend graphs pinned to the back wall. 'But you don't want the flows at Wadebridge. The river's still tidal there. You need data from further upstream – Polbrook Bridge on the Camel and Sladebridge on the Allen. Look.' Seizing his Explorer map, Sutcliffe had shown George the initials NTL – Normal Tide Limit – at both places.

'OK. So I'll need to combine the two. Can you let me have that data digitised?'

'Of course.'

George had handed over her memory stick. The scientist had fiddled with his computer and downloaded the relevant data. She wished all data could be collected so easily.

'Thank you. The other thing I might need is weather data; in particular wind strength and direction.'

'I agree. We have that, but not going back so far. Just to the 1970s. Give me your memory stick again.' And after some more fiddling the data had been transferred.

'I'd be interested to know what the numbers tell you, Mrs Gilbert. I don't have any facts on the position of the Doom Bar or I'd have tried to model it myself.'

'I'd love to come and discuss my analysis. Unlike your last visitor, I'm not under any obligations of secrecy. I'm hoping to get some Doom Bar data from the harbour manager on Friday and to work on it over the weekend. Would you be around, say, this time next week?'

George had been quietly amused that, despite his earlier frustrations, the scientist was perfectly willing to spend time in the office when he might gain from the visit. The two had parted on amicable terms.

By now the ferry was close to the Rock shoreline. George saw that on this side of the Camel there was no jetty, simply a weather beaten post in the sand. Rock was smaller than Padstow and did not have a harbour jetty. The boat drew in, lowered its hinged, broad bow onto the sand and the passengers simply walked off.

George's planned interview this morning was with Elspeth Hammond. She understood from Bill that the Hammonds ran a hardware and electrical store further up Rock's main street.

Elspeth had been at the PRAM meeting on Monday and had

put forward various ways that Rock might be modernised. She was the only one to speak for this side of the river but was very confident. George thought it was vital to touch base with both communities, hence her current journey.

As she wandered up the street, enjoying the peace and quiet – there was no Camel Trail here to bring in crowds on bicycles – George spotted a group of shops in the distance. The Hammond store was presumably one of these. Then she saw an angry-looking man storm out of one of them, leap into the van parked outside and drive off. Not all peace and quiet then.

As she got closer and could make out names she realised that his abrupt exit had been from the Hammonds' shop. She hoped nothing was awry. But Elspeth seemed calm enough when she went inside and introduced herself. The owner handed over control of the counter to her assistant and led the analyst to a living room upstairs. Obviously the Hammonds were fortunate enough to live over the shop, in the centre of the village. That was a good position for testing out new ideas.

'Could you expand your hopes for Rock that you were talking about on Monday?' George began.

'Well, James and I see the need to widen out the range of residents that feel comfortable in Rock. I mean, the place is fine for richer folk like golfers or sailors. But not necessarily younger people. There's less for them. So they tend to drift away or go off to university and then not come back.'

'What kind of things did you have in mind?'

'James and I are here all the time. OK, he's out today: it's Thursday, he's on his monthly trip to Plymouth to look for new gadgets. Normally we're both around and we've tested out many ideas. The best feedback has been on a local Leisure Centre. At the moment there's nothing nearer than Wadebridge. That would be a real boon for visitors. Frankly, anything round here that gives people somewhere to go when it's raining will get a lot of use – just like the Eden project. That's crammed in wet weather.'

'But would it get used often enough to recover the costs of the building? And how much would it get used in the winter, given fewer tourists? Would the locals come? Would it be a good investment?'

Whatever Elspeth's past, she was into logical debate. 'With organisation and good publicity it could get regular use in the winter. For example, my husband James is dead keen on coaching cricket. We have a village team here he helps with, but they never do well. But with weekly indoor coaching sessions through the winter that could make a big difference to our team's skills and to their fitness.'

'But you couldn't spend a fortune on a Leisure Centre just to develop a better village cricket team.'

'Given half a chance my husband might. But of course I agree with you. It could though help with sailing proficiency. There are many aspects where indoor courses would be useful: navigation, for example. In the warmer months the courses could be offered alongside outdoor sessions on the Camel. Together they could be very attractive and bring a lot more visitors. A heated indoor swimming pool would be popular too.'

To George this sounded like a hotchpotch of hopes and dreams. The various ideas might work but they needed to be properly evaluated. Which one was the primary fund-raiser?

'How much might a new Leisure Centre cost?'

'They built one in Bude a few years ago for half a million pounds. The Council subsidised it.'

'Let's take that figure – assume a Council subsidy might be on offer here; and that some rich local would donate land to build on. For a five year payback on that investment - which is pretty modest - you'd need £100,000 a year profit. Now, how much do you think you could charge for entry?'

'I could imagine people paying five pounds a head: more for adults, less for children.'

'So that would mean you needed, what, 20,000 visitors a year – that's around 400 per week, say 60 a day.'

'That doesn't sound impossible.'

'No; but we haven't put in any running costs yet. It assumes the Centre is unheated and unlit, doesn't pay rates, never needs maintenance and is entirely staffed by volunteers.'

Elspeth looked as though she was about to argue. George pressed on. 'But a building this size would need a full-time manager and some paid staff. Suppose you got volunteers to help run it and the total wage bill could be kept to £100,000; and the other costs were only another £50,000. That'd give a total annual cost of £250,000. Now you'd need two and a half times as many visitors as I said at first for it to break even - 50,000 a year or 150 per day.'

'I guess that might happen,' George concluded, 'in the height of the tourist season; but isn't it rather a lot for the winter?'

Elspeth looked upset. George wished she had been less gloomy. It couldn't be pleasant to have your best ideas shot down in flames.

'But maybe I'm being too pessimistic. You know the villagers much better than I do – how long have you lived here?'

'Only a couple of years, actually. Before that we were civil servants in London. Then the opportunity came to retire and move down here - and we grabbed it. We'd bought our house in London many years ago and it was worth a small fortune. This shop was for sale and we bought it: the place gave us a home and a livelihood. And even a small granny flat upstairs to let out during high season.'

It was, George noted, only a newcomer to Rock who was on the PRAM committee. Had she been specially chosen? The analyst wondered how much support there would be among more established residents.

'Might you not be simply transferring your metropolitan enthusiasms to the back of beyond?'

'I object. Cornish folk aren't stupid; it's an idea with mileage. We've bounced the idea off our customers. They're keen as well.'

'Yes, but agreeing in casual conversation that you might use a new Centre – with no thought as to how much it might cost and when you'd find the time to do so - is not the same thing as committed, regular use. Before you went much further you'd need a village survey – conducted by an outside party with real objectivity. For example, do you know how many of your customers make use of the Leisure Centre in Wadebridge?'

George and Elspeth went round these topics for some time without making much headway.

As she left, George sensed that her bucket of cold water had not made her a friend. It made her question, however, what the general level of support for PRAM was; and how she might take stock of that from more independent authorities.

CHAPTER 18

After locking horns with Elspeth, George decided that she needed some exercise to restore her spirits. By the time she left the Hammonds' shop she was pleased to discover it had stopped raining – though the sky was still overcast. Her map showed a footpath marked, running down the side of the estuary to Polzeath. It was only two or three miles and fairly level. She had no more meetings scheduled before the evening. It would be good to take time out to reflect on the various PRAM findings.

The footpath on the map was clear, but George soon found herself following a meandering path up and down a series of sand dunes. There were way markers but they were indecisive. Often the most obvious path ahead through the sandy soil did not follow their guidance. But there was no way she could get badly lost. As she broadly followed the shoreline she could hear the sea surging nearby.

What George had forgotten, until she had reached Polzeath, was that the last time she had been in that village she had been with Mark. Pressures of work had kept her from thinking too much about her recently-departed husband; but now, out of the blue, thoughts came back with renewed force. His death was just so unexpected and inexplicable.

A wave of anguish swept over her. She needed to stop and sit down. Just ahead was a sign advertising the beach-side Galleon cafe. She wouldn't have remembered the name, but now, as she stumbled along the approach decking and opened the cafe door, she remembered that her family had often gone there for cups of tea to bolster their days on the beach.

Tears not far from her eyes, she ordered a mug of coffee and sat down at a trestle table as far as she could from the door. For a few moments wave after wave of grief seemed to overwhelm her. She knew the raw facts about what had happened to her husband but they made such little sense. Why could Mark be no longer with her? Why was her intuition about what had happened to him so imprecise? How could she hope to cope for the rest of her days on her own?

'Are you all right, my dear?' A warm, sympathetic voice broke through her misery. Startled, she looked around but could see no-one. The cafe was almost empty. How bad had things got, she wondered, when she started hearing voices?

Then she realised that the voice was coming from a barred off corner of the cafe. This was presumably where the owner sat, keeping a watchful eye on his business and dealing with the finances. Looking more carefully, she saw a bearded man seated at the desk there, with a kindly face, surrounded by files; he was looking directly at her.

'I'm sorry. I'm not doing much to make people feel happy in here, am I?'

'If we provide a cafe on a popular beach like this we can't be choosy about who comes in and how they're feeling. Or how our facilities are used. If you need somewhere quiet to sit and have a good cry, please be our guest. As long as there's nothing wrong with the coffee?'

Despite her sad state, George smiled. 'No, the coffee's fine, thank you. It's a remarkably good blend, actually.'

'We don't spend a fortune on the decor here. The surfers

won't notice what colour the place is painted – as long as it's not peeling off. I do my best to make it more interesting with my picture of Volkswagon cars. But I put a lot of effort in finding really vibrant coffee beans. I drink plenty of the stuff myself. Would you like a second mug?'

George hesitated for a moment and the owner took that as a 'yes'. Before she could say any more, he had opened the door of his cage, taken her mug, walked to the counter at the other end and ordered two refills. A minute later he was sitting on the other side of the table, watching her thoughtfully. 'I'm assuming from your trim shape that you don't take sugar?'

The small act of kindness made George cry even more. All the time she was living in London she had to put on a brave front. She knew she mustn't show any vulnerability to her clients while she was at work; but she needed to look equally in control at home for the sake of her teenage daughter. She had felt little urge to go out anywhere. Her London friends, not knowing quite what to do, had largely left her alone after the early days of bereavement.

Polly, too, had been at an awkward age. She was no longer a malleable child but not old enough to be left for long on her own.

The result had been that she had put on a mask of control that had now been in place for so long it held back her deeper feelings.

Here, with this kind, older man, whom she didn't know - had never met - in an obscure place where no-one knew her, this control suddenly dissolved. For five minutes floods of tears came.

The owner said nothing but sipped his own mug of coffee. Obviously his finance work was not that urgent.

'I lost my husband, you see. Five months ago. And I've not really come to terms with it.'

'You're a visitor here, I think? Is there some reason why Polzeath has reminded you of him?'

'We used to come here for holidays – ten years ago. With our little daughter, Polly – as she was then. They were wonderful times. Mark really loved surfing.'

There was a pause. George sipped her drink. The owner was in no hurry to speak; in truth, there wasn't much he could say.

'Mark and I were so close. At least, I thought we were. It's hard to believe it has all come to an end.'

'Was he . . . was he taken by some illness?'

'No, it was nothing like that. If he'd slipped away slowly, say from cancer, that would have been terrible; but it would have given me time to prepare myself – and our daughter. No, he was killed in a plane crash in the back of beyond.'

George whimpered, 'But what I don't know is what the hell he was doing there. Some bloody town I'd never heard of. No-one seemed to know; or at least to be willing to tell me. And as time goes on that makes me wonder how close we really were.'

She stopped, suddenly too angry to say any more.

The owner felt the time had come to speak. 'There are a lot of things going on beneath the surface of life. Not all of them malign. Sometimes good things – protective things, keeping people safe, for example – are best done undercover, without any fanfare. Just because you don't know what your husband was doing on the plane when he was killed doesn't mean it was something bad or dishonourable. You were obviously close to Mark. Hang on to the wonderful memories he's left you. Those are true enough.'

George sniffed once more. She swallowed hard. 'Thank you.

Thank you for listening. It's been good to cry but I feel a lot better now. My name's George, by the way; George Gilbert. I'm around here for a fortnight. Maybe I'll drop in again.'

'And my name is Quentin; Quentin Arnold. My father started this cafe fifty years ago; I've been down here running it for the last twenty.'

'I'm glad we've been some help,' he added. 'And do come again. I promise you the coffee will still be delicious.'

CHAPTER 19

The eureka moment for Peter Travers had come when he woke at three on Friday morning. He thought about the idea and it seemed to make sense; and allowed him to sleep peacefully for the rest of the night. And next morning, when the idea seemed worthy of further exploration, it caused him to drive over once more to Wadebridge.

Only this time he was not visiting the Environment Agency office itself but the Black Nails salon below.

When he got there, soon after nine, the salon had only just opened. There was no queue of customers waiting their turn and the waft of vapours from the mixture of cosmetic creams being applied was not yet overpowering. The assistant at the front desk could see he was not a run-of-the-mill customer and quickly fetched her boss to deal with him.

'I'm interested in the tattoo side of your business,' he began.

'Yes sir. We're the main tattooing practitioner around these parts. Been in the business for over a decade. What sort of tattoo did you have in mind? We can ink into your skin animals from Africa, fish and birds from everywhere - or of course a load of black magic symbols. We can do stars and we can do flowers. Our most popular patterns are in this book here. Would you like to take a look?'

'No, no, I don't want a tattoo for myself.'

'Oh, I see, sir, it's for your partner. Does she have many tattoos already?'

'Not as far as I know. You see – '

'It's to be a surprise. Well, that's a nice idea, sir, but generally we find that the person receiving the tattoo really needs a positive attitude of their own towards it. You might like the thought of your girl's belly being covered with green mermaids, say, but ultimately it has to be her choice.'

Travers wondered how the conversation had been so swiftly derailed. He wasn't married and didn't even have a girlfriend. He knew what he'd come in for; how had he failed so dismally to express it?

While he was still thinking, the manager continued. 'After all, being given a tattoo is a painful process and not easy to reverse. In fact removing a tattoo takes longer and is even more painful than having it inked on the first place. It takes laser action to remove the ink from below the skin surface. So your partner shouldn't have one at all unless she plans to keep it.'

Unless he took charge soon, Travers could see himself leaving with a mermaid on his bottom. He held up his hand and managed to halt the flow of words.

'Can we start again please? We seem to have got off the wrong foot. You see, this uniform I'm wearing, it's not a fancy dress: I'm here on police business.'

The manager was surprised but not fazed. She met a wide range of people in this business with a variety of needs. Soon the policeman found himself in the salon's inner office with a large mug of coffee in his hands.

'I can't tell you all the details. What I can tell you is that one part of the investigation is about a lost identity. And it occurred to me that tattoo marks might throw some light on the problem.'

'Mm. Go on.'

'Well, let's assume the girl I'm interested in had a tattoo here at Black Nails, say within the last ten years. What sort of record would you keep of such a transaction?'

'You might be in luck. We keep much tighter records on tattooing than on the other aspects of our business. I wouldn't admit this to our customers but cosmetics are fairly superficial. Even when they go wrong a little patience will generally put them right.'

'Say if you give someone an orange hair dye that looks grotesque, it will eventually grow out.'

'Exactly. But for tattoos it's different. The Federation of Tattooists insists on all its members keeping records for tattoo work in case of future litigation - or new research findings. After all, injecting ink under your skin is a serious business. For example, if some dye that we injected had adverse side effects, then we'd need to know exactly which of our customers had been affected; or, conversely, to assure someone else who contacted us that the dye had not been used on them at all.'

'Sounds good. So what do these records cover?'

'First of all name, address, phone number, email; and their doctor and other contact details. And date of birth. And we ask, if they move away – which of course they often do, they're mostly young - that they tell us their new address details.'

'Would the same apply if they got married and changed their name?'

The manager nodded then continued. 'Next we list parts of the body treated in each session and the date of that session. And for each part of the body, the pattern applied, and its size, colour and the needle and ink details.'

'And if the person came back later on, for a second tattoo, would that record be connected to the first?'

'It would. It's not a computerised system; it's all on cards. Less to go wrong and it means we can't be hacked.'

The manager sounded confident. 'We keep separate sets for men and for women, mind. The men used to be more frequent visitors for tattoos, but these days both are equally common. Each set of records runs alphabetically by surname. We find that's the most useful order. But if you wanted to search for tattoos of, say, a red lion on the upper left arm, you'd need to work through the whole lot looking for that particular tattoo.'

'That sounds pretty comprehensive. The data is at least safe from hackers; but how secure are the cards?'

'They're kept in that locked cabinet over there and the office itself is locked at night. I have the only key. The new entries are put in to that in-tray over there each evening. I generally add them in to the established records once a week. There are usually a dozen new cards to go in – more, though, in the summer months than in the winter.'

The policeman did some mental arithmetic. 'So there are perhaps five hundred cards a year being added – maybe five thousand in total?'

'Something like that. Anyway, that's our records. I've told you all I can. Now, can you tell me more about this missing person and what sort of tattoo they might be displaying?'

Peter Travers sighed. 'I wish I could. And what makes it worse is that I can't even explain to you why I can't. But could I ask you one or two more general questions, please?'

'Sure.'

'For a woman, say in her early thirties, if she was going to have a tattoo, which part of the body would she tend to favour for it?'

'Fashion - and keeping up with one's friends - will be the

driving factors. They might have a tattoo anywhere on their body. But the most common starting point is one of their wrists or arms; or an ankle. Even establishment figures, like the Prime Minister's wife, have those nowadays. That way it's easy to show off. Then, later on, if they want more, they might go on to a tattoo on the shoulders or the neck – or even further down the body, out of sight of everyone except their lover.'

'And do many folk have their tattoos solely on the body?'

'I would say not many, of either sex. But having a tattoo is very addictive. Once you've got one you'll want another. That makes it very good for our business. I should say that the majority of folks with tattoos eventually have them on both their limbs and their torso. Does that help at all?'

Travers thought for a moment.

'Our problem is a white woman, in her early thirties, who's gone missing from somewhere around here. We know that she doesn't have any tattoos or any other distinctive features on her torso. But we suspect, for reasons I'm afraid I'm not able to explain, that she might have something distinctive and memorable on her arms and legs.'

The policeman paused for a moment. Was there anything else he could add in?

'And the other thing we know is that she hasn't been seen since the beginning of August.'

'Well our records could help with that. Look, it's Friday: I won't be doing anything with them today. Would you like to borrow them to look through over the weekend? That should give you long enough - if you work at it with one or two of your colleagues.

'But they are an important part of our business. Bring them back, please, on Monday morning.'

CHAPTER 20

While Peter Travers was battling with multiple tattoo records, George Gilbert was pursuing a more conventional form of data. She had discovered from Paddy Watmough that Friday would be a convenient time to revisit his office. She wanted the chance to look through his data relating to the Doom Bar.

When she arrived at the office, she found Watmough was off site for the morning and she was once more confronted by Walsh. He clearly resented the respect his boss was giving her. It was fortunate, George thought, that Watmough had been clear to his deputy what she could do or it might have been a very short visit.

'All the historical data's kept in this office,' Walsh explained, as he escorted George through a spacious main office (presumably his boss's) to the small room behind, which had no windows but had filing cabinets on every wall. 'There's a photocopier out there in the corridor. You can copy as much as you like, my boss said, but you mustn't take any of the original material away. It's our only copy.'

George saw that all the filing cabinets were labelled; the oldest one contained "Miscellaneous Channel data". She pointed to it.

'Is that where what I'm after will be kept?'

'Yes. We keep this room locked, so all the cabinets are open. The top two drawers have got the dredging details –

vessel maintenance, contracts , personnel records and so on; and also the weekly performance on moving the sand in the Camel.'

George smiled at the odd phrase; it would be more usual to talk about "moving the camel in the sand". But she doubted whether Walsh would appreciate the joke. The sour-faced man continued.

'In the bottom drawer we keep the monthly records of the Doom Bar's location. There may be a causal link between the two topics – that's what you're after, I gather - but they've certainly got something in common: sand.'

George decided to ignore his cynical tone. 'That's great. Just one or two other items and you can leave me in peace. Firstly, is there any chance I could have a chair, please? Secondly, do you have a coffee machine somewhere in these offices? And lastly, where can I find the ladies toilet?'

From Walsh's attitude, George might have asked for a luxury bed, a four course meal and a Jacuzzi. But eventually she was supplied and left alone to begin the data collection.

She decided to begin with the Doom Bar records. These were a series of hand-drawn shapes on an outline map of the shores of the Camel estuary. The charts were dated from April 1960 up to July 2008. Occasionally they were accompanied by a scribbled note.

A huge amount of effort must have gone into maintaining these. Glancing at the notes, George learned that the charts had been compiled by someone in a small boat, going out to survey the Doom Bar at a day-time low tide, around the start of the month.

She remembered Bill telling her that the position of the Doom Bar could be inferred from the line of waves in the middle of the estuary. These were caused by the shallow depth as the swell of the sea ebbed and flowed over the high sand.

Sometimes bad weather had meant the survey was delayed for a day or two – sometimes by up to a week. Once or twice the weather had been so bad that no survey had been carried out at all. But this was unusual; for most months a survey was recorded.

A massive amount of photocopying lay ahead of her: five hundred sheets. Fortunately the survey date was on the sheet, so it was just a matter of working a decade at a time, feeding the charts one by one into the machine. There was no time to do any analysis. George took care to keep the copies she had produced separate, adding them to an empty folder she had brought. The originals she carefully replaced in the drawer.

It was after two and a half hours of slog, as she reached the final year, that George came across something which was not part of the raw data. It was a one-page letter to Paddy Watmough in April 2008. Almost certainly the page had got caught between the chart itself and the note adding a few comments. It was easy to imagine how, in the hurly burly of a busy office, this could have happened.

George almost ignored it: it was none of her business. But she had been worn down by repetitive photocopying and was glad to be diverted.

The letter was headed 'Background Monitoring: Liaison'.

It said: 'Review meetings for 2008 will take place fortnightly, starting on Saturday April 5th, and continuing until further notice. This is a vital part of tracking local developments. The location will be the snug of the Fourways Inn in St Minver. Meetings will begin at 10.30 am sharp. Please come prepared to share news and to be briefed for up to two hours.'

The letter concluded with an undecipherable squiggle.

George had no idea what it was about. She thought about photocopying the letter along with all the maps, but that seemed underhand. Watmough might have said she could copy as much as she liked, but he wouldn't mean her to include this.

But, for some reason, it felt slightly less underhand for her to retrieve her camera and take a picture of the letter, before attaching it back to the map. Her only reason for doing so was curiosity: it was intriguing and she wanted to think more about it at her leisure.

Once the Doom Bar maps had all been copied, George needed a break before tackling the dredging data. She found the coffee machine and helped herself. Not like Galleon cafe but better than nothing.

The machine was in an open plan office and Walsh spotted her. 'Have you finished yet?'

'The Doom Bar maps are copied. Next I'm onto the dredging.'

'Be as fast as you can. We like to shut the office early on Friday afternoons.' George wondered if this would be true if Watmough was around, but she was not in a position to argue. She hastened back to her storeroom.

Fortunately, one of the office staff had been through the dredging records at the end of each year and copied the weekly sand-dredged totals onto a single sheet. So it was simply a matter of copying these annual summaries.

George developed a routine of opening each year's file, extracting the summary, photocopying it and returning the original to the file. She had the summaries from 1960 onwards all copied inside an hour. She was on her final year when Walsh appeared.

'We're locking up in five minutes.'

'I've just about finished.'

Walsh flipped through her folder of copied data as she put the last file back into the cabinet drawer. 'Exciting bedtime reading.'

'I hope so,' she replied. She was relieved that there was no copy of the peculiar letter to be found in the folder. She would not like to give Walsh any hold over her - ethical or otherwise.

A few minutes later, her belongings under her arm, George found herself escorted from the harbour offices into the cold light of day.

Glancing at her watch, she saw that it was only half past two. Could she turn her early exit to advantage? Maybe it was not too late to buy herself lunch upstairs in the Shipwright Inn.

CHAPTER 21

Later that Friday, Peter Travers, back in Delabole, phoned Marcus Chadwick once more in Exeter. He'd remembered that the DNA analysis on the torso had been promised to the Inspector for the previous afternoon.

The boxes he had been lent by Black Nails had been unexpectedly heavy. Travers didn't want to start ploughing through thousands of tattoo records for potential victims if pure science had already allowed the woman to be identified.

There was the usual delay before he got through. The man must have a huge number of cases under his command, he guessed, with lots of staff. How many were also under his control was perhaps more debatable. Pressure on senior police resources in Exeter must be intense.

'Good morning sir, Peter Travers here, from Delabole.'

'It may only be morning in Cornwall, Travers, but it's afternoon here in Devon. I wasn't aware there was a timeline at the Tamar. What's the matter?'

'I was wondering about the results of the post mortem and the DNA analysis, sir.'

'Oh yes; good job you caught me: I was on my way out. There's a lot going on here. Yes, I had the DNA analysis through yesterday evening. It doesn't help much, I'm afraid. We haven't got any match for it in the National DNA database.'

'That's disappointing, sir. So the victim wasn't a criminal?'

'Well, not a known one with a record. She hadn't been in a

UK prison, anyway. She could have been a prostitute, for example. We don't have DNA on all of them – they keep moving around, in any case.

'Or she could have been a minor gang character,' Chadwick continued, 'who a rival gang fell out with. A gangster's moll, for example, might never have been arrested. But if she was exceptionally pretty that might have made someone else jealous, which could in turn have been a motive for murder.'

'How about the post mortem, sir? Any more details from that?'

'They've completed the analysis of the contents of her stomach. Her last meal was fish and chips. With a couple of glasses of wine. And she smoked a little, but I think I told you that before. Hardly pinpoints her identity, does it?'

Travers eyed the boxes of tattoo records on his desk. He wished he didn't need to tackle them.

'No trace of poison, say, or anything that might have been used to put her to sleep?'

'Whatever she died of, Forensics say, it wasn't poisoning. Not a well known one, anyway. The most likely cause is some sort of head wound. The body itself seems quite healthy: nothing odd about it at all.'

'Except that it was missing a head. And then tied up and hidden in a remote pool.'

'Yes, I suppose so. If she hadn't been beheaded and then drowned she might have been quite healthy, gone on living for a long time.'

'So what are we going to do now, sir? Do we have a plan?' There was silence at the other end of the line. Travers sensed he was starting to dig himself into a hole. 'Or . . . do Forensics have any suggestions?'

'Well, we've been given some new software here recently I thought I could try. It's got a vast number of statistics about the weight and measurements of each part of the human body, based on a huge sample from different ages and backgrounds. This allows it to extrapolate statistics on the remainder of a body from whatever bits are already known.'

'So it would be able to estimate the woman's height and weight from measurements taken from our torso?'

'It'd certainly do that. But it might do a lot more. We can't expect it produce a photo-fit facial image, but it might give a broader impression.'

'Let's hope she was some sort of freak then, sir. A fat woman from a circus would be something we could get our teeth into. That would improve our chances of identifying her no end. Or a contortionist, maybe?'

Chadwick wasn't sure if Travers was joking or simply thinking so far outside the box that he'd misplaced the lid. Just trying to seem keen? Best to humour him.

'If she'd been a flame swallower I think Forensics would have noticed. They've had her throat to work on anyway. We'll have to see. The torso looked a fairly normal size to me. Anyway, I've asked the backroom boys to make it a priority. They should have something for us early next week. So give me a ring on Tuesday and we'll see where we go next.'

Travers thought, as he put down the phone, that Chadwick had not asked if he had made any progress at his end of the investigation. He hadn't even been asked about his visit to the Environment Agency, which had at least given an earliest date for the crime. Low expectations of junior staff, he thought morosely, did not do much for police morale.

But, in truth, he had found nothing earth-shattering. One

date was not much good on its own. He still had the daunting tattoo records to work through. Might he have more to offer the Inspector by Tuesday?

If his colleague didn't come back, how would he complete the mission? Back at the start – less than two months ago - there had been two of them – and they were both needed. True, it was his boss that had obtained the equipment. But it had taken them both – working as a team – to put the pieces in position.

So how on earth would he, working on his own, collect it all back, once their mission was over? And that time, he judged, was coming soon.

CHAPTER 22

George had battled with herself as to whether or not to tell Bill about the peculiar letter she had come across in the Harbour office. She probably would have told him - if she had not taken that photograph.

But if she broached the subject and, during discussion, he asked her if she had a copy of the letter, what would she say? She would find it hard to tell her relative-in-law a complete lie. On the other hand, she didn't think he would be impressed to discover that she had been snooping on a local official. It would probably confirm his worst fears about business behaviour in London. And she wanted so very much to stay on good terms with her Uncle. He was, as she well knew, the nearest blood relation to Mark.

In the end she decided to say nothing. But the letter was bugging her. What "developments" was it talking about? Did it mean someone was keeping an eye on PRAM; and if so who? The letter had been sent to Watmough; did that mean he had a foot in both camps? For her peace of mind she needed to do something.

George consulted her map. St Minver was two and a half miles up the road from Rock. There would be no harm, surely, in being at the Inn – purely as a customer - at half past ten on the following morning, just to see if anything happened. The series of meetings implied by the letter might well have drawn to a close. If that were so it would be much easier to put the letter aside: a historic puzzle, but not a contemporary event.

Fortunately the household she was staying in did not take much account of weekends. On Saturday morning a cooked breakfast was still on offer at eight o'clock sharp; Bill's naval habits had not been abandoned.

'I thought I'd go for a walk this morning,' George remarked. 'I've gathered lots of material, I could use some peace and quiet to sift it through.'

'Good idea. I'm not around much today. I've got some running about to do this morning then I'm on duty at Stepper Point this afternoon with young Toby again, bless him. He's still being trained. And he hasn't spotted a phantom swimmer for several weeks.'

George was pleased it was so easy to slip away without questions being asked. She'd feared that Bill might offer to come with her.

It was a fine-looking morning. Soon she was down on the jetty and aboard the first ferry of the day to Rock. The two-mile journey up the road to St Minver had more inclines than she had expected; but she was still able to reach her goal, a little out of breath, soon after ten.

St Minver was a small but attractive village, boasting a traditional stone church with a tall steeple. The Fourways Inn, a solid grey stone building, stood at the crossroads. George was pleased to see that free internet access was advertised in the doorway. She had her laptop with her, containing her meeting notes. This would make it easier to justify staying longer if necessary.

The analyst went inside. It was dim. There were no lights on, she presumed she was the first customer of the day. She took the opportunity to explore. After a few minutes she came across what she guessed must be the snug: a small room at the back, with an oak table and comfortable chairs, overlooking the garden. But it was not occupied.

The main bar-room itself had several alcoves. She chose one with a good view of the corridor leading to the snug and set down her rucksack to claim the chair. The alcove was even worse lit than the main room. Then she approached the bar and gave a 'ding' on the small bell at the side.

A few minutes slipped by and then someone, whom she took to be the landlady, appeared.

'Good morning, my dear. You're early. Are you here for Mr Applegate's meeting?'

'No. I didn't know there was a meeting. I'm on my own. I wondered, could I use the internet to check a few things on my computer? And could I also have a pot of your special blend Kenyan coffee?'

'That'll be fine. It'll take me a few minutes. Where are you sitting?' George pointed to the alcove. 'Have you got power and enough light? Plenty of tables to choose from.'

'Where I am is fine. It's better for me if it's gloomy. I can see my computer screen better with no reflections. It's beautifully peaceful here. I hope Mr Applegate's meeting won't be too noisy?'

'Oh no, they're tucked away in the snug. As quiet as mice, you'd never know they were here. They come every fortnight. Goodness knows what they find to talk about. They don't even drink the beer.' She bustled away and George resumed her seat.

So the meeting was on. The invitation she had come across suggested Watmough would be one of those attending. She had only met him once, at the PRAM committee, where she had been wearing her business suit. Now she was in her cagoule and walking clothes and her hair was no longer tied up. Would he still recognise her? Better if he didn't.

Hastily she arranged her scarf so it covered some of her face, sat with her back close to the unlit wall and flipped up the lid of her computer in front of her. It was the best she could do. Good enough unless the harbour manager came right into the bar – but she gathered the group weren't here for the beer. How many others would be attending?

There was a commotion outside. Then a smart-looking man, wearing a high-quality suit and carrying a leather briefcase, strode down the corridor and into the snug. He looked like the man in charge: perhaps this was Applegate?

George glanced at her watch: it was now 10.28. Clearly the meeting's convenor was a stickler for time-keeping. Who would follow?

At that moment the landlady appeared, carrying a tray holding a pot of coffee and a plate of biscuits. She headed over to George's alcove. It was, unfortunately, the same moment that the next attendees of the snug meeting arrived. To her irritation, George found her view obstructed.

Two people went in while her view was blocked. Frustrated, she shifted her position. Peering round the generous figure of the landlady she recognised a figure who from the rear looked like Paddy Watmough, striding down the corridor and into the snug. He was accompanied by someone that she'd seen somewhere before – but she could not, for the life of her, remember where.

The landlady went back behind the bar leaving George with a clear view. But in the vacated space nothing was happening. How many more would go into the snug? She poured her coffee and waited with baited breath.

Five minutes later no-one else had come. It was obviously a select meeting. The landlady did not even go in to offer them coffee.

How long before it would end? George retrieved her camera and looked at the photo of the invitation letter. The last sentence implied it could last for a couple of hours. Was it worth hanging about to see them all come out again?

Two conflicting thoughts struck her. On the one hand, the meeting might be shorter. But on the other hand, she couldn't be sure they would stay out of the bar afterwards. They might not want beer but they might still be glad of some Kenyan coffee – it was high quality.

If she didn't want Watmough to know she had been here it would be better to leave before that happened.

George finished her first cup, had a leisurely refill then put some of the biscuits into her cagoule pocket. She would be glad of them later. She walked to the bar and rang the bell. 'Can I have the bill please?'

A few moments later she was walking out. The snug overlooked the back garden so she would not be seen. Her route took her past the Inn car park. Glancing, she saw there were just a few cars there – presumably all owned by the men in the snug.

She had not much to show so far for her early morning start. George retrieved her notebook and took a note of their numbers. The nearest one, a dark blue Golf, had the number PRZ 2857.

George was a mathematician. The number was not that memorable, but it was the first four digits of 2/7, expressed as a decimal. She remembered finding on her first calculator that 1/7 was 0.142857, 2/7 was 0.285714 and so on. The discovery had made her want to study numbers more and led to a maths degree.

In her eagerness to move away from the Fourways George had set out away from Rock. It was a quiet lane through beautiful rolling countryside. In the far distance she could see a stone tower on the edge of a cliff. Consulting her map she deduced that this must be Stepper Point, on the far side of the River Camel. Somewhere near here Bill and Toby would be keeping watch that afternoon.

The analyst wandered along the lane, musing on the meeting she had glimpsed, wondering what it was all about and trying to work out a way of learning more.

There was no evidence of anything illegal. But why should anyone want to meet every other Saturday at the little Inn? If it was a bunch of layabouts she might have guessed they were betting. If they were youngsters, were they swapping song recordings? But the people she had seen going in looked smart. She couldn't believe that Applegate - or Watmough for that matter - would waste time on fruitless activity. So what on earth brought them together?

As she walked, she passed a house set back from the road which had taken the need for security seriously. It had a strong fence, the gate was closed, there was a hut beside it and there was a security camera on the entrance.

Out of line with relaxed attitude elsewhere? She knew Bill did lock his door in Padstow but it was only a standard lock: he obviously thought there was no need for anything more secure.

It was good to get some fresh air. Her plan was to go back to Bill's and work for the rest of the afternoon.

Consulting her map she saw a minor road which would lead her to a path through a golf course then back to Polzeath. From there she could take the path back to Rock and over the ferry to Padstow.

While she was in Polzeath it would be good to visit Quentin at the Galleon cafe. She was feeling more buoyant today. Good to show him she wasn't always in floods of tears.

But she was disappointed when she got to Polzeath and the Galleon cafe to discover that Quentin Arnold was not at his desk. 'He'll be back this afternoon,' the assistant told her.

Too late. She had to get back to Padstow by lunch time. Work was needed for the next PRAM committee, now only two days away.

CHAPTER 23

On the Sunday afternoon Bill seemed to realise that he had been virtually inaccessible to George for the last week.

'Would you like to go for a stroll?' he asked. 'We could walk out on the Coast Path as far as the Stepper Point and see some of the Lookout watchers in action.' It was offered as a way of making amends. But George was busy too, battling through her analysis for the next PRAM meeting.

'I'd love to,' she replied, 'but I can't spend all afternoon on it. I need something coherent to say to your next meeting.'

For a moment Bill looked despondent. Then he had an idea. 'Tell you what, I could drive us to Crugmeer. Then we could just walk round the Stepper Point headland as far as the Lookout. That would speed it all up: we could be there and back in an hour and a half.'

George felt she could hardly refuse. Uncle Bill obviously wanted to show her something of his life while she was staying with him. The trip might also give her chance to question him further about why he had asked her down.

George seized her wind-proof cagoule. Her uncle fetched his ' car from the garage down the road and the pair set off.

'Bill, I love being here but did you really need a consultant for PRAM?'

Her uncle laughed. 'I thought you'd see through the charade eventually. Why does anyone ever hire a consultant?'

'Well, they know the solution they want but they think it's

easier to achieve by using an outsider to present it. So what are you hoping for?'

'When we started off last June there seemed to be several good ideas on the table. But I soon realised Hamish Robertson was by far the leading player. He wanted to spend big money. And his Game Park would radically change Padstow. I wondered if I was the only one worrying about that. So I contrived to invite you down to get us an objective view. I thought that would give us all a chance to take stock before we went too far.'

'Thank goodness for that. I've picked up several issues and I wasn't sure how ruthlessly to pursue them. What you say gives me a lot more freedom to follow them through and see where they lead.'

Crugmeer turned out to be a minor hamlet north of Padstow on an extremely narrow road. They followed the road as far as they could, to a point where it widened and several other cars were parked. 'Two of these belong to my colleagues,' explained her uncle. 'I normally walk up here straight from Padstow – it's my weekly exercise; and a very pleasant stroll.'

They got out and Bill pointed out a track that set out left, across a grassy field. A few moments later George could see the top of the cliffs ahead of them. 'That's Butter Hole,' commented Bill, as they reached and then walked round the top of a sharply-curved inlet, with the sea swirling far below. Ahead of them, across the rough ground, George could see a grey stone stack which looked like an overfed chimney. 'And that's Stepper Point itself,' Bill added.

They pressed on. The Lookout was a couple of hundred yards from the Point, a small hut at almost the highest point on the headland with a door at the rear. George followed Bill inside.

The atmosphere inside was calm. There was never cause for panic; and hardly ever cause for alarm. Bill knew the two on duty well. Both were wearing the official, dark-blue Lookout sweaters. George was introduced. 'My niece,' Bill explained proudly, 'down from London.'

George shook their hands, then stepped forward and looked out of the tinted windows. Straight ahead was the mouth of the Camel estuary, with Polzeath and its beach on the far side. There were plenty of people out in the waves with their surf boards or body boards.

To the left the cliffs rose steadily towards the headland on the far side. She remembered this was Pentire Head. She had walked up there with Mark and Polly the last time they'd all been here.

In the other direction a low cliff led round towards another beach, more sheltered and less crowded. 'Which one's that?'

'Daymer Bay,' replied one of the lookouts. 'It's too far up the estuary for serious surfing – no big waves. But it's great for families with young children who just want peace and quiet and sand to play on. And the odd kite surfer. There's one there now. Here: take a look.'

He pointed to a pair of heavy-duty binoculars mounted on the desk beneath the window. It took George a minute to work out how to focus them. Then she saw a kite surfer, bouncing over the waves, with the two ropes to the kite above. As she watched, he adroitly completed a turn then set off back the other way.

'George, you were asking about wrecks in the estuary,' said Bill. 'Here's where some of them ended up.' He pointed to a map on the notice board behind him.

George let go of the binoculars and walked over to see. It

was a chart of the estuary, with boat names splattered across it.

'What period does this cover?'

'All the last century. Several wrecks a year.'

'Were these small boats?'

'One or two were large. The biggest was the Antoinette. You remember, I told you about her: carried a hundred tons of coal. Went down in 1895 but seen again on the Doom Bar a century later. She's mostly sunk in the sand. You can't see her except at very low tides. You can't actually see her from the Lookout, she's down below those cliffs.'

George studied the chart; then glanced at some of the other notices and equipment. By now the three men were in deep conversation. Suddenly she remembered her work for PRAM.

'Bill, I hate to disturb you but is there any chance we could go back soon? You promised me we'd be back in an hour and a half.'

'My dear, of course. My colleagues here don't need my advice. But if you like we could walk back round part of the Coast Path. It's not much further and we could see the Doom Bar from above. It's low tide about this time, so we should see something.'

This time Bill led them down a narrow footpath and onto the main Coast Path. The lower reaches of the River Camel could be seen ahead with Padstow in the distance. In the haze George could just see a girder bridge beyond. She remembered from her interviews that this was where the Camel Trail crossed Little Petherick Creek.

A short distance along Bill pointed to the estuary below. 'Look George. Can you see that line of waves? There's a second line, there, a bit further along. Those are where the incoming tide passes over the Doom Bar. It's the sand below that causes the waves.'

George stood for a minute and reflected. It seemed almost impossible that this gentle sandbank had contributed over the years to so much destruction. Obviously it wasn't always so gentle.

After half a mile they reached a cluster of houses – Hawkers Cove. 'Up to the 1970s there was a lifeboat station here,' said Bill. 'But then the Doom Bar shifted its base to this side and the main channel ran down the far side instead. So the station had to be moved to the next headland round – that's Trevose Head. No point in having a lifeboat that's cut off every low tide.'

It was far better, thought George, to have these details explained directly. It made more sense to see the Doom Bar in context than having it pointed out on the map. But when she thought about it, everything she was doing in Padstow was a crash course in one aspect or another of its history or geography. Her challenge was to help channel these details into a sensible plan for the future.

The road through Crugmeer would have led to Hawkers Cove. So now it was not far back to Bill's car. It was as they reached it that a cloud spread over George's hitherto blue-sky day.

For she noticed, as they approached the car, that it was the same dark-blue colour as the one she had seen the day before at the Fourways Inn. Then she saw the number and, to her horror, she recognised the same distinctive sequence of digits.

CHAPTER 24

Monday September 8th. Dr Brian Southgate hummed to himself as he backed his car out of his drive in Delabole and set out for his monthly Area Health meeting in Rock. He didn't especially like these meetings – most of his fellow doctors were too solemn, and dealing with the machinations of the Department of Health was hardly a bundle of laughs - but it was a relief to be away from Delabole. At this time of year his patients could wait slightly longer for their treatment.

As he drove he thought about his most recent conversation with Peter Travers. Southgate's wife, Alice, was out on her weekly visit to her family. The couple had no children and he'd taken the chance to socialise for an hour in the Trewarmett Inn.

Inevitably the men had found themselves talking about progress on the mystery torso found just up the road the week before. Travers was not one to reveal police business to outsiders but Southgate had already given part of his Sunday to help set the case in motion.

The two had been best friends since their schooldays. The policeman knew he could express his hopes and frustrations to the doctor without risk of his words going any further. And he had no immediate colleague within the police who could perform a similar role.

There was little more that could be said on the cause of death. Southgate had already observed that the lack of bloodstains on the sack meant that the body had been dead long before entering the sack – or the pool. And once he had concluded that the death had happened away from the pool, there was not much that could be deduced (so far) about the motives or circumstances that lay behind it. But the context was elusive – unknowable - until the torso had been identified.

Then Southgate had been staggered to discover that Travers was up to his neck in tattoo records. The policeman had spent practically the whole weekend working through the records borrowed from the Black Nails salon.

'Explain to me, one more time, exactly why you think this woman – one with no marks at all on her body - might have had a tattoo,' he had requested.

'Well, the process began when I asked myself why the murderer would cut off the victim's arms simply to hide their fingerprints: if that was their only motivation, why not just chop off their fingers? It'd be a lot less work.'

'And on that line, I suppose, why remove their legs? I'm sure the police don't have records of toe-prints.'

'No, they don't. Then I learned on Friday that we have no match on our database for her DNA. But if we can't recognise her DNA she can't have been through our criminal system. So we wouldn't have had any fingerprint records to match, even if they'd still been attached to the body.'

'You mean the murderer had no need to hack off her arms just to avoid her identity being revealed by her fingerprints?'

'As it turned out, no. Of course, they might not have been certain of that. And unless they'd known her for many years, that would be a gamble. But if they followed these things at all – even on a television murder mystery - they would know nothing could stop her DNA being extracted once the body was discovered.

'So, Brian, I started to ask myself why else might he (or she, I suppose) have gone to all that trouble?'

'Well, could it have been weight reduction? Her arms, legs and head together would make up a third of her body weight. Without them she was easier to cart up the hill and heave into the pool.'

'I suppose so. But it's a hell of an effort simply to reduce bodyweight. She didn't look that heavy, to be honest: certainly not overweight. More tests are being done in Exeter expanding on the measurements from the torso; we should know by next week, all being well, how much she weighed – that's before she was chopped up, I mean.'

Travers had taken another swig from his cider. 'Then I had an idea. It occurred to me that another reason for her being dismembered might be that there were marks on her arms or legs, which couldn't easily be removed by the murderer - but which might be easy to identify.'

'What sort of marks?'

'It came to me in the middle of the night. After I'd seen a salon in Wadebridge. The most obvious of those would be tattoos.'

'Come on, Peter, I'm sure that even in these security-enhanced times the police don't have a national tattoo database. What would you have done if you'd found, say, a light blue seagull on her left wrist?'

'Well, remember, we've been careful to avoid any publicity about the torso because we've so little to say.'

'Yes, the fact that the body's been found at all – and on the basis of the water quality data, within a month of it being dumped - is the police's only hidden weapon.'

'But with more facts it would all have been very different.

We could have gone public with the discovery of the torso; and had the pattern plastered across national television within twenty four hours.'

Travers had seen the doctor was still doubtful. 'You see, what I've found out this last week is that respectable tattooists keep detailed records of their customers, going back many years. So it's pretty likely that we would have had possible victims being suggested to us by the score, if we'd had a distinctive pattern we could publicise.'

Southgate remembered that he had been far from convinced. 'Peter, I read recently in the Guardian that twenty percent of the population have tattoos. They're fashion accessories, not thug status symbols. And if our victim did have a tattoo, you've no idea what it looked like. How on earth could you hope to get any further without arms or legs to work on?'

'Well, Black Nails in Wadebridge is the most likely place for someone living round here to have used. I visited them on Friday - nearly got tattooed by mistake. The manager tells me that most of their customers have got multiple tattoos on all parts of the body.'

'Yes, it's well known in medical circles that the ink they use is addictive. Arguably it should be covered by drug legislation.'

'Well, I'm just looking for the girls with no tattoos at all on their bodies, but with a distinctive pattern on the arms (and maybe the legs) that would be easy to recognise. The sort of thing an intelligent murderer would take some effort to remove.'

The policeman had taken a sip of his cider then continued, 'And then, from this list, I want any girls who've disappeared inside the last month.'

Southgate paused to consider.

'I suppose it might just work, if you're very lucky; and if we're dealing with a local girl, not someone dumped from Bristol. But it sounds a long shot to me. Surely there must be a better way?'

Southgate recalled that the two had argued round the point. But Peter Travers could be very stubborn. He remembered from their schooldays that once he got an idea into his head it was very hard for him to let it go again.

It seemed Travers' work over the weekend had produced a list of several hundred names. What he needed to do next was to find out if any of them had recently disappeared. The doctor had challenged, 'I don't see how a local policeman can check up on that lot, one by one, without raising a raft of unwanted publicity. Someone is going to be curious, aren't they?'

The doctor had suggested that Travers gave the list to the Black Nails manager and asked her to narrow it down. 'It's much more natural for her to ring each of these girls up over the next few days. She's bound to have some new manicure product she can tempt them with. At the same time she can make sure they're still alive. Then you can take further action over the few that might have disappeared.'

Even that was a long shot. But, as the doctor drove on towards Rock, that still seemed the best course to take.

It was towards the end of the Area Health meeting that Southgate, his mind wandering from the business before them, came up with a variant of his own. They were discussing the latest directive from the Department of Health. This dealt with extra measures of healthiness in young people and how early warnings might be picked up of long-term problems.

It was a meandering list and not well received. The mandarins in the Department, whatever their silky political skills, were not medically trained.

'In the good old days we doctors were simply there to treat patients as well as we could if and when they became ill,' muttered one of the older committee-men. 'Now they want us to go looking for business before half the patients are aware that they need us.'

Suddenly, it occurred to Southgate that a highly tattooed arm was not the only way a limb might be made more recognisable. He was oblivious of the next phase of the meeting as he pondered how this could be developed.

'Nearly finished; has anyone got any other business?' asked the chair of the meeting.

'Does anyone keep data on non-suicidal self injury?' Southgate blurted out.

'That's what we were discussing ten minutes ago,' replied the chair, slightly exasperated. 'I thought you weren't with it. Well, to cut a long story short, Dr Mary Ellis here offered to draw together data on the cases that each of our surgeries had on their books. Then we might do some analysis of our own which we can put back to the Department. Get them off our backs for a while. Do I take it you're offering to help?'

Brian Southgate had not intended to volunteer for anything. But it looked as if he had no choice if he wanted to take his idea any further.

CHAPTER 25

George had wrestled through the weekend with the odd meeting she had observed at the Fourways Inn, without it making any more sense. The fact that, apparently, Bill had been there too made it even odder. She had also worked hard on wider questions raised by the PRAM project, ready to give a short presentation at the next meeting.

On Monday morning she accompanied Bill down the hill to the Old Custom House. He had been out on Sunday evening, so there had been no good time to question him about the meeting in the snug.

The first part of the committee meeting consisted of progress reviews. George was not asked to make any comment, but she was relieved that the whole thing made a lot more sense than it had the week before. But some of the questions that had bothered her over the weekend were underlined. Finally, when everyone had spoken, she was given half an hour to present her observations.

'This is a very exciting venture,' she began. 'It's a real privilege to be invited here to share it with you. You've all spoken with a massive amount of enthusiasm; clearly huge amounts of thinking have gone on. But you chose to ask an outsider to help you. So what I want to do this morning is to ask you some questions that have occurred to me, as a sympathetic but disinterested outsider.'

'We need to be able to take constructive criticism,' replied the Major from his chairman's position. 'Just because we're enthusiastic doesn't mean it will all happen. Military history tells us that every worthwhile advance always had its critics. And sometimes – when the objective is flawed - those critics were right. Please continue.'

'Let me first summarise the main ideas being talked about. Then you can tell me if I've got anything massively wrong. And after that I'll give you a critique – or rather I'll sketch out some wider uncertainties.' George proceeded to summarise the various modernisation ideas, including lessons from her interviews during the previous week.

'I would say that's a good summary,' said the Major when she had finished. Other heads round the table nodded.

'Good. So here are some of the questions raised.' George looked round the table and smiled at them all. It was important they didn't take what she said next as a threat.

'I wondered, first of all, how we might summarise the overall PRAM objective. Various goals for the modernisation ideas were talked about this morning. But are we talking primarily about quality or quantity?

There was silence in the room: where was she heading?

George continued, 'To put it another way, is our vision that this area will encourage a more discerning class of visitor: one who appreciates and makes the most of the quality in what's on offer, so comes back time after time? Or are we primarily about attracting increased numbers?

'Of course, these aren't complete opposites. If Padstow and Rock are perceived as the high class end of Cornwall, that will bring more visitors as well. But if quality is the prime motive, the financial benefit will be less on extra numbers and more on the higher prices they'll be willing to pay.

'Conversely, if we're mainly interested in boosting numbers, at what time of year is that to be achieved? Are we talking primarily about ways of cramming more visitors in during high season; or about extending the parts of the year when visitors are encouraged to come? Because if Padstow is perceived as being overcrowded, that would make it harder to attract what you might term the "quality tourists".'

Some of those around the table looked unsure. But one or two others looked like they were keen to speak in response. At this stage George did not give them the chance.

'Another question that occurred to me was where PRAM stood on measures of performance: how will you judge whether or not you have succeeded? For example, are you keen on enhancing the environment around here and so attracting folk whom you might call "green"? Or are you primarily interested in maximising financial profit? Or in making more of the local history to encourage Cornish historians?'

Again there was pressure to respond. But it was an open question. George shrugged her shoulders and pressed on.

'As we all know, this part of Cornwall is very attractive – it's an Area of Outstanding Natural Beauty. But then, some might say, so is most of Cornwall. How might you stand out from the rest?

'One possible way might be to make yourselves what you might call environmentally attractive: for example, to widen the scope for bird watching in the Camel estuary.' She glanced at Hamish Robertson. 'That would be a different way of competing with the Eden Project than developing a Game Park. Or you could set yourselves to take the lead within Cornwall in addressing key questions raised by climate change.'

'Can you give us an example of what that might mean?' asked the Major.

'I've been fascinated, this last week, to learn about the Doom Bar. It provides a good name for the locally produced beer. But apart from that the sandbank seems to be regarded as a treacherous nuisance. But could we generate more of an interest in how it behaves? For example, is it a result of extremes of climate?

'I've been given access to some of the excellent data on the Doom Bar held by the Harbour authorities.' She smiled at Paddy Watmough then continued. 'I've not had long to look at it yet, but I picked out one or two points. I noticed that the Doom Bar changed its position substantially in late 1976. But if the hot, dry summer of 1976 prompted the Doom bar to swap sides, what might happen in future heat waves? If we understood what caused it to move, might Padstow be able to spend less on dredging – or to know, from the recent weather, when more dredging is needed?'

There was a still silence. George sensed the room was becoming restless. This was her idea rather than theirs. Better, she thought, to draw to a close.

'The last set of questions I've been wondering about is where the funding for all these ideas might come from. One or two of them, like the Game Park, are business ventures, which might – or might not - attract private capital. But others will need backing, either from the Cornwall Council or else from some local benefactor. Have you thought how this might happen? And have you done any work to see if the ideas are likely to be widely popular – and hence to prompt Council support?'

George stopped talking. There was a few seconds silence,

followed by competition to respond. Even for the Major it was a challenge to keep them all in order.

CHAPTER 26

So far Harriet Horsman had found no way to take her story further without some clue as to what had really happened after the fateful stag party. She had gleaned the context of the event, but none of the core.

Her encounters with Gwyneth Fry and Sergeant Travers had given her some information but not nearly enough for publication. In desperation she had even gone to see Kevin Rogers but he had been tight lipped and given away nothing at all.

On Monday evening she and her partner Janey were having a meal in the lounge of the Cornishman when she spotted Tommy Burton, on his own, perched on a bar stool and clasping a glass of cider. He seemed to be waiting for his friends but they might be a while coming. This was too good an opportunity to miss.

The aspiring journalist spent a moment working out a possible line of questioning. Then, with a muttered apology to her companion, she sidled across the bar and sat on the stool alongside him.

'Hi, my name's Harriet. I wondered if we could help one another.'

'Oh hi, I'm Tommy. Should I know you?'

'No, I don't think we've met. But we have a common interest in working out what happened to Kevin just over a week ago.'

'Well, perhaps we do. I might be willing to talk if I knew

anything but I've been baffled by Kevin's silence. I really don't know what took place. Sorry.' He turned away and looked carefully into his glass.

But Harriet wasn't so easily snubbed. 'I've been to see Sergeant Travers about the whole sequence. He helped tidy up the event afterwards, you know. He wouldn't tell me a lot but he did give me something.'

Despite his hostility, Tommy was intrigued. He turned back towards her. 'What?'

'Well, I learned it was a crime that was serious enough for him to have called out the Serious Crime Squad from Exeter: Detective Inspector Chadwick, no less. But what I can't figure out is what crime he came to look at. Did you see any signs of police tape around the place?'

'No, I didn't. To be honest, we didn't go all the way up to the Engine House on the Sunday. We could see from the road that Kevin had made his getaway.'

He paused for a moment. 'But that does sound serious: a real policeman, not just Travers. No wonder Kevin was so frightened when we caught up with him.'

'He was: told me so when I went to see him yesterday. Now I've pieced together what happened up to the point where you lads took him from the Inn, stripped him and left him tied to the railings of that Engine House. And I've met the dog-walker who found him and rescued him next morning: Gwyneth, she lives in Trewarmett. But she was as silent as Kevin, wouldn't say what happened next.'

'That's more or less where we got to from talking to Kevin. A data black hole. So as I said, we're stuck.'

'But whatever it was must have happened somewhere around the Engine House. Unless you took him somewhere else?'

'No. We went straight up the path from the road, round the back of the mound and into the Engine House. It was full moon, so we could see reasonably well.'

'And after you left him you went straight back down the hill?'

'Yes. Well, we stopped to throw his clothes over that fence into the quarry pool. Didn't want to cart them any further.'

'Course not. But did he know you'd done that?'

'Depends on how much he took in after we'd tied him up. We decided to do it before we started to walk down. I had to bundle his clothes together, you see, using his belt. We didn't bother to climb over the fence though, we just gave them a heave over the top.'

'I've had a look at that pool in daylight. There's a gap between the fence and the pool, with loads of brambles. Are you sure it went in?'

'Oh, the bundle went into the water alright. We all heard the splash.'

'But wouldn't that mean he would have to go right up to that pool next morning to rescue them?'

'It would depend on how much he remembered. Yes, I suppose he might.'

'So it's possible that it was whatever he found when he was fishing for his clothes that meant the police had to be called?'

Tommy began to reflect. But just at that moment his friends arrived. Harriet felt that she had learned all she could and it would be better to leave him in peace.

She still had half her meal to consume. But now she had something more definite to muse on.

CHAPTER 27

On Tuesday morning Sergeant Peter Travers braced himself once more for the marathon obstacle course of phoning his superior in Exeter. Even with his direct line to the Crime Squad he expected it would take several attempts before Chadwick was willing and able to take the call.

So he was pleasantly surprised, after only his second abortive attempt, when his own phone rang and he found Chadwick was on the line in person. The Inspector even sounded cheerful. That was a first, what on earth had happened?

'I've just got the report in from Forensics, produced using our new software,' he told Travers.

'Showing some urgency at last, eh. And it gives us something useful?'

'Well, it's limited, as we'd expect. But it does give us several new facts and some interesting projections.'

'Carry on, sir, my notebook is ready.'

'Hm, yes. Well, their first point is a projection of the victim's size. She was quite a tall woman, they say, around five feet eleven. And slim with it. She weighed around a hundred and forty pounds before they started her enforced trimming.'

'That's good. Better than average height and weight, anyway.'

'And they tell me that she'd not had any children but there are signs of a late abortion.'

'Can they tell if that was recent or a long time ago, sir?'

'Good question. It doesn't say here but I'll put it back to them.'

There was the sound of Chadwick turning the page. He continued, 'There are no traces of any banned substance in what's left of her blood. But they tell me, oddly, that she hadn't shaved under her arms.'

'Would the colour of that hair match the hair on her head?'

'Forensics tells me that's not certain but it's likely. In which case our victim was a red-head.'

'Or at least she would be if she hadn't dyed it to something else.'

'Quite. But why would she? A red-head is rather special.'

'Maybe to you and me, sir. But not everyone shares our tastes.'

The Inspector mused on this for a moment. Did he want to be bracketed in his tastes with the country sergeant? The trouble was, he didn't know if Travers was being subtly disrespectful or simply downright honest.

'There's just one more thing in this report. Forensics tells me they've done some detailed work on her muscles and her lungs. They say she was in good shape, in fact extremely fit. That must narrow it down.'

'OK sir, so she was tall, slim, red-haired and fit. But didn't shave under her arms. And they told us before that she was in her early thirties and smoked and drank in moderation. Do you have many missing women in Exeter that fit that profile?'

'Well Travers, that's why I'm a bit more optimistic. There are a couple of women on our system that match it, who've both disappeared from around here in the past month. And you said you'd not got anyone reported missing recently in North Cornwall. Is that still the case?'

Travers agreed. He was about to tell the Inspector about his tattoo idea – which was still being rolled out by the manager at Black Nails – when the man cut in.

'You asked last week about our plan. Well, it's not much of a plan, but I think we'll assume for the moment that the body at the quarry was dumped from up here. I've got my sergeant here talking to the contacts of these disappeared women. He's doing it very discreetly, he's good at that. Our early discovery of the body is our only secret weapon. We must make sure we keep it that way. In the meantime I'm sure you've got plenty of things to do. But keep in touch anyway.'

While the Inspector was increasingly convinced that the body had originated in Exeter, Travers still rather hoped that it was a local crime, starting and ending in North Cornwall. Mind, it was not clear that the local Tourist Offices would share this view.

And he was keen to see whether the new "facts" could be used to narrow down his suspect tattoo list. He couldn't imagine many of the Black Nail customers retaining the hair under their arms. If they were fussy enough about their appearance to go in there they would surely be happy to spend a few minutes every week applying a razor.

All the tattoo records were now back in the salon. He couldn't remember seeing any comments on the cards about body hair, or for that matter about height and weight, but he decided it was worth driving over to Wadebridge to see for himself.

Half an hour later he was once more in the manager's den, explaining the additional clues which might narrow down the list.

The manager was pleased to have anything which might

shorten the search. She wished now that she'd not agreed to help. She had diligently started to telephone the many women that Travers had picked out; but it was a surprisingly slow process. This sort of high-energy women were often out at work or socialising at the times that Black Nails was open. The manager, though keen, hadn't been prepared to stay on the task until late in the evening. And not getting through to them certainly did not mean that they were dead.

Frustratingly, Travers found that body hair was not covered by the tattoo records. 'It's too personal a detail,' the manager had explained, 'and it doesn't affect how we treat them anyway.'

But the fact that the victim was tall, thin and in good shape would certainly narrow down her search. Customers' weight, Travers learned, were part of the database. He just hadn't noticed it earlier.

Travers looked with the manager at a few of the records. Only a small percent of female customers were the victim's size. 'That'll reduce the list of possibilities hugely,' said the manager thankfully. 'I should be able to finish it in a couple of days.'

But a day which had started well was soon to get worse. Travers had not long returned to the Police House in Delabole – and was enjoying a Cornish pasty for his lunch – when the phone rang again.

It was Chadwick; and he was livid.

'Travers, I've just had someone from the media on the phone. And they've learned about our investigation. How the hell has that happened? Have you been talking out of turn?'

Travers had moved the phone some way from his ears when the torrent began. He didn't mind being partially deafened but he didn't want to be scalded by the steam. Slowly he swallowed his latest mouthful of pasty.

'Sir, I've been extremely careful what I've said to all the possible witnesses. And the location I've seen them in: I made sure I wasn't overheard. I'm as surprised as you are. Can you tell me who it was that rang you?'

'It was some woman called Harriet Horsman. Cold and clinical; she gnawed at my answers but didn't give much away. "Ratty Hattie" might be a better description. She tells me she's a journalist from Tintagel. So the leak's got to be your end, not mine.'

The Delabole policeman thought for a second. 'The name sounds familiar, sir. Yes, I've got it. She was one of the dog-walkers I interviewed last week. Now I think about it, she contacted me; and came to see me here at the Police House.'

'So it was you then. Travers, I warned you –'

'But I didn't give anything away, sir. I'm sure. There are no notes or anything lying around.'

'Well, she had my direct-line number. Could she have got that from you?'

'I left her sitting in my office while I made her some coffee. She could have seen the regional police telephone list on my notice board, I suppose. But I have no idea why she should suspect something was going on, to make her come and see me in the first place. Do you want me to make enquiries?'

'Not just make enquiries, man. What we need to know – urgently – is how much she really knows and how she's learned it. And how best to manage her from now on.'

'What did you tell her, sir?'

'Same as you: nothing. I told her I was very busy with all sorts of inquiries about all sorts of cases. Which we'd tell the media about once we were ready to do so. And I warned her that, whatever happened in London, down here in the West Country we aimed to work with the media as much as we could; but operational factors always came into play. In other words, I played for time.'

'Right sir. It's top priority. I'll find out as much as I can about her, then we can decide how best to manage her.'

'Not "we" Travers, she's your problem, not mine. A Tintagel woman. I don't care how you do it as long as you keep her quiet. Public silence is still our best tactic in this case.'

'Thank you, sir. I'll ring you as soon as I've made some progress. Any progress at all.'

CHAPTER 28

Travers wasn't used to high-speed detection but it was obviously a skill he needed to acquire if he wanted to continue working with Inspector Chadwick. He hastily finished his pasty as he wondered what to do next.

Checking his notebook he saw that, mercifully, he had taken down Harriet Horsman's address in Tintagel. He assumed that on this point at least she wasn't lying.

As he thought back to the interview, he realised he might have mentioned Chadwick's name at one point. Guilty: but that could probably be glossed over. He also remembered the dog had looked vaguely familiar. Now he thought about it, it looked very like the one owned by the landlord of the Trewarmett Inn. So maybe that was the place to start.

He knew the Trewarmett Inn landlord well; attended his quiz night most Thursdays. When he arrived the lunch time trade was drawing to a close. The policeman propped himself against the bar. Leaning forward he could see the dog, lurking in his usual place under the counter. He was almost certain it was the one that had been brought to see him by Harriet.

The landlord admitted as much when questioned. 'Harriet Horsman is in here regularly with her partner, Janey. My dog, Snoopy, knows her well and she often takes him for a walk. The two of them live down in Tintagel, but they come up here for the folk singing.'

'Did you know she was a journalist?'

'Huh. In her dreams, Peter. She'd like to be one, certainly; but she's not yet been accepted. It's always going to happen "directly". At the moment she works as a freelance, doing bits and pieces here and there.'

The landlord mused for a moment. He could see the policeman would like more. 'She's a bit of a loner. Of course, journalism, like most jobs, requires some individual skills. But it's not all like that; and Hattie doesn't get on so well when she's part of a bigger team. She's more interested in herself than in promoting the wider picture.'

The landlord concluded, 'But that's what they look for when she goes for an interview at a newspaper. And I guess that's why they won't take her.'

This was interesting, thought the policeman. She was hardly even a small cog in the media machine: more of a loose screw. The threat, properly handled, might yet be containable.

'How about her friend Janey? Any observations on her?'

'Oh, I don't know anything.'

'No, but do you have any suspicions?'

'The only complaint I've heard recently was after the Camelford Show at the end of August – that's a fortnight ago. She came home as the declared winner of the "Gateau Baking Competition".'

'What's wrong with that?'

'Well, several customers implied that the competition judges had been nobbled; incentivised to recognise her skills, shall we say.'

'As you say, that's only a rumour: it might not be true. But it's still interesting. Thanks. Maybe it's time for me to go and look up the pair of 'em.'

Peter Travers thought, as he drove into Tintagel, that he had not experienced an intense day's work like this in all his life. But there was no time to lose. If Hattie was to be deterred from spilling whatever beans she had collected it had to be done now.

He was in luck. He found the required address, and Hattie was in. Even better, from his point of view, her partner was out. Hattie didn't seem that surprised to see him.

The policeman was invited in and offered a cup of tea. His strategy was formulated as he waited for her to reappear from the kitchen.

'My boss, Inspector Chadwick, tells me that you've been bothering him. He asked me to come and see you and try and reach an understanding.'

'That's very generous of him. I've done all right on my own so far.'

'You mean, with the aid of a borrowed dog.'

'Snoopy just added a bit of local colour.'

'But you told me that you were a regular dog walker at the Prince of Wales quarry. That's not exactly true, is it?'

'I may have implied that but I never actually said so. I can't be blamed for your erratic deductions.'

'So the reason you came to me is that you'd met Gwyneth Fry?'

'That's exactly what I told you. And that was true. I met her at the Engine House.'

'And what are your other sources for this story you're hoping to publish?'

'Journalists don't give away their sources. Everyone knows that.'

'But in that case we have a problem. Because I'm investigating a serious crime. Now either you know something about it from the witnesses I've talked to; or else because you've heard about it from the criminals behind it. If it's the latter I need to interview you under caution.'

'Threats won't make me divulge my sources.'

'All journalists tell me that. But how about this for a way round? Tell me what you know or suspect. If it's just a part of the story I've also heard then we can assume you've just been very inquisitive. And that some of my witnesses have spoken out of turn.

'But maybe you can add to what I know. In that case you must have heard – or overheard – the story from the criminals. In that case you're in a much worse position.'

The policeman stared hard at her. 'So go on then. Tell me what you think you know.'

Travers judged that it had never occurred to Hattie that she might know something the police did not. She took a long time to reply.

'If you won't tell me,' he went on, tightening the screw, 'I will go round and re-interview all my witnesses and find out what they told you. It won't take me long – they're not far away. You see, the police have been keeping the media spotlight off this case for a very good reason.

'But what you also need to remember is that holding back information from a police inquiry can be a criminal offence. And I'm quite prepared to arrest you. My boss has assured me he will back me all the way.'

Hattie looked frightened. She was well out of her depth now. Then, in a timid voice, she started to speak.

'I admit that, so far, I don't know the whole story. But I don't want to be arrested. What I've learned is that just over a week ago Kevin Rogers was stripped naked and tied up in the Engine House at the end of his stag night. Next morning – the Sunday - he was discovered there by Gwyneth Fry as she walked her dog. The two believed his clothes had been thrown into that pool behind the quarry. So they went fishing. But they didn't find his clothes, they found something that had been alive and was now dead. It was an animal that has probably polluted the local water supply and given a real threat to public safety.'

There was a long pause while Travers pondered. His Inspector would rely on threats to impose control. But the Inspector wasn't here. And he'd said, 'I don't care how you do it.' So was a more subtle approach possible?

'You sound to me as if you've been talking to someone from the Environment Agency. Where did you meet him?'

'At the place where whatever it was happened. I was back at the quarry this morning, checking a few facts and taking a few pictures, and a scientist appeared. He told me he'd come to take a special water quality sample for the pool. So I took a few more pictures of him, messing about with his bottles. It's not easy to get down to that pool, you know.'

Harriet looked up and the policeman nodded. 'Then, when he'd finished, we got talking. He told me about your uncooperative approach to him last week. He looked pretty sore. Said that you'd got what you wanted from him and then just walked out.'

Travers was silent as he mused on her testimony.

'Let me make a guess, now. About motive. I believe there are two distinct reasons why you have been chasing around, trying to put this story together. The long-term one is that you are hoping to be taken seriously as a journalist; and to use this story to dazzle - or maybe bamboozle - your way onto some newspaper or other.

'The other is that, in your version of the story, there is a real threat to public health from some unspecified pollution incident at the quarry. But the police, for some reason that you don't understand, are trying to suppress the story. Maybe they need to hide their incompetence in allowing it to happen in the first place, or in not getting a public announcement about it out earlier. When what they ought to be doing in your view is not to suppress the problem but to get out and warn people; and so protect them.'

There was a longer pause. Travers breathed very quietly. Had he surmised correctly?

'I wouldn't have put it exactly like that,' Hattie replied, 'but I suppose broadly you are correct. I am an aspiring journalist; and I do believe something dangerous has gone on at that quarry which the public ought to know about.'

'OK. We're starting to understand one another. But there's something important in your story that you've got wrong. And if you don't recognise it, but go ahead trying to alert the media, you will damage your reputation, probably for ever. One thing the media won't tolerate is someone who stirs up a false storm. Not at least when it's one which the authorities can easily refute.'

Hattie looked at the policeman. She didn't trust authority, but she sensed that in this point at least the policeman was telling the truth.

'So you're telling me to drop it.'

'I'm advising you that there are key bits you are missing. Bits which I'm not going to tell you at this stage of our investigation. But if you're quiet for now, I can promise you that, as soon as I can say something, I'll make sure that you are invited to the press conference. There you'll be able to ask any questions you like. You'll be starting from much further ahead than anyone else. And if you do that well, that could make a really positive impact on all the other journalists at the conference.'

Travers looked at her. 'Do we have a deal?'

Hattie nodded, reluctantly but he judged sincerely, in reply.

An hour later the policeman was on the phone once more to Exeter. There was the usual obstacle course to reaching the Inspector but at last he got through.

'I've been to see Harriet, sir. Had a long chat. She's an aspiring journalist but not yet hired by anyone. And there hasn't been a big leak; she's just been clever at expanding the bits and pieces she's overheard. No-one's told her the full story. I persuaded her to stay quiet for now, in exchange for guaranteeing that she would get a personal invitation to the press conference when we talk to the media. I told her she could make her best impact by the questions she would be in a position to ask there.'

'Your best contribution to the case so far, Travers. Well done. Not that we'll be having a press conference for quite a while. We don't yet have the faintest idea who our victim was.'

CHAPTER 29

The previous day's debate at the PRAM committee had made George eager to see the wreck of the Antoinette that was still, apparently, littering the Camel estuary.

There was nothing she could do about it, of course. She gathered from Bill that several attempts had been made to move or destroy the wreck since it reappeared in 1996, but none had worked properly. But George was a professional. She felt uncomfortable in helping to produce a report which would have a section on enhancing the use of the estuary when a key limit on that progress was a mystery to her.

Bill was keen enough to help. Perhaps he felt embarrassed that they had spent so little time together. When they had been, usually at meal times, the two had got on fine.

Often George had been out on her interviews. When she was at home she had wanted to write these up and ponder the wider picture; or else to muse on her prospective Doom Bar model. Bill had not been home much either. He didn't say where he was going and George did not enquire.

Like many locals, Bill had a small boat of his own, with an outboard motor, moored over at Rock – the "Eilean Donan". 'That'll be big enough to take us there,' he had commented on Tuesday morning. 'If we go this afternoon the tide should be ideal.'

George gathered that the best chance of seeing any of the wrecks was when the tide was at its lowest and the sand bank not far below the surface.

'I presume that, even with binoculars, you can't see the wreck from the shore?' she had asked. 'After all, the cliffs are high towards Stepper Point; and the Coast Path runs along there. I wouldn't mind the walk if that was easier.'

'On the lowest tides of the year the wreck is visible if you know where to look. But the best way to see it at this time of the year is to sail slowly over the top and look down, very carefully of course; we don't want to capsize ourselves.'

'But if it's below the surface and out in mid-estuary how will you find it?'

'I'll use my GPS to go to the specified location. The wreck doesn't move about much. It's stuck in the sand. Its latest position is published to help boats avoid being wrecked on it.'

George looked puzzled.

'The Geographical Positioning System is similar to SAT-NAV,' her Uncle explained. 'Uses satellite signals to work out the current location. Except that when you're at sea you don't need a map of any road links. But I know roughly where the wreck is anyway.'

The pair had taken the ferry across to Rock and Bill had led the way across a series of floating jetties to the Eilean Donan. 'We could sail to it, but that would take longer. And it'd be harder to hold position over the wreck once we got there. So today we'll just use the outboard motor.'

Bill made sure George was wearing adequate protection. Fortunately it was a dry day, although cloudy and dull. There was a gentle breeze. George was surprised how much colder it was out on the water than it had been on dry land.

Bill took charge. George enjoyed the views on both sides: the extensive sand that was visible at low tide, the sand dunes behind, and beyond, varying coastal patterns. As they sailed further down the estuary the shorelines on either side slid steadily further apart.

On the Polzeath side George could see traces of the path she had walked between Rock and Polzeath. On the other she saw a group of stone houses clustered around the old lifeboat station at Hawkers Cove, then the cliffs started to rise steadily toward Stepper point.

'That lifeboat station was abandoned when the Doom Bar swapped banks in the 1970s,' Bill reminded her. 'The channel that had given it permanent access to the open sea disappeared. They had to build a station on Trevose Head instead. We're close to the Doom Bar now.'

As they chugged along the Eilean Donan had been rocking up and down on the steady swell. But looking ahead, George could see one line of white-topped waves and then another, parallel and fifty yards further on. The sand making up the Doom bar must lie between the two. Somewhere along that were the remains of the Antoinette.

Bill slowed the boat down and consulted his GPS. Then he changed course slightly as the boat moved forwards. As they floated through the line of waves the sea became calmer. Looking over the side and down, George could see sand no more than six feet below.

'Not far now. According to my instruments no more than thirty yards. Keep your eyes open, look down and shout if you see anything.'

'What does it look like?'

'It's basically the remains of the hull: about a hundred foot long. The keel is a series of black beams, running along the length of the ship, fastened together in a few places and encrusted with barnacles. But also some ribs, fastened to the keel but sticking up towards the surface. Those are what we've got to watch out for.

'Some of them will be close enough to the surface to catch our boat and make a real mess of it. I'd rather not rely on the Stepper Point Lookout if I can help it. It might be Toby on watch.'

'I can't see the Lookout. Is it - '

'Never mind that now. Just keep looking down.' George realised Bill was the naval officer once more, not the benign uncle. She dutifully peered down through the murky water.

Then, suddenly, she saw something. A dark wooden beam, a foot wide, running close to the top of the uneven sand. 'I think we're over her.'

Bill was peering over the other side. 'I can see one of the sides, too. We're more or less on top of the wreck, with our keel pointing along it. I'm going to put down an anchor.'

George continued to watch the seabed below. Looking further ahead, she could see one of the ribs, rising from alongside the beam she had seen first but reaching towards the surface. It looked to be within a couple of feet of breaking into the open air.

There was the noise of a chain running out. Bill muttered, 'That'll hold us steady for a few minutes.' He throttled down the outboard motor to a gentle chug.

George had brought her camera. It wasn't easy to take pictures with the boat rocking slowly back and forth but there was no limit on how many times she could try. She experimented with full digital zoom but the result was fuzzy. She got better though smaller pictures if she zoomed less.

She turned and saw another rib sticking up, only twenty feet away. This one was almost vertical. And she saw something metal had been added: a tube, about six feet long. It was fastened to the rib near the top and pointed vertically. She took several pictures of the arrangement.

She was about to ask Bill what it might be when he gave a shout. 'We're drifting towards a fierce-looking rib. We'll have to move away.'

George watched with respect as he expertly and simultaneously hauled up the anchor and revved up the motor and then steered the Eilean Donan sideways away from the wreck.

'It's dangerous to stay over the wreck for long,' explained Bill. 'And that's in good weather and in a boat of shallow draught. Imagine what it would be like to drift over the top at night in a storm. That's why the Doom Bar is such a threat – even today.'

George was going to ask Bill about the metal tube, but thought it would be better to wait until they were back on dry land.

And once they were back at Rock she decided she would examine her pictures more carefully first. She had some advanced software on her laptop to expand parts of pictures. She didn't want to make a complete fool of herself by asking about something that turned out to be labelled. And she still had doubts about Bill from what she had seen on their last trip to Stepper Point.

But there was no doubt that she had added to the mounting pile of oddities that were collecting in the neighbourhood.

159

As the days passed he was missing her more and more. He'd looked everywhere. Walked tracts of the Coast Path in both directions; searched surrounding villages; even hired a bike and cycled the Camel Trail.

If she'd been called away to another project, she would surely have let him know? Maybe not straight away, but she'd been gone for a month. Even a message by carrier pigeon would have reached him by now. For someone of her skills communication would not be the problem.

He would have to recover the equipment single-handed. There was no choice. But he knew it was a much more risky operation.

CHAPTER 30

Reflecting on his conversation with Harriet Horsman the day before, Peter Travers decided he had to do something to improve his relationship with the Environment Agency scientist in Wadebridge. It was dangerous for the pair to be at loggerheads: better ways to maintain secrecy were needed. He'd no idea the man had been so upset when he left him a week ago.

A careful, non-confrontational phone call brought him an invitation to call on the scientist again in Wadebridge. 'I've got to be here today anyway; got someone coming to see me this afternoon.'

The visit would also give him chance to visit the Black Nails salon and check on progress. It was fortunate he thought, as he drove over, that Harriet Horsman was not a woman who took great care in her appearance. He didn't want her encouraging staff at the salon to speak out of turn. Before he knew it she'd be concocting a tale of an over-tattooed sheep being found in the quarry pool.

'I realised, when I thought about it, that I wasn't very fair to you last week,' Travers began, once he was seated in the Agency office with a mug of coffee. 'I left you knowing that there was a water quality problem at the Prince of Wales quarry, but not telling you what else we knew. I did give you a few hints. But now I've come to realise that disinformation is also dangerous.'

For Martin Sutcliffe light began to dawn. 'Oh, I see what's

happened. It's that nosey woman I met at the quarry yesterday who's been talking. Spreading gossip and expanding the raw facts. Looking back, I suppose she did coax me to say too much. I was just so annoyed at the way it was left when you last came here.'

'I'm truly sorry. I'm not used to handling media-sensitive cases. They don't come up very often. I need to be a lot more thoughtful about who I can trust. You have a right to know more than I told you last week and to know why it has to remain a secret.'

'I'm sure there are some aspects you can't tell me - how the investigation is going, for example, or if an arrest is imminent. But it would be good for you to tell me what you can. I promise I will be very careful not to pass on anything to anyone outside this office.'

Travers gave a sigh of relief; it was going to be alright. 'Fine. The key fact is that someone found a body in that pool, just over a week ago. Not just someone who'd fallen in but some-one who'd been murdered. We got the body out straight away, of course. But their head had been cut off and we can't match their DNA. So we're finding it very hard to identify the victim or make much sense of the crime.'

'Gosh. No wonder the stream's been polluted. The sample I took yesterday will show that, no doubt. I suppose it's an operational decision by the police not to publicise anything until you know who it is, or rather was. So is that the cause of the secrecy?'

'That's right. You told me your sampling proved the water was fine at the end of July. So the body must have been dumped at the start of August. The condition of its skin tells our forensic scientists it's been there at least four weeks. That's why I was asking if you happened to have seen anything last time you were there.'

'Well, I can give you something, as it happens. As you've gleaned from the busybody, I was there yesterday taking another water sample. Your question last week made me have a good look at the place to see if anything had changed.'

'And?'

'There wasn't much different around the pool. It looked as if it had been trampled over by a bunch of boy scouts, but I guess you knew that already, probably knew the boy scouts by name. But you know the car park at the bottom? The entrance to it has a white height barrier to prevent large vans parking there. I guess that's 'cos they don't want lorries making use of it overnight.'

'But that's been there for years.'

'Yes. But what I noticed is that there is now a large gash and a purple paint mark about three feet above the ground, on one side – as though an impatient driver had bumped into it on the way in or out. I tend to notice these things at our sampling sites – my boss thinks I take them too personally. Anyway, I'm pretty sure the mark has only appeared in the last month.'

This was potentially a huge lead.

Travers pondered. 'When the body was dumped, whoever humped it up the hillside wouldn't want to be seen. So it's almost certain it would have been done at night. I mean, the place isn't overcrowded in the daytime, but there are a few dog-walkers, as well as the occasional visitor to the Engine House. You couldn't be sure you'd have the place to yourself.'

'But if you drove in at the dead of night,' said the scientist, 'you could easily imagine knocking against the entrance height bar.'

'They'd probably be in a panic – and in a hurry.'

'And what's more, they might well turn their lights off when they pulled up the slope to park, and keep them off until they were back on the road. It would be easy to hit the post in the dark.'

There was pause of mutual satisfaction.

Travers smiled. 'Thank you. This could be a real break-through. I'll get over there as soon as I've finished here and have a look.'

Coming over here had been well worth the effort. Travers started to pull himself out of his chair. 'Unless you have any more clues you can tell me?'

'There is one more thing, actually.' Sutcliffe was basking in the glow of having contributed to the investigation and was eager to do more.

'Go on.'

'I noticed it after you'd gone last time. But I was so mad with you I couldn't be bothered to ring you to say so. And I didn't realise how important it might be until you explained about the body earlier on.'

'I'm intrigued. Please, do tell me.'

'It was the date on the water quality sample I took last July – July 31st. Or to be more precise, what struck me was that this date was less than five months since the previous sample there, on March 4th.'

The policeman counted on his fingers to check. 'Yes, that was almost five months ago. Is that not just natural variation? You told me the samples are taken around every six months.'

'It could be. But the shortened gap prompted me to check my diary. And I found that it wasn't just random. I'd been rung up on July 26th, and asked to bring the sample date forward.'

Travers could hardly contain his excitement. 'And does your diary record who made the call?'

'I didn't keep the name I'm afraid, but I recorded that it was someone from Cornwall Council. A man with a posh voice. He claimed some sort of military title. He said the Council had been contacted by one or two people who lived down the Trebarwith valley, saying their water was starting to taste odd. So could I take a sample please, to check everything was OK?'

'Do you often get calls like that?'

'We get that sort of phone call from time to time. So I agreed to bring the sample date forward; that's why it happened so early.'

Travers thought for a moment.

'This is dynamite. It has major implications. It could just be the biggest coincidence in criminal history – a change of date that helped a criminal. Or else . . . or else it means that this crime was very carefully premeditated. And not only that, it was planned by someone who knew a great deal about local arrangements.'

It was time to go. 'Do you have any more clues for me? If not, then I'd better be on my way. You've given me a lot to follow up. Thank you, Martin. Thank you very much indeed.'

CHAPTER 31

On Wednesday afternoon, Martin Sutcliffe had his second visitor of the day. But this one was more welcome. He was more partial to attractive and articulate women than he was to burly policemen.

'I'm glad I've got someone sympathetic to talk to,' began George, once she had sat down and been given a mug of coffee. 'And someone with a scientific mind. I'm fed up of being told about curses from enraged mermaids and insoluble mysteries. In my view there's a reason for everything: the challenge is to find it. I haven't done nearly as much as I'd hoped but I've had a good look at the data; and I've got some ideas which I'd like to run past you.'

'Go ahead. My routine tasks are straightforward, except during emergencies. But it's the wrong time of year for floods. It's good to wrestle with something more meaty. So tell me, what you have discovered about the Doom Bar?'

'Well, I discovered that the Harbour Office had got data on the sandbank's position, going right back to the Second World War. They had monthly charts, produced by a small boat that went out to track its location. I can show you.'

George reached into her briefcase and produced a huge folder of charts.

'I decided the first thing I needed to do was to concoct a notation to summarise each of these diagrams - some way to reduce this lot to a sequence of numbers.'

'Sounds a tough challenge.'

'I'm not aiming for a detailed model. I just want to make some sense of the broad sandbank movements - to see if they can be linked to other factors like tide and weather.' George took a sip of her coffee.

'So I really did start with the basics. If I had to describe the Doom Bar's location to someone over the phone, how would I do it? The most talked-about aspect is the shoreline which the sandbank starts from. Another is the grid reference of its outermost location, which is towards the opposite side. The third is its overall direction, the deviation from north, the line on which it lies. And the fourth is the grid reference of the place where the sandbank reaches the shoreline.'

'Even those numbers you've just listed will have some redundancy,' commented Sutcliffe. 'They're not all independent. Because you could compute the direction in which the bank lies from the coordinates of the two ends. It's what used to be O-level trigonometry.'

'Yes, I realised that. But I wasn't sure which would be the best numbers to model. So while I was plodding through the charts I noted them all.'

'There are hundreds of charts here. It must have taken you ages.'

'It's not as bad as it looks. Often there was no trace of movement at all. So I only had to take fresh measurements where the bar had moved, which is about thirty charts. I created a template of the estuary on a clear piece of plastic, together with a set of grid lines. Then I laid the template on top of each chart in turn and took the readings.'

'Hm. I can see that would be manageable - for a first attempt. And what did you do next?'

167

'Then I wrote a small program, to convert my readings into a series of lines on a graph; lines that we could step through on the computer. Would you like to see?'

Assuming the answer would be yes George turned to her laptop case, unloaded the computer and switched it on.

'Here we go. I spent a few minutes getting coordinates of the sides of the estuary to give us a context. That's the pair of wiggly lines shown on each side in brown.'

'Ah, now you've told me what I'm looking at, I see what you mean. I was expecting to see the shape of Pentire Head on the eastern side. But the Doom Bar never reaches that far.'

'Now watch. I'll show you the changes in the sandbank over the past half-century.' And George slowly clicked the arrow keys on her computer.

On the first click, a thick red line appeared. It started on the eastern shoreline, just north of Rock; and ended in mid-channel, over towards the coast north of Padstow. 'That's where the sandbank was in April 1960.'

She clicked the computer again and the red line representing the Doom bar moved north, still starting from the same side. 'That's the movement which happened in July 1966'.

Another click and a further shift north. 'That was in September 1969.'

Sutcliffe was fascinated. 'You and I are much too young to have seen this for ourselves. But the older generation saw it. And it does explain why the main lifeboat station for the area was based at Hawkers Cove. There's a clear channel out to sea from that side for all these years.'

'Right. Now watch the 1970s.' And, as George continued to click, the red line suddenly altered from minor adjustments to a major change, switching to the other side.

'Stop right there,' instructed Sutcliffe. 'When did that happen?'

'It's shown on the charts as being October 1976.'

'Wait a minute.' Sutcliffe was fully alert now. He stood up and walked over to the charts he had shown George a week ago: the history of flow rates into the River Camel. He examined them for a moment.

'Yes, it's as I thought.' He turned back to her. 'Do you remember that 1976 was the year of the massive drought?'

'I was six years old at the time and living in London. I can't remember any detail, but it was a glorious summer. I spent most of my time in the paddling pool. It didn't rain in London for months. So are you saying the Doom Bar shifted because of the drought?'

'Not on the numbers you just showed me. But what is less well remembered is that after the months of drought in 1976 we had the wettest autumn on record. No sooner had the government appointed a Minister for Drought – Denis Howell, he used to be a football referee - than it started to rain; and, once it started, it rained for months. As you can see in these flow histories.'

George joined him to look at the charts. There was a big increase in both tributaries to the upstream River Camel flow between August 1976 and the following months.

'So are we saying that the big switch in Doom Bar position resulted from a huge increase in flow down the Camel?'

'A huge increase in flow could change the equilibrium point, where the incoming tide comes up against the river flow. And if that happened, steadily for a few months, the sand bank would be forced to move as well.'

'But why would it swap sides?'

'Well, maybe there was so much water in the River Camel that the extra flow broke through the sandbank on the eastern side. So for a very short time there would be channels on both sides. But once that happened there would be less flow on the western side. So that would start to silt up instead.'

'So the sand dredging would concentrate on the other side?'

'I guess so. After all, Padstow didn't need two channels. One deep one is worth more than two shallow ones. So at some point the dredged channel would swap to the other side. You know, this could be really important.'

George felt buoyed by his enthusiasm. It seemed that, until her efforts, the data on the Doom Bar held by the Harbour Board had never been set alongside the data on river flows upstream of Wadebridge.

But there was much more still to do. Sutcliffe had several more ideas which she needed to test out on her data.

Later, as she pulled together her various collections of data and prepared to leave, George remembered that, last time she had been there, Sutcliffe had had a run-in with a policeman. 'Have you seen that policeman again?'

'He was here this morning, actually. More or less apologising for not telling me what was going on when he came before. Far more conciliatory. Even gave me chance to make a contribution to his investigation.'

'And no doubt binding you to secrecy at the same time?'

'Oh, he did that on what he told me. But I don't see why I can't sketch out my contribution. As a mathematician you'd appreciate it. It was about dates between samples. You see, I happened to notice that the crucial six-month sample he was interested in hadn't happened at the right time compared to the previous one. It was early, brought forward by over a month.

And all as a result of a phone call to this office. Which he seemed to find very suspicious indeed.'

It didn't seem suspicious to George. What was a month? It was far better, surely, to be investigating something like the Doom Bar over half a century, using publicly collected data.

At least, it was when progress could be made. George headed back to Padstow; she was itching to develop her simple model further.

CHAPTER 32

Seldom had a working day contained so many contrasts of highs and lows. Peter Travers was to remark on this philosophically to his friend Brian Southgate later that Wednesday evening.

After leaving the Environment Agency office, the policeman had called once more at the Black Nails salon. There, to his delight, he was given a short list containing just three names. Each of these identified a local customer of the salon: girls with the required combinations of tattoo and more or less the target height, weight and age, as indicated by the torso.

And all of them, apparently, had gone missing during the previous month.

As soon as he had reached his car, Travers called Inspector Chadwick in Exeter. When he eventually got through, he started with his findings from the Environment Agency.

'So you see, sir,' he concluded, 'it looks as if this was a premeditated crime by someone of intelligence. Planned with care, with the dumping pool already identified, to take place soon after July 31st. And it seems likely the body was taken there in some vehicle which was coloured purple. We need to get Forensics to come and take a sample of the paint left behind as soon as possible.'

'Hm. Good work, Travers. I told you to go and interview the Agency last week, if you remember. So what do you conclude?'

'Well, sir, it seems to me that this points to a local crime. One based in North Cornwall. Someone who knew which Agency would be taking water samples of that pool and where that Agency was based; and who was prepared to modify the date when the sample took place so as to delay the risk of discovery.'

'OK. I accept that it's almost certain the phone call to the Agency in Wadebridge was part of the crime. Otherwise it's an amazing coincidence. But can I ask you a question: how did you find the Agency you've just been to?'

For the minute Travers couldn't see where this was going. 'I looked it up in the phone book, sir. A lot of Environment Agency sites were listed. I just picked the office nearest to Trewarmett, which was Wadebridge, and gave them a ring.'

'Was that in some special police force phone directory?'

'No sir. Just the standard one from British Telecom.'

It was the giveaway answer and Chadwick pounced. 'And are you saying that this task would have been beyond our murderer? Suppose he had come across the quarry pool some time earlier and planned to use it. Why d'you suppose he could only make the call from a phone in North Cornwall?'

Travers was silent. There must be a reply to this, but he couldn't think what it was.

Chadwick took his silence as acquiescence. 'What you've found out will be vital one day, helping to prove that the murder didn't just happen in a moment of passion. But it doesn't narrow down where the victim came from or who they were. That's our first problem. And as far as I'm concerned, Exeter is still a plausible location.'

Travers was about to go on to tell the Inspector about his progress on identifying missing tattoo girls. But some instinct warned him that this finding would not be taken as convincing either. And worst of all, there was a risk that he would be ordered not to waste his time on what Chadwick might well term "another futile chase".

He decided to postpone passing on any more news. At least until he had made a few enquiries about the three names he had just been given. Fortunately the Inspector was far too busy to give him anything else to do.

The first name, Travers, saw, was that of a woman whose address was in Wadebridge. He decided he might as well call there straight away.

The house, when he had found his way to the far end of the estate, was modestly-sized but in reasonable condition. It looked abandoned. The policeman knocked firmly at the front door but no-one answered - even when he knocked a second time, harder and louder.

But his efforts had some effect. A neighbour came to the door of the house next door. 'Can I help you?'

'I was hoping for a few words with Angela Missan. Have I got the right address?'

'Angela certainly used to live here. Her family moved away at the start of August.'

'Do you know where they went?'

'She gave me her new address in case anyone wanted her. Hold on a minute.'

The woman disappeared but returned a few minutes later, holding a piece of paper. The policeman was pleased to see it contained a new phone number as well as an address in Scotland.

'Scotland's a long way to go,' he remarked.

'Her husband used to work on an oil refinery in Dubai. Then his contract came to an end and he got made redundant. So when he got a new job, up at the BP refinery in the Firth of Forth, they were pleased to move. The summer holidays is a good time to move house if you've got any children at school, as they had. A little horror, to be honest, aged six.'

The policeman made a note of the address and the neighbour's comments. It sounded genuine. One phone call to Scotland should be enough to confirm the story. Or at least, to make Angela's absence seem no longer odd.

The second address was for a house in Trebetherick, a small village overlooking the sea, close to Polzeath. The policeman decided to visit there on his way back to Delabole.

That meant he needed to buy lunch. After a moment's thought he drove to Polzeath, parked on the beach and headed for the Galleon cafe. He knew the manager, Quentin Arnold: they had helped one another in the past.

The two men nodded as Travers went in and ordered his hot pasty and mug of chocolate.

'Everything OK?' asked Quentin.

'I'm here in search of somebody. But I can't say any more at this stage.'

'If you need any reinforcements, I'm around.'

After his lunch, Travers went on to Trebetherick and, after some effort, found the address he had been given. It was an isolated house at the end of a muddy track. No chance of helpful neighbours here.

Once again the policeman knocked, repeatedly and loudly, on the front door but no-one answered. He could, though, hear a faint noise. It seemed to be coming from inside.

He stood back from the front door and eyed the house carefully, window by window. As his gaze reached the upstairs rooms he thought he saw something move; then drop out of sight.

The policeman was in uniform. Whoever was hiding must be aware who they were trying to dupe. Even for policemen there were rules about forcing entry to someone's home; but there were also exceptions. He was investigating a savage murder: that was pretty exceptional. What would Chadwick do?

He suspected the Inspector would try and break in as quietly as possible to get an answer out of whoever was hiding there and then straighten out the "due process" of law afterwards. Travers decided he would take responsibility and do the same.

The policeman strode forward and hammered hard on the front door once more. But nothing happened. He tried to open the door but it was firmly locked.

Was there an easier way in? Travers circled the house until he came to the back door which he found also locked. But the window beside it had been left open.

It was an invitation to action. With no pause his hand had reached through, seized the door key on the inside and unlocked it.

'That's careless,' he said to an imaginary superior, rehearsing his lines for any future inquiry. 'Shouldn't leave a back door unlocked on an isolated house. Better go in and check everything's in order.'

Travers opened the door and entered. Now, for his imaginary inquiry, he needed to be bold and transparent. He shouted the name of the girl he was after. 'Joanna Wisdom. Police Sergeant Travers here. Is anyone around?'

But there was no answer.

Carefully he went through each downstairs room in turn. There was no-one at ground level and no sign of a cellar. That just left upstairs.

Slowly, deliberately, the policeman mounted the stairs, repeating his announcement clearly. He wondered what he would do if the person he suspected of hiding in the house was not some fragile female but a muscular male - one determined not to be found. The starting point for this case, he reminded himself, was an exceptionally brutal murder.

Maybe he should have brought reinforcements. But it was too late for that now. As a precaution the policeman eased out his truncheon and prepared himself for a struggle.

The bathroom was empty. Now all that was left was a choice of bedroom. It was a small house and there were just two. After a second's thought he identified the one he had seen movement in when standing outside.

He pushed the door open.

Slowly he stepped inside. He was confronted by a young woman, quivering with fear, standing at the far side of the room. She was tall and slim and had bright red tattoos down both arms. In her right hand she held a cricket bat. But he was relieved to see she didn't look that keen to use it.

It was instinct rather than any training course which told him what to do next. The natural courtesy of a rural policeman took over.

'Good afternoon madam. I'm Police Sergeant Peter Travers. Are you, by any chance, Joanna Wisdom? I believe you left your back door unlocked.'

The woman looked shocked then relieved and burst into tears. 'Oh, thank heavens. You're a policeman. I couldn't be sure: I couldn't find my glasses. I feared you were Julian Hereford. He's a very unpleasant bookmaker from Bodmin that I owe money to. Hereford warned me he knew where I lived; said that if I didn't pay he would come here to collect it. I haven't dared go out or answer the phone. But I haven't got enough money to pay him.'

It took a couple of hours to sort it all out. The woman was indeed Joanna Wisdom; so that was another suspect victim who could be taken off the list.

But Joanna was a victim of sorts; and action was needed. After talking to the woman at length, Travers spoke to a colleague at the Police Station in Bodmin. He learned that a case was being constructed to deal with Hereford, who had apparently dealt with other women in the way he was threatening to behave with Joanna. A policewoman from Bodmin who knew the details of the case so far would come over and interview her. And he gathered Hereford would soon be under arrest.

A result of sorts, thought Travers; but not one likely to impress Inspector Chadwick.

The third name of a missing tattoo customer came with an address in Tintagel. Since this was only a couple of miles from Delabole, Travers had left her till last.

This time, when he knocked at the door of the specified address, there was a response.

A woman came to the door whose arms were heavily tattooed. This looked promising. But she looked much older than the thirty five Travers had set as the upper bound. Could the tattooing have prematurely aged her? Maybe - but surely not by that much?

'Good afternoon, madam. I'm Sergeant Travers. Could you help me, please, with some enquiries?'

The woman looked surprised but nodded.

'Is your name Sylvia Trumper?'

'It is.'

'And do you use the Black Nails salon in Wadebridge?'

'No. Never been there.'

This was not the answer expected. Travers pondered and then protested, 'But they gave me your name.'

'Doesn't matter what they gave you. I've never been there.'

'And not just your name, madam, but they gave me your address as well.'

There was a pause as they both considered this collision of authority. Then Sylvia's face lit up.

'Oh, I know what's happened. It's my daughter they've told you about. She's Sylvia Mary Trumper. I'm Sylvia Marigold. Yes, I can well imagine her going to a place like that. Sorry, I can't help you.'

'But can you tell me where I might find your daughter?'

'No idea.'

'You mean she's no longer living here?'

'She left about three weeks ago. August 10th to be precise. Said she'd had enough of Britain and would take her chance in Eastern Europe.'

'And she's not been in touch since?'

'I don't suppose she's got there yet. Or not for long enough for the post to have brought back any letter. But given the scale of the row we had before she left, she probably won't be in touch for months.'

Travers couldn't think what else to say. Sylvia's mother sounded sincere and plausible. And, if her daughter had been seen on August 10th, that was only three weeks before the body was discovered. Which meant it was too late for her to have

179

been the torso in the pool.

That evening Peter Travers begged the company of Brian Southgate for a consoling drink. 'I can't stay long,' the doctor told him, as they met at the Trewarmett Inn, 'my wife is threatening to register me with Alcoholics Anonymous if I'm out with you much more this week.'

Once they had claimed their traditional, discreet table at the rear, Travers poured out the story of his day, with all its highs and lows. First he shared the news from Martin Sutcliffe at the Environment Agency about the purple paint on the height barrier; and about the peculiar call prompting him to take the water sample at the quarry well ahead of schedule. 'That suggests a premeditated crime,' commented the doctor. It was the one point about which everyone was agreed.

Then the policeman waded through his investigation of the suitably-sized, locally-tattooed ladies who had disappeared in the last month. 'I really thought, when I got to the tattooed woman in Tintagel, that I'd found the home of the victim. But it wasn't her either. So all that work last weekend, chasing through tattoo records, has yielded me absolutely nothing.'

'Look on the bright side,' his friend advised. 'At least Chadwick knew nothing about it. He can't accuse you of wasting police time. It didn't work but that didn't mean it was a bad idea.' The doctor decided he would not raise the policeman's hopes with his own variation on the theme. He would know more about that tomorrow.

As they stood up to leave, a young man, having a drink at the bar on his own, hesitated about whether he should approach them. But he was not confident enough. By the time he had built up courage the two had disappeared. 'I guess it's not that important,' he muttered to himself. But, deep down, he knew that it was.

CHAPTER 33

On Thursday morning Brian Southgate was eager to meet his colleague, Dr Ellis, in Rock. By now she should have assembled the raw data on patients from all the local surgeries who had symptoms of what was more commonly known as "self harming".

As far as the local Area Health Committee was concerned his task today was to help Dr Ellis organise this data and to draw some lessons for the Department of Health. But following last night's discussion with Peter Travers he also had another goal: to see if any of the women on the list (they would be mostly women) could possibly be the victim he'd seen taken out of the pool at the Prince of Wales Quarry.

For self-harming – slashing one's arms or wrists as a silent cry for help – was another distinctive identifier on limbs that a risk-averse murderer might want to remove, at least if he wanted a corpse to stay unidentified.

His meeting started promisingly. Dr Ellis was one of the younger doctors on the Area Health committee. She was mustard-keen and had already done preliminary work on the data. The use of matching surgery computer systems across the area, together with the power of the internet to move around selected segments of data, meant that the raw data now downloaded onto her computer was ready for analysis.

Southgate's first task was to help his colleague react to the data she had obtained and to suggest how it might best be organised.

As he had hoped, standard identifiers and the medical history of all those with symptoms of self-harm had been downloaded. The data was private and confidential, but as doctors they had privileged access. Patients' names would be removed before it was sent any further.

The data came from a dozen local surgeries, from Boscastle down as far as Rock, each with several hundred patients on their books. Typically each had a score with symptoms of self-harming. Only a few were current self-harmers attending surgery for help. For most it was an affliction that had happened a long time ago which was still on their medical record.

As he looked at the list, Southgate started to feel sympathy with Travers and his search through tattoo records. The big difference though was that those records had all been held on card and had to be analysed by hand; whereas he could use the computer to narrow down the possibilities.

The question for the Area Health Committee was whether there were any common indicators that arose before the patients sought help for self-harm. Could the medical profession anticipate this need and so to be ahead of the game, calling in potential victims rather than waiting for them to appear?

Dr Ellis had several radical ideas, but as far as Southgate could see the data did not strongly support them. He was more interested in new lines of treatment as hinted at in some of the cases they had assembled.

Eventually Dr Ellis went to organise some refreshments and Southgate had the computer to himself. This was his chance. How many of these sufferers were in the right age bracket to match the victim at the quarry? It turned out there were relatively few: most of the women in the cases downloaded were much younger.

Then he spotted that height and weight data had also been included. Travers had passed on this projection for the torso the evening before, claiming that 'it was one of the few useful things to come out of Exeter.' Fortunately the doctor had noted the values down.

It was as well that the victim had been tall and slim. Only a small minority fell into this category. Applying this further constraint narrowed the possibilities considerably.

Dr Ellis was rather a long time. He assumed that she had been nabbed by one of her fellow-doctors and snared into other surgery business. But he didn't mind: it gave him longer to search.

There was a printer attached to Dr Ellis's computer. Quickly he ran off all the details for the four local patients in the "potential victim" category. Then feeling only marginally guilty he slipped these into his briefcase.

His young colleague was still out of the room. It would be a relief not to have a dispute over the conflicting confidentiality obligations of the police and the Health Service for these patients.

Half an hour later their meeting had finished. Ellis had come back with coffee but acknowledging that a new crisis had arisen. As usual, short-term urgency trumped long-term significance. They agreed it would be sensible to reflect and to meet again in a week's time.

A few moments later Brian Southgate found himself sitting behind his wheel in the car park next to the Rock surgery.

He wasn't due back until the afternoon and was in no hurry. He might as well have a look at his short-list: it was impressively short. Fortunately the medical records assembled by Dr Ellis had been comprehensive and he had printed out everything. They even included dates of medical appointments.

Glancing, he saw that of the four women he had identified, two had been seen by their doctors within the past couple of weeks. Neither of these could be the victim. That just left two. The doctor recalled his law enforcement friend's experience the day before and wondered if he was going to suffer a similar fate.

One of the two had given an address in Rock: over a shop on the main street. But she had had an appointment with her doctor on August 8th. He checked his notes. Yes, that was outside the submersion date range: it was practically certain the torso had been dumped in the pool before then. Even so . . . he thought he could justify a short chat with her, which would also be a check that she was still around, as part of the self-harming study.

George Gilbert had decided that she needed to collect views on the need or otherwise to modernise Padstow and Rock, taken from random visitors. And this might as well begin by catching the ferry to Rock.

She was growing in confidence now; her bouts of self-pity were starting to diminish. The wait for the ferry and the voyage over to Rock – the boat was again only half full - gave her an opportunity to talk to several passengers. She could detect no strong sense of any desire for change, either among locals or visitors. Was PRAM simply chasing a mirage?

Now she was in Rock, George decided she might as well visit the hardware/electrical shop again; but she would try and leave on a better footing this time. And this time she hoped she might be able to meet Elspeth's husband, James.

As she reached the shop there was someone coming out

with a frustrated look on his face. He looked familiar, but from a completely different context. She stared. Where had she seen him before? Oddly, her mind took her back to her late husband's funeral.

Obviously the feeling was mutual, for the man stopped dead in his tracks, staring back at her.

'George Gilbert, what the dickens are you doing here? I haven't seen you since . . .' He swallowed hard. He had been about to say Mark's funeral, but managed to stop himself in time.

'Brian. I'm sorry, I lost your address in all the confusion. It was a bad time. I'm staying for a couple of weeks in Padstow with one of Mark's relatives. I knew from his uncle that you were a doctor around here, but he didn't know where. He just knew it wasn't Padstow. So though I knew this was your part of the world, it wasn't obvious how to find you. How amazing that we've met – this is providential.'

'Are you in a hurry? Could we go for a coffee or something?'

'I'm sort of working. But not to a tight timetable. I've certainly time for coffee. But how about you? Shouldn't you be at some patient's bedside?'

'I'm sort of working as well. But I don't do bedside visits any more: the patients are too healthy for that down here, or too ill. My surgery is over in Delabole. I had to come here to meet a colleague: we're doing some research on new methods of diagnosis for self-harming. But I've finished that for the day. Look, I've got my car; where would you like to go?'

George assumed the offer was limited; he wouldn't take her to Lands End. The nearest place where she'd been served high quality coffee on this side of the estuary was the Fourways Inn in St Minver. Soon the two were in the doctor's car and heading up the road, talking intensely.

Brian had been Mark's friend rather than hers and a friend from school days at that. But it was a friendship that had run on into adult life. Because the doctor lived in Cornwall while she and Mark had been based in London she had never seen much of him. But he had taken the trouble to come up to London for Mark's funeral and she was grateful for that.

The Inn was declared to be open for business but was deserted when they walked in. George 'dinged' the bell on the counter; the landlady whom she had seen last time appeared.

'Can we order a pot of coffee please? We'll be sitting in the snug – unless Mr Applegate's booked it again?'

He hadn't; and George led them into the cosy room at the back.

'For a newcomer who is staying the other side of the estuary you seem remarkably well informed. Who's Applegate?'

George hadn't planned to say anything, but she was glad of the opportunity to talk to someone whom she had reason to trust about the oddities which had piled up in the past two weeks.

Being a doctor made Brian a practised listener. He learned about the regular meetings in the snug, about George's discovery that Uncle Bill was among the attendees and about the odd phone calls she had taken or overheard in his cottage. Finally, the analyst told him about the strange tube she'd seen attached to the wreck of the Antoinette on the Doom Bar.

'That's all very odd. I wouldn't have thought your Uncle Bill would have been up to any funny business. Through Mark I've known him since childhood. He's as straight as a die. Why don't you just ask him about it directly?'

The landlady came through at this point with their coffee.

As she fussed about, unpacking cups from the tray, this gave the doctor time to ponder what it all might mean. It also gave George the chance to frame some questions in return.

'As a matter of interest, what were you after in the hardware shop when we met? You looked a bit frustrated.'

If George had not been so open about her anxieties and suspicions, Brian would have batted the question away. He might well have cited medical confidentiality. But his companion's vulnerability made it hard for him to refuse to say anything.

'It was "who" actually, rather than "what"; a person, not a piece of kit. I was hoping to interview a patient I'd learned about in my earlier meeting. But the shopkeeper claimed that no-one of that name lived there.'

'Did you talk to James or to Elspeth?'

'How long have you been down here, George? And how many local names have you picked up in that time? If that's the choice I guess it was James I talked to.'

'I've only met Elspeth, but she told me about her husband and referred to him as James. I was hoping to meet him this morning. Elspeth is the only Rock representative on the committee I'm working for. That's the only reason I know their names.'

George paused: did she know something relevant to help her newly-contacted friend? 'Now I think about it, she told me they had a small flat in the attic over their living quarters above the shop. But it was no longer occupied, she said. So maybe your patient's moved on.'

'But if that's all that's happened, why did James tell me something different? I mean, he must have known the name of the lodger they'd just had living above them. Why on earth lie about it?'

'It's another mystery. Talking of mysteries, I haven't told you yet about the Environment Agency man in Wadebridge. He had a run-in with some policeman from Tintagel - that's near to Delabole, isn't it? Probably you'd know him. About something poisonous he'd found in a water source there, which he refused to tell the scientist what it was. All this secrecy, it's not very helpful is it?'

The doctor had to agree. He thought he had better not add to her suspicions by admitting that the policeman was his best friend.

Then he wondered if he ought to warn George, on the basis of his conversations with that friend, that she might be in some danger.

'Do you really need to meet James?' he asked. 'I can't explain why, but my instinct is that you should stay away from him for the time being.'

George did not offer any commitment. She was sure the doctor was sincere but she was not in the habit of being frightened off – not without more information, anyway.

Soon their coffee break was over. The doctor realised that he had to be getting back to his surgery.

The two exchanged business cards, giving their phone numbers and Brian scribbled his address on the back. 'I appreciate that you're down here to work. But if you could spare the time, my wife and I would love to have you over for a meal. We could show you the delights of Delabole. It wouldn't take long. Do let us know. But, for now, let me take you back to Rock.'

CHAPTER 34

Sergeant Peter Travers thought hard, and with a glimmer of satisfaction, about what his friend had told him over lunch at the Trewarmett Inn. They had a possible name for their victim. At last!

A tall, thirty-year-old woman, Cécile Ferrier, with symptoms of previous episodes of self-harming down both arms, had not been seen at her short-term address in Rock since August 8th. That was promising in itself. But, adding to the suspicion, the owner of the flat where she was staying denied he had ever heard of her.

Only the evening before he had been in despair over their lack of progress. Now he had a possible victim; and even a possible suspect. Though all this had fallen rather suddenly into his lap, he reminded himself that the idea of looking for reasons for chopping off limbs had been his own. And it had made use of official records, though in this case they had relied on the Health Service rather than the tattooist or the police's own data.

The last-seen date bothered him a little. It was outside the range he had been working to, but not far. It was surely worth a look.

Then he remembered the media blackout Inspector Chadwick had insisted he worked under. If he dragged the Rock flat-owner in for questioning about a dead body and there was some innocent explanation – maybe Southgate had simply misunderstood his reply - he might not be so keen to keep quiet afterwards. Travers had managed to silence the local journalist in Tintagel, but this man might not be so amenable.

But on the other hand, if the man was guilty he might have found Southgate's approach suspicious, even though it was more or less genuine. There really was a study being carried out on self-harmers living in the area. Was there anything the policeman could do to make sure the owner – James, was it? - didn't suddenly disappear?

When he thought about it, he had spent all his efforts so far finding the identity of the victim. He had no real evidence of anything beyond a savage death. Or to be precise, the savage dismantling of an already-dead body. The proper investigation to find the criminal had hardly begun. And what there had been was mostly in the hands of the Crime Squad up in Exeter.

But there was the purple paint just below bonnet level on the height barrier. He wondered what coloured vehicle James owned; or, if he'd changed it in the last month, what colour it had been.

Southgate had also talked about meeting the widow of his school friend, Mark. She had also been in the shop and talked to James' wife.

He peered into his notebook; he had taken a note of her name and mobile phone number. His friend had said that George – odd name, why not Georgia or Georgina? – was reliable and sharp. Could she give him one or two more details?

Half an hour later he sat back, pleased. It had been a productive phone call. First of all George had given him the surname and address for James and Elspeth: Hammond. It was "blazoned over their shop". In a few minutes he would look up what vehicles the couple owned, using the police vehicle database.

But George had been thinking about the situation as well. He was sure Brian would not give much away to her directly, but she was a canny business woman - no doubt good at reading between the lines.

She told him that on her own visit to the shop, a week ago – the first Thursday of September – Elspeth had mentioned that her husband was normally away on the first Thursday of the month. He went looking at the latest electrical gadgets in Plymouth.

So if he had done that a month ago . . . he checked his diary, that would be August 7th . . . then that would be a suitable date for someone who had dumped a body at Trewarmett a day or two earlier. Provided he had a car of the correct colour.

His computer whirred. He didn't often have to use it to link owners to cars; normally the question came the other way round - either making sense of cars which had been found abandoned, or pinning down the owners of vehicles reported to him for dangerous driving.

At last an answer appeared. But it was not what he had expected. According to the police database, James Hammond of Rock did not own any vehicle at all.

But that didn't make sense. He must at least have access to a car. How else did he travel to Plymouth every month? It would be a miserable journey across Cornwall: a series of buses in each direction. After a few seconds, though, he remembered he hadn't completed his search.

Once again Travers' computer whirred, this time with the name Elspeth Hammond. And this time there was success. Elspeth was the owner of a small green Astra. But she was also the nominal owner of a small van.

And, hey, the van's colour was down on the database as

"magenta". Which, after a moment's thought, Peter Travers realised was an official-sounding word that could mean pinkish-purple.

His first instinct was to speed over to Rock and take Hammond in to the nearest Police Station at Bodmin for questioning. But again he remembered Chadwick's warning. Were there any other preliminary steps he could take before he alerted Hammond?

One possibility remained. Vehicle paint-spraying businesses were not that common. Assume Hammond really did go regularly to Plymouth to keep himself up to date on gadgets. Then it was most likely that he would have tried to have his van paint-spraying done while he was there. Of course, he might have the job done elsewhere, say Launceston, but the work would probably take two or three hours. He was unlikely to choose to be stuck in a small town, without transport and without much to do.

Travers had been issued with a set of "Yellow Pages for Cornwall and Devon" as part of his police equipment though it was seldom needed. He found their best use was as doorstops. Now he seized the volume dealing with Plymouth from beside his study door and started to search.

Eventually he came across one place that did the kind of business he was interested in, located in the docks area. He guessed that much of their business would be re-spraying boats.

The policeman thought about the geography of Plymouth. Yes, the docks were a strolling distance from the middle of Plymouth – no more than a mile away. Hammond would be able to look at new televisions and satellite receivers and the rest to his heart's content while the repair was being done - assuming he took the van there. It was worth a phone call.

This was painstaking detection work, thought Travers. He battled past the youth-opportunity lad on "reception" at the firm, who seemed to think his job-title was "rejection"; past the personnel lady (why on earth did they need one of these in a paint shop?); and finally on to the manager. Fortunately the man had been on duty on Thursday August 7th and had access to the firm's records for that day.

There was a pause while he hunted down the customers served.

But the name of James Hammond was not on the list.

Travers grimaced. He was about to ring off and start looking through Yellow Pages again, seeking any similar establishment in the Plymouth area, when one more question came to him. 'Do you keep a record of the registration numbers of the vehicles you deal with?'

'Course we do. Especially if the vehicle is to be given a different colour. The police often want to know about that when they're after stolen cars. All the car-thieves know we keep that data now, though, so we don't usually have them coming here.'

Travers told him the registration number he was interested in and held his breath.

'Yes, that vehicle was here with us on August 7th. It was a van. Brought in by a Mr Simmonds, it says. Maybe my lad misheard. According to our records there was a gash at the front, just under the bonnet lid. It wasn't a big job, the rest of the vehicle looked fine. We just had to knock out a small dent and then re-spray that part to match the rest. By the time we'd finished it looked as good as new.'

'Thank you, sir, that's really helpful. Could I ask you, please, not to say anything about this phone call to anyone - especially

not to Mr Simmonds. This is part of an ongoing inquiry.'
Travers rang off and tried to work out what he should do next.

Reluctantly, he decided he had done as much as he could
without higher authority. He reached for his phone to dial his
boss in Exeter.

CHAPTER 35

George Gilbert decided the advice she had been given by Brian Southgate was sound. It was ridiculous to think that her Uncle Bill could possibly be involved in anything crooked; she felt ashamed to think she had let the suspicion even cross her mind.

Random surveys of visitors for her project could wait. Her peace of mind was more important. She resolved to return to Padstow as soon as possible and wring the truth out of him.

Crucially, what was going on in the Fourways Inn snug every fortnight? It was an odd place for a serious meeting. Whatever it was, she wanted to know. Like the Environment Agency scientist in Wadebridge, she was fed up with being fobbed off by official confidentiality.

Brian had dropped her off on the road in Rock down by the estuary. She joined one or two tourists on the Rock beach, awaiting the next ferry back. She'd obviously just missed one. The twenty minute delay was irritating (maybe there was a case for enlarging capacity after all?) but gave her time to plan a provisional line of questioning; to guess how her uncle might react; and to work out alternative responses. Now she had braced herself to act she wanted to do so quickly.

So she was pleased, after she reached Padstow, tramped up the hill and arrived at his cottage, to find that Bill was at home. She had feared she might yet again find him absent.

'I've just got back from shopping. Haven't had my lunch

yet,' he greeted her, 'do you want to join me?'

George hadn't realised it was already two o'clock, well past her lunch time. But it would be much easier to talk over a meal. Soon two plates of cheddar, a jar of pickled onions, a bowl of salad and a basket of rolls had appeared on the kitchen table; and a proper conversation could begin.

'Bill, I've come across various peculiar items while I've been down here. And I'd like your help to make sense of them.'

'You make it sound very mysterious, m'dear. But if it's local I may know something. What sort of things did you have in mind?'

'Well, first of all, am I right that you were at a meeting last Saturday morning in St Minver?'

Bill looked surprised. But as George had calculated while waiting for the ferry, whatever his training or instinct might dictate, he wouldn't be able to bring himself to tell his invited guest a direct lie.

'Well, I was, as it happens. And what's so odd about that?'

'But they're regular meetings, aren't they – every other Saturday?'

Again she had given him little scope to obfuscate. 'I've no idea how you know this, m'dear, or why you're interested, but, as a matter of fact they are regular gatherings.'

George could see he was looking more anxious now. His initial confident openness was being challenged. If she wasn't careful he might simply refuse to answer any further; then she would be stymied.

'I didn't want to overhear anything. I'm just a guest here. But once or twice I couldn't help it. I walked in and heard the end of your phone calls. They all sounded very secretive; and they stopped abruptly once I made any noise. It was clear that you didn't want me to hear any more. And I also took that very short phone message that I left on the table here – a rather odd message, from someone who didn't give his name. Tell me: are these anything to do with your meetings in St Minver?'

Bill looked troubled. Now his guest had laid out the various incidents, he could see why she had become so curious. Were all females so inquisitive? But just because the question had been asked didn't mean he was at liberty to explain. He recalled being advised a long time ago that a good evasive response to an awkward question was to ask a question in return.

'And have you any suggestions for what this might all mean?'

George had given this some thought, most recently on the ferry. She took a deep breath. 'I wondered if it had something to do with your previous work in the Royal Navy, or maybe the Ministry of Defence?'

'Go on. That's an interesting idea.'

'I've never had anything to do with national security. I watch Spooks and I've read John Le Carré and that's about it. I'm a business analyst. But the only thing I could think of that might pull together the items I've just listed, and that would also account for their secrecy, would be some sort of security operation. But I've no idea what that could be.'

'Of course, I'm not saying anything. If it's secret then how could I? But let's carry on guessing for a moment. No – I know, I've got a better idea. How about you telling me how you found out about those meetings in St Minver?'

George had feared that she might have to disclose this. But she could hardly expect her uncle to give her his secrets if she wouldn't do the same in return.

'I came across a letter to Paddy Watmough when I was

going through the harbour records on Friday. It had got caught between two charts I was photocopying. I was bored and I skimmed it. And I saw it talked about regular fortnightly meetings on Saturdays at St Minver.'

'So what happened next?'

'I was intrigued. I thought I might as well wander up there last Saturday and take a look. See how many came and what sort of people they were and whether the meeting was quiet or rowdy. For all I knew it could be a bunch of Scalextric enthusiasts. Of course, I didn't expect to recognise anybody.'

'And that's when you saw me?'

'Oh, no. The landlady must have blocked my view as you came in: she's well built. I was sitting in the darkest corner, wearing my cagoule and scarf and shielded by my laptop. I did see Applegate though, arriving first. He looked very smart, like a top-level civil servant. If he was hoping to blend in as a tourist he was grossly overdressed. And I saw Watmough creep in – he was a whole minute late. Black mark! I didn't recognise anyone else.'

George paused to recall what else had occurred to her. 'The only reason I knew you were there is that I saw the number plate of your car parked outside as I left. But I didn't even recognise that at once – I'd never seen your vehicle. It was only when you took me to the Stepper Point Lookout on Sunday that I realised whose car it was.'

'And that's the sum total of the mysteries you've been worrying about?'

George paused to check her mental list. It didn't seem so long, now she'd spoken it all out.

'There was just one more item. I saw it when you took me to see the Doom Bar on Tuesday.'

Bill looked puzzled now. 'Go on.'

'When we were anchored over the Antoinette, I saw something odd about the wreck.'

'You're intriguing me. How do you mean, odd?'

'There was a metal tube, about six foot long, firmly attached to one of the ribs. It pointed vertically.'

'That sounds very bizarre. Are you sure? Was it an old tube?'

'No, it looked very modern. Would you like to see my pictures?'

Half an hour later George was still feeling confused; but no longer excluded. For Bill had shown a great deal of interest in her pictures of the tube on the Antoinette. It had helped that she could also show him the cropped and expanded close-ups; and that one of these had displayed a peculiar device at the top end of the tube.

Once he had examined the pictures, Bill had been pensive for a while. Then he had asked for them to be downloaded onto his computer. 'If you don't mind, I'd like to send them on to someone.' And after that he had made a phone call to Applegate.

Her uncle had made no attempt to make the call in private. George had been sitting in the lounge; but Bill had deliberately left the door into the hall wide open as he made the call. George guessed this was the nearest he could come to telling her what was going on without explicitly betraying his secrets.

She didn't yet know everything. But she listened hard. And, if Bill was prepared to let her make suggestions, she now had several more ideas she was keen to test out.

CHAPTER 36

Peter Travers had not expected too much praise from Inspector Chadwick when he finally got through to him at Exeter. He knew the man was too frazzled to have much energy left for personal appreciation. But he had hoped his efforts would at least be acknowledged before being taken further.

What he had never expected was that Chadwick would tell him that, as far as the police were concerned, the investigation was closed until further notice.

'I'm sorry lad. I got my orders half an hour ago. I was first shutting down the activities I knew were taking place here. Then I was going to tell you. I hadn't realised you were still actively pursuing the investigation today or I would have come to you first.'

'Sorry, sir, I don't understand. We both saw the sawn-up torso. It's a serious crime. Why on earth are we closing the case?'

'It's politics, Travers. National Security Force trumps Regional Police efforts. Bloody high-level, inter-departmental politics.'

'Could you explain a bit more, sir. That sort of thing may happen all the time in Exeter but I've not come across it before down here –at least, not at my lowly level.'

'Basically, I got hauled in by senior management. They asked me to give them a progress report. I didn't have much to tell them. As you can imagine, that didn't go down too well. They beat me up over that for a while. Went on about crime-solving statistics in the South West and how I'd let them down. Then, when I was just starting to argue that the work was only ten days old, they told me that the case had been shown to have wider security connections. So that it would be taken over at once by the Security Forces. I was to stop working on the case immediately.'

'But . . . '

'I don't like it any more than you do, Travers. I may be grossly overloaded but I take my cases seriously. I don't like having them taken off me. I want to solve them not drop 'em. And no - I've no idea how they can know it's a security issue when you and I've spent a week and a half on it and not even found out the name of the victim.'

'That was what I was going to tell you, sir. I think I may have found the name of the victim.'

'Bloody hell, Travers. I wish I'd known that an hour ago. Mind, I doubt it would have made much difference. Top brass had already made up their mind that this was one to set aside. How on earth have you done that?'

'Well sir, do you remember Dr Southgate – he was guarding the body the first day, when you came down to Trewarmett. We met him at the quarry. He had to help with a local Area Health study about women who had self-harmed. And he spotted that one of the girls on his list was the right sort of age and build for her to have been the victim. So, purely for his health study, he tried to interview her. The health records he'd obtained showed that she used to live in Rock. But he found that she had disappeared –at the start of August.'

'Travers, that doesn't prove she was the victim. She might just have gone on holiday. Evidence, man, we need evidence.'

'Quite so, sir. So when he told me this, a couple of hours ago, I got the address where the girl had been staying, it was a hardware and electrical shop in Rock. Then I found out what vehicles they owned, using the police vehicle database. And one of them was a purple van. You remember, sir, I told you that the Environment Agency scientist told me he'd seen a purple mark on the height barrier – one that wasn't there the last time he visited.'

'Travers, we can't arrest a man for murder because he has a purple van. There must be thousands of vans like that – dozens in your part of Cornwall.'

'I agree, sir. But I gathered from the lady at the shop that her husband always went to check on new electrical products in Plymouth on the first Thursday of the month.'

'This is getting worse . . .'

'Hear me out, sir. You see, I looked up paint re-spray businesses in Plymouth in the Yellow Pages; there were only a couple that were within walking distance of the main shops. So on the off-chance I rang them.'

'To ask them if they'd ever repainted a purple van?'

'Not as general as that, sir. I had the van's registration number from the police database. So I asked if they had dealt with this particular van on August 7th – that's the first Thursday of last month. And they had.'

There was silence at the other end of the phone. Inspector Chadwick was thinking hard; no doubt weighing his recently-received orders to curtail his inquiry against the real prospect of making significant progress. 'So you were ringing me to suggest we interview this chap?'

'It gets better sir. The chap is called James Hammond. But when he took his van in for repairs in Plymouth, their records show that he lied about his name. Said he was called Simmonds. So what I was hoping to discuss with you, sir, was what we should do now?'

Half an hour later an angry Peter Travers, having been rebuffed by the sanctimonious telephone guardians at Brian Southgate's surgery, decided that he would ring George Gilbert.

He wanted to unburden himself to someone. And to be fair, George had given Brian the information about the granny flat over the shop. She'd also given him the crucial information on the dates when James went to Plymouth – dates which, it seemed, had moved the case substantially forward.

George had been friendly and lucid when they talked earlier. And there was no point in registering his frustration to someone else within the police force. A sympathetic female would be much better to listen to his woes.

The phone seemed to ring for ages. She was obviously busy with something – or someone. By the time George had answered the policeman had started to realise that this was not an appropriate action. But he still needed to say something.

'Mrs Gilbert? Police Sergeant Peter Travers here again. I was mainly ringing to thank you for the information you gave me about James being away on the first Thursday of the month. It was really helpful.'

'I'm glad I could be of help. Does it mean you can make an arrest or something?'

'It's really odd, actually. I rang my boss in Exeter to discuss how we should proceed. But it turned out he'd just been told – by his boss - to close down the investigation. I'm gutted.'

'That doesn't make sense. Not if you were making progress.'

'It makes no sense at all, Mrs Gilbert. I've bust my guts over this case for the last week and a half. Almost been tattooed on one occasion; had a massive turf war with a man from the Environment Agency on another. And now it's closed. But what I also wanted to warn you about was to be careful over James Hammond. In fact, I would strongly advise you to keep well away from him. Of course, this is all unofficial - I can't say more at this stage - but please take me seriously.'

'Who was that?' asked Bill Gilbert.

'It was my local policeman friend, Peter Travers, not that I've met him yet. He's based in Delabole. Apparently he's a good friend of Brian Southgate – that's Mark's old school friend that you mentioned.'

'Oh yes, I know Travers. Good man; solid and down to earth. Been around these parts for years.'

'He was ringing to thank me for some information I gave him this morning. And to warn me to stay away from someone I had planned to interview in Rock. He'd been hoping to arrest him, I think, but he'd just been told to close down the investigation instead. He sounded fed up.'

'How odd. Police investigations aren't usually asked to close down. Not unless there's some overlapping security angle or something.' Bill puzzled for a moment. 'What was the chap's name that you have to avoid? I might even know him.'

'He was called James. James Hammond. He and his wife run a hardware and electrical shop.'

'Oh, I know James. He's . . . well, perhaps I'd better not say. How extraordinary.'

CHAPTER 37

George Gilbert sat in her room that Thursday evening pulling together the various pieces she had managed to make Bill divulge about his 'other life'. She remembered thinking that being "retired" simply told her what he no longer did; and that she had not pressed him too hard on what he did. Maybe that was as well.

He had not "told" her anything. She presumed that was because he had obligations to his colleagues and maybe was bound by the Official Secrets Act? She remembered Mark storming on once about its draconian powers. But given that her uncle had strongly denied some of her more outlandish guesses, yet smiled serenely at others, she presumed that many of her suggestions had been close to the mark. So what did it all add up to?

She gleaned that Bill was part of some loose security ring around Padstow and Rock. It acted as a "Hidden Extra Layer of Protection" – or HELP for short. All the members of the ring had a relevant background, either in one of the Armed Forces or in the Ministry of Defence. He and the rest of the ring met fortnightly, for briefing and sharing, in the snug in St Minver.

Bill had effectively confirmed that Applegate was the smartly-dressed man she had seen arrive first; he was the focal point for the ring and the person to whom they were each answerable.

So what was HELP for? She gathered that there was some

important member of the establishment, a senior politician, who brought his family to spend part of his summers in a cottage around these parts. He had come here regularly before he mattered to anyone and continued to come even though now he did. Was that because his children and wife insisted?

Of course, there was a core of protection provided by the state – as for all such high-ups. His cottage had been thoroughly checked for any explosives or listening devices before he arrived. Once he had come there would be a couple of armed guards keeping permanent watch; and another who would accompany him and his family on their outings to the beach - or wherever they chose to go. The politician might not much like this intrusion and his family certainly wouldn't, but he probably shrugged and accepted it as a necessary part of the public life he had chosen.

But the politician did not know about the outer ring, comprising Bill and his colleagues. There was no reason why he should. They were all background people, locals who had taken on extra responsibility for modest remuneration. Their task was simply to keep an eye out for anyone behaving suspiciously, or who was asking too many questions. If they saw something suspicious they were not to intervene but to act as a back-stop, contributing the new facts to Applegate and hence to the intelligence pool.

No-one expected trouble. The same arrangement had started the summer before, when the politician had first become significant; nothing untoward had happened then. The biggest risk, probably, was some sort of eavesdropping - picking up snippets of conversation or plans only intended to be heard in private; or wicked asides about fellow-politicians. Or even potential scandals that had so far remained hidden to the outside world.

Bill was no kind of political animal, George realised. But he believed that politicians, like everyone else, were entitled to some privacy. She thought that on the whole this was a sensible viewpoint.

The politician entertained many visitors over the summer: other politicians, sponsors, supporters and even opposite numbers from countries in Europe and beyond. He was generous in his hospitality and on occasion would invite the visitors to stay on to enjoy the Cornish coast and beaches, while he travelled elsewhere. After all, the security was in place. It was better to make the most of it than to stretch a creaking National Security budget even further.

But this year, during the summer, leaks had started to appear in overseas newspapers. These had included suggestions of radical ideas; new ways of doing business that had never previously been considered; and ways of handling opposing forces - across other parties and in their own.

It had taken a couple of weeks for these to be spotted in the UK – during the "silly season" the national papers were always full of odd items, most of which their own reporters had made up. Many security staff were on holiday at this time too – they had children as well.

But eventually the leaks' provenance had been traced to the politician's cottage in North Cornwall. And then the pressure on security staff and on Bill's HELP ring had become more intense. This was exactly the time, George realised, that she had arrived in Padstow.

George gathered that the earliest leak which was certain, a new fact about immigration not in the public domain, had occurred at the beginning of August; and the leaks had continued regularly ever since.

She tried to imagine what might have occurred to make the leaks suddenly available. But she did not know enough about the process by which a leak could be induced. Could the politician be advised that less outrageous remarks be made? No, the thought was ridiculous: she guessed that no Security Force man would dare tell a politician that he could no longer speak freely in his own home.

Now she could understand why Bill had been so busy since her arrival and was out most evenings. He and the rest of his ring had no idea how the leaks were happening either or how they could be stopped.

While George was grappling with new information on her own, fifteen miles away Peter Travers was doing much the same; but he was in the company of Brian Southgate in a secluded corner of the Trewarmett Inn.

He felt no guilt in sharing his professional frustrations. The policeman was baffled by what had occurred; and unlike Inspector Chadwick he did not have a mountain of other cases he could move on to. How could he return with any enthusiasm to community policing, when there was a vicious murderer on the loose in the area, possibly running a shop in the centre of Rock?

'Trouble is, Peter, that though you had enough data to question the man – James - you've got nowhere near enough to bring a case against him. Not on what you've told me, anyway. This embargo from on high that's brought your investigation to a grinding halt might be a blessing in disguise.'

'If it is a blessing the disguise is bloody good, I'd say.'

'No, look. You don't even know that the paint on his car is the same as the paint on the barrier up the road here. It just happens to be roughly the same colour. How much of his car was painted over in Plymouth? And even if it was only a fraction on that day, he might have had the whole van repainted somewhere else later on. Do you know what colour it is now?'

The policeman had not thought of that.

His friend continued remorselessly, 'Even if your Forensic lads can show by clever analysis that it's exactly the same paint as found on his car, he can just suddenly remember he visited the quarry in the past month. He could freely admit he was there – but not at the time that matters. Claim an interest in industrial archaeology or something. It would give a faint link to the body-discovery scene but it's not overwhelming proof of anything else, is it?'

'He's admitted the woman had stayed in his house; and then he visited the scene where she was dumped. Isn't that suggestive?'

'Peter, you haven't even proved it's the same woman. That might not be too easy. OK, she was the right size and age and had self-harming marks down her arms. It all fits, as far as it goes. But that's not proof, is it?'

'If Forensics could get access to his flat they could probably find traces of her DNA – couldn't they?'

'It's over a month since she was staying in Rock. I bet James, or let's be honest his wife, has cleaned the flat since she left. She might even have re-let it. Unless Cécile left a towel or something behind and they've "kept it in a bag in case she reclaims it", it might be hard to prove forensically that she was ever there at all.'

'But,' continued the doctor brutally, 'if Hammond has anything at all to do with her disappearance, keeping her towel is the very last thing he'll do. And that's the only link to James that you've got.'

Peter Travers sighed and took a big swig of his cider. He was starting to see why the Crime Squad took so long to solve their cases.

'But we've got the name she used to register with the local surgery. "Cécile Ferrier". Assuming she wasn't making that up, doesn't that give us a start? I mean, if the torso we found is that woman then someone, somewhere must be missing her. In France, maybe? Hey - were there any other details on her medical record?'

'I re-checked the medical stuff this afternoon. There's not much. She just gave the flat over the shop in Rock as her address. That's a fault in the system, incidentally – we should have had her long-term address. She should have been forced to give it when she registered. Somewhere in France, I would guess. Ferrier is their equivalent of "Smith". She only registered with the Rock doctor in mid July. And her last visit to the surgery was on August 8th.'

The policeman gawped at him. 'But that's too late – '

'All those end-of-life dates from Forensics are best estimates, Peter. The torso might not have been dumped till then - even though that's a few days later than they thought possible. If the water in the pool was cooler in August than on the day we measured it, for instance.'

'No, no, I don't mean that. The date when Hammond took his car to Plymouth and had it re-sprayed. That was a day earlier than that - August 7th.'

The policeman explained, 'I feared it was all far too good to be true. James can't possibly be the murderer after all.'

CHAPTER 38

Though Bill Gilbert preferred the familiarity of his landline he did own a mobile phone. An elaborate one, in fact, with many security features – too many, he often thought. And when he did not want to risk being overheard, even by his house guest whom he trusted, he was prepared to use it.

Jeremy Applegate was not used to receiving calls from members of the HELP team but when they occurred he gave them his full attention.

'Jerry, I'm very concerned about a police investigation embargo. One I've just discovered that you've imposed in the past twenty four hours. Can you give me some background, please? Does it affect me? Is there anything I should know? And for how long, do you think, will it be in place?'

Applegate was a smooth operator. He hadn't expected Bill's call but he had faced sharper questions than this in Whitehall.

'Bill, I know you have a great attachment to the honest and straightforward, which of course I respect and admire – and indeed share. The law of the land does apply equally without fear or favour to the great and the small. It's the hallmark of a mature democracy. It's just that the 'greater good' sometimes requires unusual methods to achieve and maintain it. Anyway, how do you know about this – it was meant to be top secret?'

'There are benefits in being a long-term local in the area. I'm built in to the village gossip grape-vine. I hear an awful lot and that's why I'm some use to HELP. I gather the local policeman felt he was making progress on some case or other and was very frustrated to be hauled off it.'

'Hm. This was all supposed to be low key. Exeter assured me there was nothing to lose: the police were stuck for the time being, anyway. They'd plenty of other cases for the senior detective to work on.'

'Jerry, how can a police investigation possibly affect our security operation?'

'To be honest, it was James who asked me to take action. He told me he was worried that he was being drawn in to some police investigation. He feared he might be spending days answering damn-fool questions from some plod in Bodmin Police Station when he should be on the track of this leak.'

'There seems to be a discrepancy between Exeter's notion that the police were making no progress at all and James' fear that he was about to be arrested.'

'Yes, I did wonder about that. I asked James if he wasn't being paranoid. But he seemed convinced there was a real threat. He feared they might end up searching his shop and also the flat above. That could uncover more than we would want to reveal – even to the police. Once the police know something the media won't be far behind, first extracting it and then announcing it to the world. "The public's right to know" and all that. There's various bits of advanced surveillance equipment we've got installed over that electrical shop that I would rather we didn't have to talk about – or to move.'

'Do you know what the police were investigating?'

Applegate wondered for a second whether he should refuse to answer this; maybe appeal to the "you don't need to know" principle. He had already said far more than he'd intended.

But Bill was the senior member of his team here down in

Cornwall. The naval man would probably find out the answer in other ways if he didn't give the information himself.

'I understand it was some woman's body, found in a pool near Trewarmett. Apparently she was murdered.'

'How on earth can that link to James?'

'James believes the woman may have stayed for a time in the flat over his shop, so he was her landlord for a few weeks.'

'But in that case he should go to police and offer to help. I'm sure he would be a civilised landlord, tell her about special tickets for the Eden Project, local red wine deals and so on. I can't imagine him charging an excessive rent. Why on earth would they suspect him of having anything to do with her death?'

'It was a bit more complicated than that, I gather.'

'Because?'

'James told me that he had discovered that the woman was an overseas journalist. Working in an underhand way. He had confronted her about it and then she left very suddenly.'

'But surely it would help the police to know that?'

'It might. And one day soon we'll tell them. The trouble is that James strongly suspects that if something happened to this woman, after he rumbled her and moved her on, the most likely culprit will be her colleague. That's whoever she was working with on her undercover journalism. If the colleague learned that she'd been found out, worst of all by someone with links to national security, that might cause a massive row between the two of 'em. Maybe one with fatal consequences.'

'You mean, when we finally solve the leak we might also solve the murder?'

'We might well. Or at least give the police inquiry a push forward. And of course, that's the answer to another of your questions earlier. Given what you told me this afternoon about the mysterious metal tube on the wreck, we've now got some idea on how the information is being taken from the protected household.'

'But we don't know yet how it's being recorded.'

'No, but we're on the trail. And as soon as we've found the leak, Bill, I promise we'll end the embargo. To be honest, I'm not that comfortable about it either. Whether or not there's any connection between the leaker and the murderer. I'm not going to stop James answering police questions for ever. None of us are above the law, not for long, anyway.'

There seemed to be nothing else to say. Bill felt he had registered a protest and made some progress on having it resolved. He ended the call and switched off his phone. He was by no means satisfied, but for the moment could not see what more he could do.

CHAPTER 39

Later that Thursday evening Jeremy Applegate's computer clattered into life as it picked up a highly classified document from the Cornwall Internal Security Team. At the same time his security phone rang. It was his colleague from Internal Security.

'Following your note earlier today, we've just sent you the final section of an interview transcript. We picked the man up wandering about on the beach near Trebetherick earlier this afternoon, where our major client and his wife had been surfing. He was wearing a wetsuit and carrying a body board. We strip-searched him – that didn't take long – but he wasn't carrying anything. No explosives, drugs or listening devices. Not even a phone. And his body board was perfectly normal. Even so, I think you'll find it interesting. We're holding the guy here for the present.'

Applegate was tempted to retort that you couldn't just hold every surfer who went near the client. But he needed some facts. Turning to his computer, he downloaded the document and applied the decryption software with the latest password. There was a new one each day: he was sent page and line number and had to look up the first word of the line from Thomas Hardy's 'Far from the Madding Crowd'. Sometimes he wondered if this wasn't overkill.

After a few minutes a readable document appeared. He spent a minute fiddling with font size so he could browse it on his monitor without excessive squinting. Then he settled down to read.

TRANSCRIPT OF INTERVIEW THURSDAY SEPT 11TH 2008 (PART 3)
INTERVIEWER: INTERNAL SECURITY
SUBJECT: ALLAIN CHAUSSEUR

[IS] Monsieur, this afternoon you were found on the same tract of beach as [our major client] and his family. You were on your own. You had a body board but there were no signs it had recently been used. And the body board was green, the same colour and size as [our client's]. Have you any explanation?

[AC] Explanation? It's a coincidence. I have had my surf board for several months. Green is a common colour. And it was not a private beach, just a quiet one. Some way from the crowds at Polzeath. Is that not correct? Why are you holding me here?

[IS] Monsieur, we have security cameras in place on this beach. Hidden cameras, mounted among the rocks at both ends. And since we arrested you we have reviewed their footage carefully.

[AC] And what did you see? Rien! Nothing happened this afternoon.

[IS] That's right. We could see nothing unusual, anyway. So then we looked back to the film of the beach from earlier days this summer. And we have seen that it is not the first time you have been there.

[AC] [AC Shrugs] No. It's not. As I say, it's a quiet beach. So what?

[IS] We had to go back some time to find it: the previous occasion was the start of August. But do you know what? [Our client] was there with his body board on that occasion as well.

Was this another coincidence?

[AC] Maybe it's a popular beach. Or else we have common tastes.

[IS] I would say it's rather a quiet beach. Maybe we can agree that it attracts quality rather than quantity. But on that occasion you were not alone. There was an attractive lady there too. Early thirties, tall and slim.

[AC] Like I said, it's a popular beach.

[IS] This lady was with you. And she wasn't wearing a wetsuit but a skimpy bikini. Half of which she discarded once the sun came out. Giving pleasure, incidentally, to our security guards when they later watched the film. I believe that's how they found it again so quickly. You and she definitely arrived together. So can you tell me her name, please?

[Pause: AC seems distressed at this news.]

[AC] That was Cécile, Cécile Ferrier. She is a good friend. Yes, we were together on the beach for that one occasion. It was the only time. But I don't know where she has gone. Do you have any news of her?

[IS] When did you last see Ms Ferrier?

[AC] At the end of that afternoon – Saturday August 2nd – she came back to my flat in Padstow. That was quite an adventure.

[IS] Why? What happened?

[AC] After we'd been on the beach I went swimming in the estuary; and got into difficulties.

[IS] What sort of difficulties?

[AC] There was a storm; it blew up suddenly. Cécile wasn't with me; she'd started walking back to Rock. By some miracle she saw I was in trouble. She managed to hire a small boat in Rock. She piloted it out, located me in the swell and pulled me on board.

[IS] So you were a fortunate man. What happened next?

[AC] I was almost finished: the waves were massive. I lay exhausted in the bottom of the boat. I don't know where she took me, I think to a tiny harbour on the far side of Stepper Point. It was hard to see in the storm but she seemed to have an instinct for the sea. I think she was brought up in Bordeaux. Anyway, wherever we'd landed, we got a taxi back to Padstow. When we finally got to my flat I was wiped out.

[IS] And Cécile stayed with you that night?

[AC] No. As I told you she was just a friend. We were both just wearing swimming gear and wetsuits. But Cécile had a set of spare clothes – underwear and a smart dress - which she had stored in my flat. She got changed and then set off back to Rock. I was too tired to go with her. But I never saw her again.

[IS] Never saw her again . . . I see. That sounds rather odd. But you must have talked to her on the phone? Did she ever reach her flat?

[AC] Yes. I mean no. I tried ringing her – many times - but her phone did not respond. It was dead. I would have liked to visit her flat to check, of course, but how could I? She hadn't told me where it was.

[IS] And as your stay here was all innocence you reported her disappearance to the police? We have a fine police service in this country. Just because they have no guns does not mean they are ineffective.

[AC] No. I am sure your police are fine. But . . . I was busy. I decided to wait and see if she turned up again. The only thing I could think of was that she might have been called away at short notice to another job.

[IS] Called away? To what sort of job? And by whom?

[Pause while AC assessed his options]

[AC] Cécile and I are journalists. With the Paris Lumière - it's a bit like Private Eye. It is a hectic profession. We move about a lot to find the stories. We both like to probe below the surface – to find out what's going on beneath the façade. That's why she and I were working together.

[IS] Hm. We will need to know more about this. But there is one other matter you can help us on. We have examined your wrist watch. It shows the right time and is waterproof – it's still working and we don't believe it will explode. We noticed it also could act as an alarm clock. Fine; but the alarm is set to go off at two o'clock in the morning. Can you tell us, please, why you need to be woken up in the middle of the night?

[AC] Um . . . I'm not sure. Oh yes, I had it set to that time to catch a plane when I came here in July. Just because the time is set on my watch doesn't mean it goes off every night.

The transcript continued in this vein for several more pages. Applegate studied it carefully. Then he reached for his phone and dialled Bill. It was late but this might be the breakthrough they were after.

He could simply have given his Internal Security colleagues his ideas. No doubt they would take the action and claim all the credit. But it would be much more impressive if he could give them some hard facts. Especially if his own team could provide them.

CHAPTER 40

Bill Gilbert was not happy with Jeremy Applegate's cavalier approach to the legal system. In his view no-one should be above the law – full stop. And he was not so inclined to give James Hammond the benefit of the doubt. Of course, like anyone else, the man was entitled to be presumed innocent until proven guilty. But that did not mean he should be immune to investigation.

He recalled that James and his wife had only come down to Cornwall a couple of years ago. Although he met James regularly at HELP and Elspeth at PRAM committees, he didn't know either of them that well: neither of these gatherings spawned much social interaction. Before that they both worked in London as high-level civil servants.

Bill guessed it was likely that Applegate had known them in that time. He had been a major player in Whitehall for years. Maybe it was that inside knowledge which made him reluctant to believe the worst of them and allowed the embargo to happen?

But if James was not to be investigated by the police that did not mean he could remain completely in the clear. There were several points of his story needing to be clarified. Bill thought that he himself could find ways of asking the awkward questions, and could pass on any interesting results to Applegate.

The first problem was how and where the conversation might happen. Obviously he could not contrive a formal, taped interview. But Bill didn't mind that, he had a good memory. It was an overall impression he wanted, not fine details. But if new facts started to emerge he didn't want James just to be able to walk casually away.

His first idea was to arrange to meet in a room with a secure door, which he could lock and then pocket the key. But it was hardly subtle. James was by no means stupid and would immediately realise he was being interviewed, forcefully if not formally.

It was unclear how he would then behave. He might simply refuse to talk and there would be stalemate – completely unproductive. Or he might turn nasty or even aggressive. Once or twice at HELP meetings there had been strong disagreements and James had lost his temper: it had not been a pretty sight.

Bill was not sure whether he could hang on to the key in that case. He was fit for a man in his sixties but not as strong as someone who coached the local cricket team. On his HELP remit he wasn't expected to take part in active conflict.

Then he remembered the Eilean Donan. If he could lure James out on to the Camel then there would be no-one to interrupt them. The man would have little choice but to converse for a couple of hours. He could hardly walk away from there.

Suddenly he remembered the metal tube on the wreck of the Antoinette, out on the Doom Bar. He had an idea what it might be there for but James was, after all, the HELP technical expert. So it was perfectly natural that he should take the man out to the wreck. He wanted his opinion on what it was - and what they could do about it.

He had just reached this point and was about to look up the times of the tide – there was no point in going out to the Doom

Bar to see the wreck at anything except low tide – when his phone rang. It was Jeremy Applegate.

Swiftly Bill was told about the apprehension of a French journalist, Allain Chausseur, by Internal Security; and his apparently genuine grief at the sudden disappearance of his friend, Cécile Ferrier, at the beginning of August. Applegate thought that it would be interesting to compare this with the story so far pieced together by the police. And it would need to be stacked in due course against James's own version of what had happened.

But the most startling fact was that the journalist got an alarm call at two in the morning. Might this be linked to the tube which Bill had seen on the wreck? Did something odd happen to it at this time of night? And was this a key part of the eavesdropping mechanism?

Bill had certainly not planned to take out his boat with James in the middle of the night. A gentle daytime voyage was what he had in mind. But he had the boat lights needed for a night voyage, it was technically possible. This remit from Applegate could apply to both of them and would make it harder for James to resist coming with him. They could still talk on the journey.

And from his point of view the darkness would make one or two refinements possible.

Now there was a real urgency about the need to gather the Doom Bar intelligence. As well as his personal mission to interrogate James.

Two hours later the two men were sailing out from Rock on the Eilean Donan. At Bill's suggestion, Applegate had been the one to get in touch with James. It was after eleven but fortunately he was still awake.

It had not taken much persuasion for him to come and have a look at the peculiar tube, even though it was the dead of night. The time of low tide was the determining factor. And they all knew, when they signed up, that HELP didn't work standard office hours.

James had heard talk of the wreck on the Doom Bar but never been out to see it, so for him this was a double win.

Bill had computed that the tide would be low enough for them to see the wreck at half two in the morning. This was probably the earliest Allain could get there if he was awakened in his Padstow flat at two, so from either angle it was a sensible target. The only doubt was the weather: the forecast showed a thunderstorm brewing. But Bill thought they could be back to Rock before it took hold. Carefully he set his various instruments for the voyage ahead.

The former sailor was not sure of James' boating skills so he took complete charge, as he had two days earlier with George. He wasn't going to conduct a boating lesson in the dark. And, with that storm imminent, speed was of the essence.

'Jeremy Applegate was telling me that you'd prompted him to ask for a police embargo,' Bill began, as they left the paltry streetlights of the Rock waterfront and started to weave their way down the estuary. A bit abrupt, but he wanted to make the most of their limited time together.

James looked surprised. 'I didn't realise he'd tell anyone within HELP. It was just a precaution. I didn't want to get sidetracked by the police while we were on the trail of the leak.'

'Applegate said you thought you might know the woman who was murdered? Might even have been her landlord?'

'In truth, I've no idea. I never talked to the police. I don't know what the dead woman looked like, I haven't seen photographs or anything. There's been nothing in the papers, has there? But I had got rid of my tenant at short notice in early August – after a major row. I gather she was about the same size as the dead woman – tall and slim; and a similar age.'

There was a pause. Bill had to concentrate on keeping his boat inside a sharp bend in the narrow channel. There was not much light; it was a cloudy night with no moon, but with a rising wind. The tide was now fairly low and the channel's path meandered through a wide expanse of rippled sand.

'So even if it wasn't the same woman,' James continued, once the navigational test was over, 'I feared the police might take up a lot of my time before they could confirm that. Once the police get an idea into their heads it takes a long time for them to replace it with anything else. And all that time I'd be hampered from helping HELP with our search here. Which if we're fortunate we may make progress on tonight. How on earth did you find this tube, by the way?'

Bill did not want to change the subject but if he was to maintain a two-way dialogue he had no choice. So as they cruised slowly down the estuary, with the pitch of the waves steadily stretching as the wind speed rose, he told James about his niece George and her interest in the Doom Bar wrecks.

By the time he'd finished they were approaching the line of waves marking the edge of the Doom Bar – though these were not as gentle as they'd been earlier in the week. The wind was much fiercer now.

'This is where I need my satellite positioning system,' said Bill. 'Otherwise we'll never find her. The Antoinette's not far below the surface, she only shows above it at exceptionally low tides.' As he spoke, checked his instruments, slowed the boat and fine-tuned its direction, he wondered how he could turn the conversation back to James' lodger. Suddenly their location gave him inspiration.

'Was your tenant interested in the Doom Bar?'

'She was, as it happens. Elspeth told her about the wrecks in the estuary when Cécile first arrived and was asking us about the area. We showed her some pictures on the internet, including the Antoinette, and she got very excited. She asked where the wrecks were and if she could go out in the estuary to take a look. She even suggested I should take her out there.'

His narrative was interrupted by the distant rumble of thunder. The storm was going to be here sooner than predicted. Rain began to fall with gathering intensity. It wasn't the best of nights for viewing anything. James continued his story.

'I wasn't having that. I'm not an expert sailor, as you can see. But I did look up the grid reference for the Antoinette and marked it on the map for her. She took it away to look at more carefully. For some reason it seemed to enthuse her even more.

'Meanwhile Elspeth asked her if she was used to boats and then, when she said she was a good sailor, advised her to hire a small boat for the day in Rock. As you know, you can borrow anything from a sailing dinghy to a motorised inflatable through the Rock Sailing Club. I don't know if she ever did.'

'Is that what you had your row about?'

'What row?'

'You said you had a big row with her that made her leave.'

'Oh – oh yes. Well, the let hadn't gone too well. She was quiet enough but she had a dog which she kept leaving in the flat. The damn thing would howl for hours. You could still hear it, or at least I could, in the shop two floors below. It used to drive me crackers.'

'But you can't have given her notice because of a dog?'

'No. It wasn't just that. It all came to a head one Saturday. I had to go up to her flat to find her. She had a phone call, from France I believe. She'd told me earlier that her mobile had come to the end of its useful life. So I went upstairs, knocked and then walked in – I thought she'd invited me to do so. It was all a misunderstanding.'

'Was she practising yoga in her underwear or something?'

'Chance would be a fine thing. She was a pretty girl, dressed or otherwise. No, she was fully clothed, but she had some electrical equipment laid out on the bed. Her dog was just sitting there with its head on one side listening.'

'You make it sound like a French version of "His Master's Voice" – Le Voix de Son Maître. How touching.'

'I thought it was a device to provide her with French music and plays while she was abroad. She was very proud of her culture. Then I realised it was surveillance kit. To my horror I realised she was part of the group who were eavesdropping on our politician.'

As if in shocked response there was a flash of lightning across the estuary, followed a few seconds later by a crash of thunder. They wouldn't miss the thunderstorm and it wouldn't miss them. It would be upon them within minutes. But their dialogue was equally intense.

'So you interrogated her?'

'I tried to. But she wouldn't answer my questions, not in English anyway. And my French isn't too hot, Elspeth is the linguist. When I threatened to call the police, she said that would be good: she wanted to complain about me invading her bedroom. She started taking her clothes off to underline her story. The row got much worse then.'

227

'Did she sound more French as she became more angry?'

'She certainly did. We were both shouting at each other in a mixture of languages, including in my case coarse Anglo-Saxon. In the end I seized all her kit, marched downstairs and slung it outside the back door. I was shaking with anger.' He swallowed hard.

'Then I went back upstairs and seized her by the ear. Really grabbed it. I forced her to come back down with me and follow the luggage outside. She picked it up and slunk away; I never saw her again.'

'What did Elspeth make of all this?'

'Oh, Elspeth. Hm. Elspeth went away for a three-week writing holiday in Crete at the end of July – with the daughter from her first marriage. She didn't come back until the end of the first week in August so she missed the whole drama. It was probably as well. I'd allowed myself to become really angry. Here we are as HELP, being paid to watch out for leakers, and I'd allowed a key one to stay under my own roof.'

There was another flash of lightning and this time the thunder followed almost immediately. In its light Bill saw that one of the mooring ropes at the bow had unwound. He pointed it out. 'James, would you mind wriggling through to the bow and securing that rope. We don't want to lose it.'

As he did so, Bill reached into his pocket. There was another task that he wanted to complete while his companion was occupied.

'The trouble is,' continued Bill, once positions had been restored, 'that your action didn't stop the leaks. Even if the dead woman whom the police are interested in is this Cécile, we can see with the benefit of hindsight that her partner was able to continue the surveillance on his own, using whatever scheme they'd set up beforehand. It's a pity you couldn't make her give you any details. Did she not say anything helpful?'

James did not answer at once. But as Bill looked past him, there was another flash of lightning, followed at once by a crash of thunder. The whole estuary around them lit up. And Bill saw a clue that gave him part of the answer to the question the HELP team had been grappling with.

For it was clear they were now right over the Antoinette. And in the light from the mast, behind James, Bill could see a slender rod, sticking out of the water and rising twenty feet into the sky.

'Talking of which, I think we can see the French surveillance gear in action.' As he spoke Bill knew it was time to draw the interview to a close.

James turned to see what on earth he was talking about.

And as he did so there was an even bigger flash of lightning, this time simultaneous with a huge, deafening crash of thunder.

It was a flash which did the Eilean Donan no good at all.

CHAPTER 41

When George awoke next morning, slightly later than normal, she had an almost imperceptible feeling that something was wrong. Then she realised what her senses had picked up: the usual noise and smell of breakfast being grilled in the kitchen below was missing.

A moment later she had worked out why this disturbed her. It meant that, for some reason or other, Bill was not at home. It was Friday morning but she knew the day of the week never affected his schedule.

At first she had assumed that her host had simply overslept. She had heard him creep out, for some reason, not far off midnight, so he must have gone to bed very late. But wandering round the unusually-quiet cottage in her dressing gown she saw several signs that he was still out. Crucially, his waterproof cape and sailing hat that he had worn for their trip on the Eilean Donan were no longer hanging in the hall.

This morning George was to have her final meeting with PRAM. She now had many questions about the scheme and whether any of it could really work. She had some exercises that might help the committee to grasp this. But she needed to give them her full concentration. So for now she could not give much attention to the whereabouts of her uncle.

She hurried through her own breakfast – cereals and toast did not take long. Her workshop material, drawn together the evening before, was laid out on her makeshift bedroom desk.

Soon it was bundled into her briefcase and she was striding down to the harbour.

As she walked George turned on her phone. She always turned it off at night to avoid being woken by someone offering her a special rate top-up. She did not want a remote chance to win a holiday in the Seychelles. She was surprised to hear a voicemail from Bill.

'George, I'm with James. Can you find out when Elspeth went on holiday this year and when she came back? I need to check some dates, it's to do with the police embargo.'

It was a peculiar message. George assumed he would explain later. Her first task was to do as he had requested. Fortunately it would be quite easy to learn what he wanted by augmenting the exercises she had already planned.

'Today is my last day down in Padstow – for now,' George began. 'I'll certainly be coming back here for my holidays. Once this meeting is over I'm off back to London. So this is my last chance to give you a sympathetic outsider's observations on what you are doing and how it might possibly be done better.'

The group was silent, awaiting her verdict.

'As I told Bill after my first meeting,' she went on, 'I think that what you are aspiring to do is, in its own terms, impressive. I can't fault any of you on enthusiasm or discipline. Your presentations were fine. Any small business would do well to be run as efficiently as you are.'

The Major looked particularly proud. Good, she thought, he's done well to hold it all together.

'Over the last fortnight I've been to see each of you indi-vidually; and I thank you for your hospitality. We've had some interesting discussions. What I want to do now is to bring together some of the questions into an overall critique. Because these are the questions that the outside world will ask when you go public. You don't need any answers for me – I'll be gone. But I strongly advise you that you will need answers for others.'

The group rustled. This is where their cosy world would hit the wider reality. They needed to brace themselves.

'One of the questions that I've brought up repeatedly is the numbers that your schemes would need to attract, week by week, in high season and low season, to make them financial successes. Just because you personally like an idea doesn't by any means make it viable.

'You've done well to aspire for strength in numbers. Half a dozen distinct schemes, each attracting new visitors, could help one another along. Tourists who came for one might be enthused by others.'

'But that argument cuts both ways. Unless each of the schemes works on the scale needed you're going to be sharing failure rather than success. And I challenge you that the numbers required – and the numbers likely to be attracted – are substantially different.

'Take the Game Park. It's a clever idea; and Hamish is a charismatic champion. But how many could play at a time? Let's say two hundred, who would occupy the Park for, say, two hours of contest plus relaxing afterwards in the restaurants. You'd do well to attract five hundred a day. Now that might work at weekends. But even so that's only a thousand visitors a week and only for the summer season.

'Hamish spoke of the restaurant overlooking the estuary. I agree there's a niche for snacks along the Camel Trail. But you need to take account of the competition. Like the Pickwick Arms above Little Petherick. I went there for supper earlier this week: it already offers stunning views over the estuary.'

George noticed Hamish Robertson was starting to look disgruntled. She hastened on.

'If this was Newquay, with coach loads of student visitors celebrating their exams, the Game Park might have a chance. But do you want to emulate Newquay? Do you yourselves go there? Or do you prefer to stay here with your beautiful coastline? And if you do that why do you think others might not feel the same?

'At the end I've got some exercises that will help us explore these issues at a personal level. I'll take your answers with me and let you have the results with the rest of my report next week.

'As for other schemes . . . I spent a couple of hours with the Tourist Office. They tell me your Camel Trail is the most successful cycling trail in the country: a thousand visitors a day. The manager was horrified when I asked about replacing the trail with a railway line to Bodmin. You'd get a huge amount of opposition - from all sides. There's a bus from Bodmin to Padstow anyway. Accessibility is not your problem.

'In general, you've dreamed up your schemes in ideal circumstances. What you each need to do now is to imagine the worst that could happen to them, not just the best. Look for similar schemes elsewhere in Cornwall and how many visitors they attract. From what I've been able to pick up in a few evenings browsing the internet, all the numbers you're cited so far are highly optimistic.'

George paused to let her point sink in. There was a rather sombre silence. Then the Major responded. 'OK, we need to apply these questions to ourselves earnestly. Maybe we have been over-optimistic. But I'm sure you want Padstow to succeed too. Do you have any positive ideas of other things we could be looking at?'

George looked around and glanced at Watmough. 'Your deputy is dead keen on the local bird life – he's a real twitcher. If I was prepared to let him he would have taken me to various creeks in the Camel estuary and shown me all sorts of waders. You'd need to work on his interpersonal skills but there's an enthusiasm there that's worth harnessing. Could you risk him on other visitors?

'And there's the Doom Bar. You all seem to treat it as a nuisance. But I've talked to the Environment Agency scientist in Wadebridge, Martin Sutcliffe; he'd be keen to make much more of it. And for just a few moments I'd like to show you something that he and I developed which might help.'

George stopped talking and fiddled with her laptop. She had been impressed to learn that the hotel could project her computer onto a bigger screen. Even though it had meant arriving early George had been keen to use it. It gave her one tiny chance to give the committee something more than words.

'I'd like to show you the Doom Bar's position over the last half-century. This is based on the excellent data kept by Paddy Watmough.'

George ran through the display she had already shown Martin Sutcliffe. The group were fascinated to see a feature of their daily lives in Padstow summarised so succinctly.

'And now I'll show you data on the flows in the River Camel over much the same period.' A series of time charts appeared.

'Finally, I'll put the two together.' As she said this George superposed the two sequences then stepped through the events of 1976. Now the Doom Bar movements could be seen side by side with changes in river flow.

'Hey, that's when the Doom Bar switched sides. It was *after* the drought had ended - when the river flows were high for months on end.' Paddy Watmough was excited now. She could see she had caught his imagination at least.

'That's what Martin Sutcliffe and I thought. Martin was keen to give talks on the Doom Bar's behaviour and maybe link these with a commentary on climate change. It could become a regular feature. Many people who cycle here from Wadebridge might want to make it part of their visit. And over time it might attract new visitors.'

The demonstration concluded and the meeting progressed. There was a lot of discussion of George's challenges; and some acceptance that they needed to fear the worst.

As the meeting drew to its scheduled close George decided it was time to conduct her exercises. 'Whatever else happens here we're all agreed that the primary role of the Camel estuary will be associated with holiday-makers. But as residents are you in tune with what holiday makers want? So what I want to do is an exercise to find out about your own holidays and your own hopes for crowds in Padstow.'

There was a murmur of unease. But most were happy to go along. After all, they'd hired George precisely because she was an outsider. They might as well make the most of that.

'I'm going to hand out a sheet of paper to each of you. Then I've got a list of questions which I'll put up on this flip-chart. I don't want you to discuss them with one another. I just want you each to answer the questions individually, in terms of your own holidays this year; and your own aspirations for Padstow and Rock.'

'Please miss, do you want names on the top of the paper?'

George smiled. 'It's up to you. But if you don't, say you've spent an undercover fortnight gambling in Las Vegas, could you at least say male or female?'

George strode to the flip-chart and turned the top sheet over. Below was the sheet she had prepared beforehand, which she wanted them to answer.

She glanced round the room as the committee members started to respond, memorising their positions. She did not know if Elspeth would put her name on her paper. But she would make sure she took back the papers in the order they were seated. And she had also given a small corner-fold to Elspeth's sheet. It shouldn't be hard to work out which was hers.

At least she would have something to report back to Bill.

CHAPTER 42

Later that Friday morning, when the various exercises had been carried out and her presentation completed, George returned to Bill's cottage to pick up her luggage; and to see if he had returned. She didn't want to slip away without saying goodbye.

But there was nobody there. She was in a hurry and had to be off. In the end she just wrote him a note of thanks. She was more anxious now; should she report his absence? And if so, to whom?

Bill had not explained his various trips out before though, with what she had gleaned about HELP, she could now see why he might have been so secretive. She'd heard him ring Applegate after they had talked yesterday. That was the person he answered to within HELP. But she didn't know what number he'd rung, or where the super-suave Applegate might be found.

On a Saturday she would have driven round to St Minver to catch the end of the HELP meeting; it was virtually certain Applegate would be there. But George did not want to wait twenty four hours: she was due back in London that evening. Polly was desperate to see her again.

In the end she decided to tell the only other person she'd met with family connections, loose ones admittedly, via Mark. Suddenly she realised that she was thinking of her dead husband for the first time with some distance. Maybe her time here had begun to give her a new life of her own.

She found the card Brian Southgate had given her in her handbag and rang his home number. It was just an off-chance he'd be there late on Friday morning. But she couldn't face the battle to get through to the surgery.

A rather strict-sounding female answered. 'It is his day off, you know.' Presumably his wife being protective. George remembered she used to be like that with Mark on his days off. That now seemed a long time ago.

Eventually, when she'd explained who she was, she was allowed to get through. Brian was out in his vegetable patch; he had to come in and remove his boots. It sounded from the background dialogue as though leaving a mess on the kitchen floor would be a criminal offence.

'Hi,' the doctor greeted her. 'Good to hear from you. So you've found time for a meal: when would you like to come?'

'It'll have to be another time, I'm afraid. I'm driving back to London this afternoon. My daughter wants me home again. But something odd has happened; and I didn't know who else I could talk to.'

'I'm used to being told secrets - and keeping them. On all sorts of topics and from all sides. What's the matter?'

There was a pause as George considered how to begin. Brian picked up her hesitation.

'Or if you'd rather talk face to face, why not come for a light lunch on your way home? Delabole isn't far out of your way. You'll have to pass through Camelford on your way to Launceston.'

George had been slightly apprehensive about meeting Brian's wife. On the phone she sounded fearsome. And how would she take to her husband inviting single women home to lunch?

But her fears were groundless. Alice, she learned when she reached the doctor's house, was the head teacher at the local primary school. If today had not been an "inset day", she would have been at the school chalk-face. She'd been working at home when George rang but was now back in her head teacher's office. So Brian was on his own, which made it easier to talk.

George had wondered, as she drove over to Delabole, how much she could share with Brian about HELP and Bill's role within it. What she most wanted to pass on, really, was to warn someone about Bill's absence and maybe to start to look for him. She would rely on Brian's judgement as to whether that "someone" was the local police.

She was held back from too strong a sense of betrayal by the fact that Bill had told her nothing about HELP directly. All she had were her own deductions and inferences.

Brian had laid out rolls and cheese for lunch. He offered her a glass of wine, but she declined: she'd be driving again within the hour.

'It's my Uncle Bill,' George began, 'he's disappeared.'

'Last time we talked you main complaint was that he kept disappearing. Your grouse then was him not telling you where he was going. So how is this different?'

'This time he's been away all night. And hadn't come back by the time I left Padstow.'

'I assume that once again he didn't tell you where he was going?'

'No. The only clue was a voicemail on my phone this morning.'

'But that means he was alive, anyway. I don't think you should worry. He can take care of himself.'

'But it was a very odd message.' George realised the message was still on her phone. She handed it over and Brian listened carefully.

'Elspeth, eh,' he commented, 'the first time I've heard her name mentioned. So did you find out her holiday arrangements?'

'I believe so, via an exercise for the PRAM committee. I made it as general as I could. I've not had chance to look at them yet. I wanted to get home so I didn't hang about. I set off from Padstow straight after the meeting.'

The analyst reached into her briefcase and produced a pile of hand-written answer sheets to the questionnaire presented that morning. A further rummage produced the list of questions posted on the flip chart.

Brian picked up the pile of responses and started to glance through them. 'They're good questions. Now all you've got to do is to pick out Elspeth's answers. It's a pity none of them gave their names.'

'Don't alter the order, please. I took them back as they were seated round the table.' George seized the pile from him and started to deal them back to an imaginary committee seated round the kitchen table. Eventually she came to the one from Elspeth.

'This must be hers. Even though she's not given her name - or even admitted to being female. That's naughty: I told them all to give their gender. Look, the corner of the sheet is ear-marked. I only did that to the sheet I gave to Elspeth.'

'But she must have spotted that: it's been straightened out. Anyway, what does she tell us?'

George glanced at the sheet. 'She went away on holiday on Saturday July 19th. "To a writing course," she says, "on a remote Greek island.""

'It's a pity she doesn't say which one,' mused the doctor. 'That'll make it much harder for Peter to check.'

George looked at him – no he wasn't joking. "Peter" must be the policeman Peter Travers who had talked to her on the phone. And they were talking about cross-checking her survey answers. There was something important going on here - something that she was not party to.

She looked down the sheet. 'And Elspeth says she came back on Saturday August 9th. Is that a significant date, too?'

'It's highly significant. It means she was away for the whole shenanigans. She can't help us at all.' The doctor looked disconsolate.

'Can you tell me what you're talking about? Or is this all part of the embargoed police investigation?'

The doctor shook his head. 'I'd love to explain the whole thing. But as I said before, lots of people tell me things in confidence. And I have to respect that. So for the moment I can't tell you anything.

'But I hope that, before too long, that will change. You deserve to know more. I promise you I'll give you a ring as soon as I'm allowed to share anything.'

George wrestled with the conundrum as she drove back to London. As a mathematician she enjoyed all sorts of puzzles but this one seemed to have too many missing pieces. Or rather, she might have enough pieces, but not all of them were correct. No wonder they didn't fit together properly.

It was the information on holiday dates which she'd brought to Brian which didn't fit into whatever pattern the doctor was constructing. There must have been some reason for Bill to have raised that question. But she had no idea what it was.

By now she had been driving for three hours and was well along the M4. She decided she'd stop at the next service station – Membury - for a cup of coffee and a break.

It was as she locked her car, making sure nothing valuable was left in view, that she noticed a folder among the pile of files and notes sprawled across the back seat. It was one she had been given by Martha Singleton: the minutes of every PRAM meeting to date.

She picked it up to take into the cafe to skim as she had her coffee. The committee, she'd been told by Bill, had met from early June. Which meetings had Elspeth Hammond missed? And at which ones had she been present?

Half an hour later she was on her phone to Brian. A wait before he picked up – no doubt he was back in his vegetable patch. It was an enthusiasm that reminded her of Mark – maybe a result of being brought up in Cornwall. She gritted her teeth and hung on. Finally the doctor answered.

'Brian, I can prove it, she was lying.'

'Slow down a minute. I take it we're talking about Elspeth. How on earth have you learned more while sitting in your car? Hey, you're not trying to talk and drive at the same time, are you? Because –'

'Shut up Brian. I'm at Membury Service Station, sitting in the cafe. I've got a file containing the minutes of every PRAM meeting since June. Which always start with a list of those present. Minutes which are corrected and signed off at the next meeting.'

'Yes?'

'I'm looking at the meeting which took place on Monday August 4th. Among those listed as present is Elspeth

Hammond. And not only was she there, the minutes state that she gave an update about a new Leisure Centre for Rock. Does that help your investigation? And if it does, please give Peter Travers my regards.'

CHAPTER 43

'Peter, I've just received some information I think you'll be interested in.' Brian Southgate had just come off the phone to George. He wanted to make sure action was taken on what he had just heard as soon as possible. And the only source of official action he had direct contact with was the local policeman.

The embargo imposed by the Security Forces still held and Peter Travers was back to his duties as community policeman. This meant wearing his high-visibility jacket over his uniform in one of the tourist honey-pots of the area. His usual role was inhibiting crime rather than solving it.

This Friday afternoon he had decided to wander round Boscastle. He had a pleasant chat with the artist in the Old Forge, Helen Setteringham, who painted and sold dramatic water colours. It was all very pleasant but didn't give him much sense of impending crime.

Travers glanced at his watch; it was five fifteen. 'Hi Brian. I'm almost off duty. When do you finish healing the sick and halting the lame? If whatever you've learned is significant I'd much rather hear it face to face.'

The pair arranged to meet at the Trewarmett Inn. The Inn was partway along the road from Boscastle to Delabole, as good a place as any for a discussion leading on from the torso in the nearby quarry.

'You see, Peter, what you found out yesterday about James Hammond – all the details of his van being repaired and so on - might not be what you think.'

'But we got stuck, anyway. The potential victim was still around on August 8th – which was the day after the van was repaired.'

'That's the detail that might not be quite right. I made enquiries this morning from my colleague in Rock where our patient had her appointment. My colleague tells me that they're always hard-pressed in August. Many of their own staff, all the ones with children, go on holiday themselves. But because of all the tourists here getting sunburnt and so on the practice's own workload increases.'

'Sounds like an annual headache. How do they sort it?'

'They have a couple of locum doctors who come to work with them for the month. Trainee doctors from less beautiful parts of the country who are happy enough to put in extra hours here. After all they still have the evenings and weekends to enjoy themselves.'

'How does that help our inquiry?'

'Well, I persuaded my colleague at the surgery, Dr Ellis, to tell me who Cécile saw when she came to the surgery on August 8th. At first she wasn't keen, bleating about patient confidentiality. So I reminded her that the woman was a self-harming victim. I happen to know that's Dr Ellis's latest hobby horse.

'After a bit of debate she looked it up in the surgery records; and sure enough it was one of the locums. It was surgery policy, she said, that newer patients were handed to the visiting doctors. Who, of course, would have no reason to know their real names. So the patient might not have been Cécile at all, just some other woman claiming her identity.'

'But if it wasn't Cécile, who was it?'

The doctor rubbed his hands together and wrinkled his brow as if in fierce concentration. 'I've been giving that some thought . . .'

'Stop mucking about. You've got an idea. Tell me.'

'Well, I think it could have been Elspeth Hammond - James' wife.'

'Mm. She was around then, was she?'

'This is where it gets interesting. Elspeth is on this Working Party that's trying to produce some sort of modernisation plan for Padstow and Rock. My friend George, who's been acting as their consultant for the last fortnight – the one who told us about James going away on Thursdays - asked the whole committee this morning to tell her when they went on holiday this year, and where they went to.'

'And discovered that Elspeth was at home then?'

'No. Exactly the opposite. Elspeth told George she was abroad from mid July until August 9th.'

Peter looked puzzled. 'I'm missing something here. How on earth does that help us?'

'Well, if that was all we'd been told it wouldn't help at all. But George is a perceptive and a persistent lady.'

'I wouldn't disagree with that. And?'

'She'd earlier been given a copy of the minutes of this committee. It's a very formal group with accurate minutes, duly agreed and signed at the next meeting. And these show that Elspeth was actually around and present at the meeting on Monday August 4th. Must have been there, George tells me, she gave a presentation to the Working Party. So firstly, that means we've broken her alibi – she wasn't abroad at the time, as she claimed. But more importantly, why did she lie about being around at the crucial time?'

It was a good question. Peter Travers went to the bar to refill their glasses as he pondered, trying to imagine what might have happened.

What motive might be in play? Why should a middle-aged woman, returning from holiday, have any reason to feel malice towards a young lady staying in her upstairs flat? While her husband was living on his own down below. Even as he asked himself the question, he realised that there was one devastatingly plausible answer.

'Do you think we might be looking at a crime of passion?' he asked, as he returned to their table carrying two more halves of cider. 'I mean, suppose Elspeth came back from her holiday ahead of time. Maybe came home and found her husband having a fling with Cécile. Perhaps caught the two of them hard at it. Could that cause a massive row, which ended up with Cécile being killed?'

There was a pause as both men supped their drinks and pondered the scenario.

'It might,' replied the doctor. 'In that case James and Elspeth would have an equal interest in disposing of Cécile's body and then chucking away all her belongings.'

'Doing that, they might have found her diary,' mused Travers.

'They'd want to check on her plans: how long before she'd be missed? So they could have found an appointment with the surgery. Because there was an appointment: the surgery has already told us about it. That would be a shock: their whole strategy was to make out she'd moved on several days earlier.'

'Her diary could well name the doctor she was booked in to see.'

'But when James and Elspeth saw the name, they would know it was a short-term locum. They could have gambled that it would be less of a risk for Elspeth to go, pretending to be Cécile, than to risk the doctor reporting her missing.'

It was only conjecture; but by no means impossible.

Travers summarised the scenario. 'So their first line of defence would be to hide the body. It was sheer luck that it was found so quickly.'

'Next,' said the doctor, 'they made it hard to identify the body. Cutting off the head stymied the whole investigation. Chadwick retreated to his gangs in Exeter. You and I tried local tattoos and local self-harming. It was their good luck, I think, that Cécile was French.'

'Chadwick consulted the UK national DNA database and drew a blank. I'm not sure though if he went through the hassle of looking at DNA records for countries abroad.'

'Being French meant there was no relative close to hand who would notice she'd gone and report her missing. Matching a complete corpse to one of a list of missing people – however long - would be much, much easier than identifying one with no head.'

The policeman nodded. 'But despite all these obstacles progress is made. So finally, when James realises that the police are closing in, he pulls strings to make sure the investigation is stalled. The only way that could be done, you know, is if he has some connection with the security services. I could ask Chadwick. He wouldn't know, but he might be glad of some ammunition that his bosses could fire back at the security people.'

Southgate concluded, 'I think we've made a good case for investigation against the two of them. The trouble is, that's nowhere near the same thing as hard proof. It's all indirect and circumstantial. We still need something that directly connects the pair with the quarry up the road.'

Soon afterwards Brian Southgate realised what the time was and declared that he had to be home. He had just remembered that Alice had invited friends for dinner. She would be cooking beef Wellington and he had promised to produce a suitable matching dessert.

With the time left all he could cook would be a basic blackberry crumble. But maybe he could still get some double cream on the way home. That would make it special for their household. He swigged the rest of his drink and was gone.

Peter Travers was left to finish his drink on his own. He was in no hurry and was still meditating on the case. Maybe a further glass of cider might help? As he stood up, he was aware of someone coming towards him – a young man with a worried expression. 'Can I have a word, please?'

'Sure,' the policeman replied, sitting down again. 'Take a seat.'

'Am I right that you've been making inquiries about that quarry up the road, about whether anyone's seen anything odd going on in the car park?'

'That's right. I've talked to several dog-walkers, anyway. They haven't given me anything. Why, do you know something?'

'I might. I saw a couple up there, pushing something in a wheelbarrow. Would that be the kind of thing you were after?'

Peter Travers went from being superficially polite to being very interested indeed. His desire for another drink faded. He reached for his notebook and then turned to the newcomer.

'Let's start from the beginning. Can you tell me your name, please.'

'Sure. I'm Tommy Burton.'

The policeman had heard the name before. He frowned. Then it came to him. 'You were the best man at that stag party here, a couple of weeks ago?'

'That's right. You interviewed the bridegroom, Kevin, but for some reason you didn't come and find me.'

'No, I didn't think there was any need.' Peter Travers wasn't going to explain the convoluted police logic which had led to him being barred from doing so by Inspector Chadwick. 'Maybe that was a mistake. Was there something you wanted to add?'

'Not about the stag party itself. I think Kevin gave you the full picture. But the events in the Engine House didn't just happen by accident. I was up there much earlier, checking out how much light there was in the Engine House during a full moon.'

'Earlier? You mean earlier in the week?'

'Nah. If you're going to have a classic stag party, where the bridegroom is really embarrassed, you need to plan better than that. No, I was up at the Engine House at about one o'clock in the morning on the previous full moon – four weeks earlier. Saturday, August 2nd, to be precise.'

The hairs at the back of Peter Travers neck suddenly felt as if they were standing to attention. This was the weekend when, on all that he had gleaned, the body had gone into the pool.

'So you were up at the Prince of Wales Engine House on a bright, moonlit night on August 2nd. And what did you see? Take your time please, this could be very important.'

'It wasn't what I saw, first of all, as much as what I heard. I was in the Engine House, checking on whether the moon would be bright enough to let me tie the knots I would use, when I heard people talking. It sounded as though they were down by the quarry pool.'

'So what did you do?'

'Well, I didn't want to be discovered. As far as I knew there was nothing illegal about me being there, but I didn't want to take any chances. I'd decided the Engine House would be ideal for my stag party climax a month later. For all I knew the people I'd heard could be policemen. So I kept very quiet and got ready to leave. Then I crept down the path towards the pool.'

Tommy was silent as he recalled the experience. The policeman did not hurry him. He was thankful that he and Southgate had earlier chosen a table at the back of the dining room bar which was not close to anyone else. It was a relief that Harriet the aspiring journalist was not around. Without her it was an ideal spot for a quiet conversation.

'Then I saw them.'

'Them? There was more than one?'

'There were two people, a man and a woman. Talking to one another quietly. I'd been worried about being seen but they weren't keen to be spotted either. Both wearing dark jackets and trousers and both with gloves and woolly hats. The gloves seemed strange in the middle of summer. It wasn't a heat wave by any means - but it wasn't that cold.'

'Hold on a second, I want to make sure I get this all down.' Travers scrawled away in his notebook, thankful that his handwriting was still legible despite years of pressure from computer keyboards. 'And where exactly were they standing?'

Tommy seemed encouraged that he was being taken seriously. He had wrestled for weeks with these memories, not sure whether to speak out or to stay silent. His instinct had told him that he had stumbled on something suspect; it was a relief that someone else evidently thought the same.

'When I first saw them, they were both just inside the metal fence. I expect you know there's a tall fence around the pool.'

'Yes, I know the one you mean.'

'I don't know what they'd been doing inside there. By the time I saw them they were on the way out. They had a piece of carpet over the top of the fence and they both climbed out over that. It was then that I saw the wheelbarrow.'

'The wheelbarrow was outside the fence?'

'Yes. As far as I could see it was empty. So I guess it must have been full of something when they walked up to the fence in the first place. Anyway, their business was over and they weren't hanging about. The man seized the wheelbarrow and then they set off down the path back to the road.'

'What did you do?'

'I needed to get down to the road too. It's the only way out from the quarry. I live in Treknow, just down the road, so I hadn't used my car, I'd walked all the way. By now I'd done all the research I needed. So I followed them, hanging back so I wouldn't be spotted. Mind you, it's a good job it's a grassy path. If it was stony the crunch of my footsteps might have given me away.'

'So what happened once the pair reached the road?'

'They had a vehicle waiting in the car park.'

'What sort of vehicle? A car?'

'No, it was a small van, actually. A dark colour, not black maybe blue . . . or purple? The moon made it hard to say exactly. They opened the back doors and put the wheelbarrow inside. Shut the doors gently and quietly. Then they got in and drove away.'

'Without any difficulty?'

'No . . . Hold on a minute, there was something – a bang. I think they hit the side bar of the height barrier on the way out.'

'And can you remember anything else about the van – its registration number, for example?' Travers held his breath.

'No, I was too far away to see the number plate. The moon light was bright but not that bright.'

It had been too much to hope for.

Then Travers remembered that they'd been in a van . . .

'Any other memorable features?' he asked. 'Take your time. Try and imagine yourself back there again.'

Tommy shut his eyes, thinking hard. The policeman waited once more, hoping . . .

'It was a commercial van, I think . . . Yes, that's right: there was a name on the back door. It was something like "Hammond". But I can't remember the initials.'

Once again there was a pause as the policeman transcribed what he had just heard. But this time he was quietly exultant. 'Brilliant. And would you recognise the couple again?'

'I wasn't close enough to see their faces. And they were well covered up. But I saw them climbing back over the fence. They seemed to make heavy weather of it. I would say they were both middle aged. And I remember the woman had blonde hair.'

'All this is really important, sir. Thank you for coming forward. What I'd like to do is to repeat this interview, in a Police Station where we can record it and maybe help push your memories further. And get you to sign a statement.'

Travers paused then continued. 'But since we're talking about an event that took place six weeks ago, a few hours is neither here nor there. How would Monday morning suit you?'

CHAPTER 44

Though Peter Travers wanted a celebratory drink as Tommy Burton moved away he was still more in need of a clear head.

Before he contacted Inspector Chadwick he wanted to set down as fully as possible what he now knew, and more importantly what he could prove about the murder uncovered at the Prince of Wales Quarry pool, less than a fortnight ago. Before he spoke to anyone he wanted to be sure there were no major gaps in his thinking.

A few moments later he was back at his Police House in Delabole, settled in front of his computer. He had never been part of the team on a murder case before and did not know if there were standard ways of setting out suspicions, accusations and evidence. But he could at least begin with a narrative of the crime.

Even this was a salutary process. He had come home on a high, given what he had been told by Tommy Burton. But starting to write a narrative made him increasingly aware of what he did not know. The story quickly turned into a long list of questions.

Why had Cécile come to Rock in the first place?
When did she arrive at the Hammonds' flat?
How long had she planned to stay?
Had Elspeth been at the flat when Cécile arrived? OR

Had she moved in after Elspeth had gone to Greece, leaving James to mind the shop, and act as landlord, on his own?

Had Elspeth come home when expected, or had something brought her home early?

Did James know when she was supposed to come home?

How much of a shock was it when, on coming home, she found something going on between James and Cécile? And

What, exactly, had Elspeth found?

Had anyone else been involved?

As he listed the questions, the policeman reflected that he could not rely on any answers given by the Hammonds. Both had issued lies already, one to Southgate and the other to George, and seemed to be consummate story-tellers. Clearly finessing the truth was a skill honed in Whitehall.

So how could he assemble reliable answers, to these and other questions, from alternative sources? Who else knew what?

Peter Travers decided he needed some inspiration from Brian Southgate. He reached for the phone – then remembered that his friend had rushed off to a dinner party. His wife would doubtless make sure that interruptions were not tolerated. He would have to persevere on his own.

So far his questions had been about the mechanics of the crime. But what about motivation? Crucially, was this a spontaneous crime of passion or was it carefully premeditated?

With something of a shock, Travers remembered what he had learned from the Environment Agency a couple of days before. Martin Sutcliffe had told him he'd been pressed to check the water quality in the pool where the body would be found and to take the sample earlier than usual. He had been certain – and both Chadwick and Southgate had agreed - that this meant the murder was premeditated.

But if that was the case, what was Elspeth's role? The story he had come home with from the Trewarmett Inn - in his imagination - was that Elspeth Hammond was the prime mover. The crux of the case was that the murder was a spontaneous response to some compromising situation she had discovered on her return. It was the only way he could find to account for her deliberate lying about the dates when she was away.

The murder could either be pre-planned or it could be spontaneous. But whatever happened it couldn't be both.

So was his whole thesis erroneous? Had someone else planned and carried out the murder – and then used the Hammonds to remove the body? Were James and Elspeth just the ancillaries to some deeper crime that he had not yet even touched on?

Travers felt his elation slipping away. There was still plenty of work to be done. Perhaps he needed that drink after all.

CHAPTER 45

Early on Saturday morning Peter Travers was woken from a deep sleep by the insistent ringing of his phone. Whatever did or did not happen on the murder case, he would be needed today as community policeman.

The call was from the harbour manager at Padstow, Paddy Watmough – he knew the man slightly. Paddy reported that there had been a shipwreck. The boat had come ashore on the cliffs north of Bude, been spotted by a group walking the Coast Path and was now under investigation by the local coastguards.

It was the Padstow man who had been alerted, the policeman gathered, because the boat was normally moored in the Camel estuary.

'Do we know of any casualties?'

'I'm afraid so. There are a couple of bodies on board. I don't know yet who they are. And I don't know if anyone else was on board and was washed out to sea.'

The deaths made it a police matter. The policeman took the details of the location and hastened to put on his uniform. This was an unexpected development and might take some time. It was as well the murder inquiry was on hold.

On the other hand, fifteen minutes delay on his getting there would not make any difference to bodies that had been dead for some hours. Better to eat now, he might not eat again until much later in the day.

Travers gulped down a bowl of muesli, a couple of slices of toast and a mug of coffee. There was no time for a cooked breakfast.

Fifty minutes later Peter Travers had driven up the main A39 up past Bude – the so-called "Atlantic Highway" - and taken a minor road off to the left after Kilkhampton. This led, many bends later, to the cliffs near Morwenstow. He was still in Cornwall, he reckoned - though only just.

Travers didn't often come this far. It wasn't a huge distance from Delabole – no more than thirty miles - but the coast here had a more sinister character. The cliffs were no higher than those further south, but there were many serrated rocks sticking out from the base of the cliffs into the sea. The place had a reputation for shipwrecks and, looking down, he could see why.

Below was the wreck he had been called to. It was a small boat firmly jammed onto the rocks, with a couple of coast-guards clambering about. He gave them a hail. Once they saw who he was, they pointed to a place to his left, where a rough path down began between gorse bushes. A few minutes later he had joined them beside the forlorn remains of the little vessel.

'Hi. I'm Phil Turner,' said the first coastguard. 'And this is Alan Peabody. We're based in Bude, got here half an hour ago. Glad you could join us.'

'I'm Police Sergeant Peter Travers - from Delabole. I'm sorry that any of us need to be here. So what can you tell me?'

'We've had a quick look. It's been here for some time,' Phil Turner told him. 'Do you remember? There was that massive storm on Thursday night; this boat almost certainly got caught in it. It looks as though it was struck by lightning as well – see there, those could easily be marks from the mast being scorched.'

'We've had a quick look in the cabin; the radio equipment is all burnt out,' his colleague continued. 'That could well happen if lightning struck. They wouldn't be able to send out any distress signals as they were battered to and fro. Finally, after a massive buffeting, Phil and I think the boat was washed up here sometime yesterday evening. It couldn't have been earlier or someone on the Coast Path would have seen and reported it yesterday.'

'And the crew are still on board?'

'Well, their bodies are. Two of them, anyway. They'd roped themselves to the stays on the deck, otherwise I'm sure they'd be in the sea – and maybe not washed up for another week.'

Peter Travers followed the coastguards onto the boat. He saw the bodies of two men, both in full waterproof gear, nestled close to one another in the tiny cabin. For his records he took a few photographs of the scene and the victims.

'Any reason to suspect foul play?' he asked. It was the routine question that always needed to be answered before any work began to remove the bodies.

'Nothing at all from what we can see. They were probably both exhausted by the storm – and huddled together for warmth,' suggested Turner.

'I would say it's more likely that they were both electrocuted when the boat was hit by a bolt of lightning,' opined his colleague.

There was silence for a moment as they each tried to imagine either sequence of events. What a way to go.

'OK then, how are we going to remove the bodies?' asked the policeman.

'There's no easy way down these cliffs – and certainly no

easy way back. You'll find that out for yourself soon enough. There's no obvious boat access either – without risking a second shipwreck. It'll have to be done using a helicopter.'

It was not a common method of taking away bodies, but not that rare on this rugged coastline. Travers had expected, when he had looked down the cliffs and seen the location, that it might come to this. 'OK. Are you going to call them or am I?'

While the coastguard called on his mobile, Peter Travers crouched down beside the two men. It would be useful to establish identity as soon as possible. Relatives could then be informed.

Gently he moved the two men apart. He unzipped their waterproof jackets and then, reaching behind them, felt for the back pockets of their trousers.

'This older one was Bill Gilbert,' he announced, after finding a wallet and looking at the name on the bank card inside. While he was at it, he had better take care of the dead men's other possessions. He pulled a dark plastic bag out of his own jacket pocket and dropped the wallet in.

Then, for completeness, he checked the man's other pockets. A mobile phone and one or two other items were added to the bag. When there was no more he sealed it shut and slipped it into the pouch of his jacket.

'Hey, I know that name,' said Phil Turner. He stepped forward to examine the body more closely. 'Yes, I recognise him. He's a great bloke, helps with the Stepper Point Lookout. Or rather, did. He's averted many potential accidents. What a shame no-one was around to help him. It's a real tragedy.'

Travers continued his search, this time on the pockets of the second man. 'And the other one . . .' he opened the second wallet and took out a card, 'is James Hammond. Hell's bells, I was wanting to talk to him and his wife. I need to think about this.'

As he spoke he continued to go through the man's pockets and assembled a second bag of possessions. This, too, he stashed safely away.

'If you like, Alan and I can wait here for the helicopter,' offered Phil. 'Two will be enough to guide it in then fasten the bodies, one by one, on to the lowered stretcher.' He turned to the policeman.

'You've got their names, Peter. Can you get back and make sure the relatives are informed as soon as possible? That's the worst part of dealing with accidents like this.'

With some effort, Peter Travers climbed steadily back to the top of the cliffs, pausing once or twice to catch his breath and thinking hard. Both of the dead men's names seemed familiar.

"Hammond", of course, was his prime murder suspect. If the case had not been curtailed he would have interviewed him on Thursday – and maybe averted the accident. But "Gilbert"... where had he come across that name recently? Then he remembered: his most recent source, George, was also a "Gilbert". Was there some family connection?

And why on earth were Hammond and Gilbert out on a night cruise together in the first place – especially during a storm?

Puffing more than he would have liked as he reached the top, the policeman flopped into his car to recover his breath. His next official job, he knew, should be to go back to Padstow and Rock and break the sad news of the shipwreck deaths to the next of kin.

But at this moment he was the only one who knew who the

dead men were – and no-one in authority, least of all his various police bosses, knew exactly where he was. It followed that no-one would know if he took a few minutes to go through their belongings more carefully.

In particular, he had found a small tape recorder in the pocket of Bill Gilbert. He had not remarked on it to the coast-guards but he thought it was an odd sort of item to take on a boat trip. Of course, it might just have been something the man happened to have in his pocket when he set out. But he guessed Bill was a diligent and well-prepared sailor, so that seemed unlikely. He wondered what memories it held.

It took only a minute's work to check that, despite the storm, the tape recorder had been kept dry under several layers of waterproofs; and its battery was still working. The recorder had presumably been switched off some time before the lightning struck – but maybe not long before?

Peering, he saw that the tape had run about halfway through. So there might be half an hour's recorded conversation to listen to.

He arranged it carefully on the passenger seat. He would make sure there was enough time to hear whatever was on it as he drove steadily back towards Padstow.

CHAPTER 46

As Peter Travers drove the Atlantic Highway, it was with amazement that he listened to the dialogue recorded less than forty eight hours before on the Eilean Donan, between Bill Gilbert and James Hammond.

It was a high-performance recorder. The sound at the start of the voyage, when the key part of the conversation had taken place, was excellent. Towards the end the noise of the storm and the surging waves made it harder to pick up every word; but overall it was of excellent quality. Travers had little doubt that it could be used in a court-room.

After listening to the whole recording once, there were still some gaps in his knowledge. It was clear, though, that the Security Force that had blocked the police inquiry was known to these two. Reading between the lines he could imagine how Brian Southgate's relatively innocent query, into the self-harming lodger once living at James Hammond's flat, could have led to their inquiry being embargoed.

Another name was mentioned in this part of the conversation: Jeremy Applegate. Winding back to the beginning of the tape and listening to this section again, Travers gathered that he was the boss of these two; and had been the one who formally requested the embargo.

Applegate must have a lot of authority but also plenty of knowledge. He also seemed to know something about "Cécile". Maybe he should be the first to know about the deaths of

Hammond and Gilbert? Perhaps, Travers thought, he could trade information with him?

What he needed was Applegate's phone number. No doubt it was ex-directory and not available to the likes of him. But he had Bill's phone . . .

Travers saw a convenient lay-by just ahead. Once he had parked, he seized the first pocket-contents bag from his jacket and pulled out the dead man's phone. As he had hoped Jeremy Applegate was on its phone list.

Travers paused for a moment to make sure he was clear in his mind what he wanted; and what he was prepared to trade. Then he dialled the number.

Despite his suave tone, Applegate sounded flustered and anxious. 'It's not a good time to talk, actually, Sergeant Travers. I've got a regular meeting starting in a few minutes time. Could you ring me later, please?'

'I thought you might like some information on Gilbert and Hammond, sir?'

'What? Yes, I very much do . . . In fact they're supposed to be at the meeting I'm about to go to -'

'I can assure you, sir, they won't be there. But I'd rather not say any more over the phone. If you give me your address I'd like to come and see you. Straight away if possible.'

Applegate paused to weigh competing priorities. Now that the French journalist, Allain, had been detained by Internal Security, he was confident that the leaks which had so bothered him for the summer were on the way to being dealt with. So the forthcoming meeting at the Fourways Snug was mostly routine – dotting i's and crossing t's.

It would be easy enough to call Watmough and ask him to

take charge and report back afterwards. Whereas Travers . . . the policeman sounded as if he might really know something that the security supremo didn't. Applegate did not like the idea of being relatively ill-informed in any context. Changing that had to be his priority.

'Very well, then. As I guess you can understand, I would prefer to meet in a secluded public place rather than tell you where I'm based. That's an Official Secret. You must know the pubs round here better than I do. Name one and I'll meet you there in, say, half an hour.'

They settled on the Cornish Arms at Pendoggett, a village on the road from Delabole to Rock. Travers knew it had a side room. The landlord, whom he had known for years, would let him use it for a private meeting in the day-time. The pub would hardly be open yet, it was still only half past ten in the morning.

Pendoggett was five miles down the road. That gave him a few minutes to plan his strategy. He could play the official policeman, but he doubted that would achieve much. This man had already blocked their inquiry once – in fact, he needed to be careful what he admitted doing, it was still officially blocked.

But he would not simply go as a poor supplicant, seeking help from a high-placed expert. This was, after all, his case: he had personally unravelled the body from the sack. The best outcome would be some form of cooperative action. After all they were both officials in authority.

Travers got to the Inn with five minutes to spare but even so the smart-suited Applegate was ahead of him and had already claimed the small room for their exclusive use. Clearly he liked to appear to be in control.

But despite his reservations the policeman's impressions

were positive. This man was used to authority and willing to make decisions. He was top dog: there was no bureaucracy he needed to consult or satisfy. He would be answerable for whatever he did.

On the other hand, he was sharp; his dark eyes were piercing and alert. He might want to be captain of the team but at least he recognised that a team was needed - in this kind of work. And he accepted others might have something to say as well; and if it was fresh and valid their input would be welcomed.

He shook Travers warmly by the hand as they introduced themselves.

'I've ordered a large pot of coffee,' he stated. 'I assume you're not a tea-drinker? We'll wait until they bring it in before we start on the details.'

Applegate's eyes sparkled. He had more charm, Travers thought, than the senior policemen he had occasionally come across. Maybe that was more use in the circles he moved in – whatever they were. 'When we start I'll be intrigued to learn how you got hold of my name and my private phone number. I make sure it's not widely available. My methods can't be as secure as I'd hoped. Tell me, how long have you been with the police? Have you always been based in this area?'

'I joined straight after I left school, sir. I wasn't an academic child but I wasn't stupid either; I wanted to do something useful. Apart from Police College I've always lived in these parts. I have family responsibilities here with my mother and it's not a bad part of the country to be based, is it?'

The landlord's wife knocked at the door and brought in their coffee, then carefully shut the door behind her. Travers was pleased to see that she had also provided a plate of chocolate biscuits; he helped himself to a couple. Applegate started to pour the coffee.

'Let's get down to business. I gather you're the policeman who's been so assiduous in tracking this corpse in the quarry, just up the road – and her murderer. And I'm the miserable high-level official who's been throwing spanners into the works. Maybe you could tell me what you know first. After that I'll explain what I can, then do my best to help move things along. I want to get at the truth as well.'

Travers recognised that he was in the company of a powerful man. There was no way as a lowly policeman that he could impose his own agenda. From now on, for better or worse, the die was cast. He would have to trust Applegate that his findings would be well handled.

'Well, first of all, sir, I regret to have to tell you that both Bill Gilbert and James Hammond are dead. They were drowned in a boat accident – probably struck by lightning on Thursday night. The boat was washed up on the rocks north of Bude sometime last night.

'I've been up there this morning,' the policeman continued, 'and seen the bodies and wreck for myself. The coastguards were still with the boat when I left and will make sure the bodies are properly dealt with.'

Applegate's face saddened. 'What terrible news. They'd both gone out of contact. I talked to them late on Thursday evening but I couldn't get through to either yesterday. I knew they'd planned to go sailing so I feared something like this might have happened - but I hoped I was wrong.'

He paused then continued, 'But how did you find out my name and number? Oh – from their phones, I suppose. They would still be carrying them. But how did you know that I, Jeremy Applegate, was the person they reported to? You can't possibly have worked through every name on their phone lists. Or even checked which numbers the two had in common. Not working alone, anyway. You're a resourceful man, Travers, but I don't have the impression of a vast team behind you.'

'No sir, there's just me. There was an Inspector from Exeter, but he's been taken off the case.'

The policeman checked Applegate had picked up this reference to the embargo. With his point made he continued.

'You asked me how I knew, sir. Well, I found a small tape recorder in Bill Gilbert's pocket. He was wearing waterproofs so it hadn't got waterlogged despite the storm. He'd used it to record his conversation with James Hammond on the boat. My guess is it was a deliberate plan on his part to ask questions without the other man being able to walk away. Maybe he didn't approve of the embargo which had been imposed on the police either, and wanted to carry on the investigation himself.'

Applegate looked stunned. By requesting Bill and James to go out on this boat trip he had played right into Bill's hands.

'Would you like to hear the tape, sir? I've got it with me. That's why I wanted us to meet face to face. It lasts for half an hour. But then, I hope, you'll help me to unravel it.'

As the recording concluded, Peter Travers reached over and switched it off. 'So what do you make of that, sir?'

Applegate looked distressed. A solemn expression came over his face. 'Sergeant Travers, I owe the police a sincere apology for the embargo I've imposed on your investigation. The reasons that Hammond gave me for it were false. He knew much more about this woman – Cécile - than he admitted to me. Indeed, the fact that he asked me to intervene at all in the case is suggestive of his guilt.'

'We had got quite a long way, sir, before we were halted - even before we heard this tape. But we hadn't got final proof – and still haven't. Either James is lying, for at least the last part of the conversation; or else he's in the clear, in which case the murder is very peculiar indeed. So this recording, even if admissible in court, isn't final proof of anything.'

'But now James Hammond is dead. Drowned, you say. Doesn't that bring the case to a conclusion?'

'It might, sir. Except that I don't believe he was the only one involved.'

'Someone else - as well as James Hammond? Who?'

'His wife, sir. Elspeth. Do you know her?'

'Elspeth? Of course I know her. She used to be a civil servant in London. I knew them both. So what's the evidence against her?'

'Again it's not complete. But I have a witness who saw two people, a man and a woman, humping a big sack up to the quarry one Saturday night in early August. My witness couldn't identify them. But he told me they were using a van with the name Hammond painted on the back doors to carry the sack there.'

'And of course you've not been able to interview her yet because some high-ranking cretin has frozen your investigation.'

'Yes, sir. I mean –'

'No, Travers, you're absolutely right. I've been an arrogant and gullible fool. But, look, we can cancel the embargo straight away. I just need to phone -'

'With respect, sir, if we're after justice rather than the niceties of procedures, I think we need to play this very carefully. Right now Elspeth may be worried about him but she doesn't know what's happened to her James.'

'Yes, I guess she's used to him disappearing without warning.'

'But once she does know he's dead, she'll surely find a way of putting all the blame on to him and end up walking away scot free.'

'Yes, I can see that's a risk. So what do you suggest?'

'I think what we need is an informal interview to try and incriminate her before she's told about her husband's death. Of course, as we speak, the police investigation is frozen. But if you're with me then I don't see how I could be accused of breaking the embargo.

'And you say that you know her, sir. She would trust you and would believe whatever you told her about James. So would you be willing to come with me with another secret tape recorder and see what we can learn?'

CHAPTER 47

Peter Travers' interview with Elspeth Hammond was booked for twelve thirty. 'That's fine for me,' she told the policeman. 'Mandy can cover the last half hour of the morning here. On Saturdays the shop closes at one anyway. No-one wants to buy electrical or hardware goods on a Saturday afternoon, at least not in Rock.' She sniffed. 'They're too busy sailing or playing golf.'

As Travers and Applegate drove over to Rock together in Travers' police car, tactics were finalised.

'This is an official police interview,' said Travers, 'so I need to take the lead – and if necessary to ask her the hard questions. But you know her and her husband so you can be more supportive – and maybe trap her. She might be less guarded for you than she is for me.'

'Whatever happens,' replied Applegate, 'we mustn't admit that James is dead. It's a bit underhand but we need to keep that from her for as long as possible. But we need to say something about him, don't we? Or else why am I there?'

'Would you mind hinting that he's been arrested for something? That would give a reason for his absence. Then I could begin the interview trying to gather facts relating to him – and see where it leads.'

As they drove along, Applegate set his recording device. Glancing across, Travers could see it was a high-calibre piece of equipment. The policeman was not sure of its legal status but it wouldn't do any harm to have the interview on tape – if only for their own use.

A few minutes later they had parked outside the parade of shops on Rock High Street and were entering Hammonds' hardware and electrical store.

Elspeth seemed surprised to see Jeremy Applegate alongside the uniformed policeman but made no comment as she led them upstairs.

Coffee was offered but courteously refused. Both men had drunk plenty while listening to the recording in Pendoggett. They were awash with caffeine. Now the moment had arrived both were keen to get on. Travers extracted his notebook and prepared to take notes.

Applegate began. 'Sergeant Travers suggested I joined him today because I know both you and James. And it's really James that's brought us here.'

'James – oh, is he alright? He left late on Thursday evening for some reason. I haven't seen him since.'

'As far as I know, he is not in any discomfort. But I'm afraid he's no longer at liberty.'

Elspeth looked shocked. But before she could question him further, Travers took up the narrative.

'That's why we're here, madam. There are various points where we need to confirm and amplify James' answers.'

'I'll do my best to help. Mind, I was away for a while earlier this summer.'

'James did mention that. That was one of my points, actually. Can you tell me, first of all, when you went away and when you returned?'

Travers sensed that beneath the surface Elspeth was anxious, but her fears were well-hidden. 'You want exact dates, I presume? I'd better consult our calendar. In this household it's our first point of reference.'

She stood up and walked over to the monthly calendar, hanging in the kitchen area. She flipped the pages back to July and peered at the grid of dates set out below an attractive Cornish coastal landscape.

'I went away on Saturday July 19th. For about three weeks.'

She flipped the calendar forward to August. 'And it seems I came back on Saturday August 9th.'

Travers knew he would come back to these dates. They were certainly in conflict with other evidence. But first he had another question. 'And where did you go for this holiday?'

'I went on a writing course on a Greek island. The Island of Patmos. The course wasn't running every day mind, so there was plenty of time for relaxing - and writing, if you wanted. Poetry is my new passion since I retired. But mostly I enjoyed the warm sea. It's warmer than here, anyway.'

'Have you got the name and address of the course?'

She glanced at her reference. 'It's not on the calendar so I probably didn't keep it. But there can't be many courses on the island. I'm sure you could find it via Google if you really needed to.'

There was a pause as Travers consulted his notes. It was time to change tack.

'I think you had someone to stay in the flat upstairs during the summer?'

'Not while I was here. It was a woman, I think. She only came for a couple of weeks and that was while I was in Greece.'

'Are you sure, madam? That's not what James says.'

Travers took Bill Gilbert's recording device out of his pocket and placed it on the table. He had decided beforehand which part to play and set the tape accordingly. He pressed the switch and a male voice was heard: 'Was your tenant interested in the Doom Bar?'

There was no mistaking James' voice as he replied: 'She was, as it happens. Elspeth told her about the wrecks in the estuary when Cécile first arrived and asked about the area. We showed her some pictures on the internet, including the Antoinette, and she got very excited. She asked where the wrecks were and if she could go out in the estuary to take a look.'

Travers reached out and zoomed the tape forward. He certainly didn't want Elspeth to hear the thunderstorm which came next. 'I'll skip a bit to save time.'

He pressed "play" and the tape began again. James was still speaking.

'I did look up the latest grid reference for the Antoinette and marked it on the map for her. She took it away to look at more carefully and for some reason it seemed to enthuse her. Meanwhile Elspeth asked her if she was used to boats and then, when she said she was a good sailor, advised her to hire a small boat for the day in Rock.'

Travers leaned forward once more; this time he switched off the tape.

'And do you still say, madam, that you never met your guest - Cécile?'

There was a long silence. A look of panic swept across Elspeth's face. She obviously hadn't expected that James would betray her carefully prepared story so blatantly.

'Oh, Cécile. I was thinking of someone else who stayed here not long ago. Yes, of course I met Cécile. That was before I went to Greece.'

'And did you meet her again when you came back?'

'Oh no – she'd gone by then.'

Quietly, Peter Travers reached forward for the recorder. A moment of sheer terror swept across Elspeth's face.

'No, maybe she hadn't gone. It's very confusing when you have a guest flat. Fresh people, coming and going. Yes, I remember. Cécile was still here when I got back. I saw her go. She left the day I returned.'

'And was that a pleasant farewell?'

Elspeth stared at the recorder, then back at the policeman. She was almost in tears: she did not know what further confessions were ready to be replayed. And she did not know whether to proclaim her ignorance or to do what she could to protect her husband.

'It was dreadful. Terrible. An awful accident. James was angry but he didn't mean to push her downstairs – I'm sure he didn't. But however it happened, Cécile fell. Head first, she went. Bump, bump, bump. Down thirty, wrought iron, fire-escape stairs. James reckoned she was dead long before she reached the bottom.'

'And that's when you decided to implement the emergency plan?'

Elspeth looked at the policeman. By good fortune added to careful guesswork he had hit on a key phrase.

'It was. It was a game we'd played one winter evening when we were bored. How would you dispose of a body around here, we asked, and where would you hide it?'

'And what had you decided, in this game of yours?'

'When we first came down to this part of Cornwall we did a lot of exploring. Especially places off the beaten track. One of the places we visited was the Engine House near Trewarmett. When we were there we also saw the quarry behind it, with its fenced-off pool. "That's the place to put a body," James said, "it wouldn't be found for years."

'My husband kept on building up the plan in his mind. He looked at the quarry every time we drove that way and observed that the car park was always deserted. Another time he spotted the waterfall there; and worked out that it might be sampled. So he'd planned that the Environment Agency would need to be approached, to prevent a water quality sample being taken soon afterwards.'

She stopped for a moment, her face melancholy. 'But we'd seen the pool was up a slope. And Cécile was a tall woman. So we decided to chop the body up first, to get her weight down.'

Elspeth was no longer just answering the policeman's questions. In her imagination she was replaying the terrible events of a few weeks ago – events that must have bitten deep into her soul. It was a form of "confession", but not the sort the policeman was used to. Maybe it was Applegate's silent presence in the room, he thought, that was making her behave as she did.

'We sell power saws in the hardware shop downstairs. So I drove my car out of the garage behind the shop and we dragged her body in there instead. It was a late summer evening; by now it was practically dark. Then James brought in the saw he had chosen: Black and Decker's finest. We took all the rest of Cécile's clothes off and wedged her into our workbench. Then James took the power saw to her.'

Elspeth paused as the terror of that night seized her. 'It was horrible - but James said I had to stay. I was needed to hold her limbs firm as James hacked them off one by one. Her long, heavy legs; then her badly hacked arms. And finally her dread-fully-gashed head. That was gruesome. As he carried out the last of these cuts, James acknowledged it would be much safer if the body could never be recognised.'

'And then?'

'We put the torso into the biggest sack we could find . . . James made sure it didn't carry the Hammond name. Then we put the sack into the van – followed by a wheelbarrow. We left the rest of the body parts in the garage. We drove steadily over to Trewarmett, parked below the Prince of Wales Quarry and then slowly pushed the wheelbarrow and the torso up the hillside. The tall fence round the pool was the biggest problem. We'd both forgotten that in our mind-games.'

Elspeth paused, lost in thought. Neither men spoke. Travers hoped that Applegate hadn't screwed up on tape recording this interview. He looked across to check but he couldn't catch the man's eye. Applegate simply looked distressed as so much evil was gradually exposed, committed by people he thought he knew.

'When we saw we would have to climb over the fence and through thorn bushes we were glad we were wearing old clothes,' Elspeth continued. 'James had a piece of old carpet in the van. I was sent back to fetch that, we'd use it to cover the top of the fence. Meanwhile James took the wheelbarrow to collect some large pieces of slate from the spoil tip that we could use to weigh the sack down.

'Once I was back we heaved the sack over the fence and down towards the pool. Finally, we added the slate weights inside and tied lots of rope around it and then pushed her in. There were lots of bubbles as the whole thing sank ever so slowly below the surface. It was heavy work – and a good job we were both fit.'

There was another lull. Elspeth took a deep breath. But

Travers wasn't going to let her stop now.

'But you still had the rest of the body to dispose of?'

'We did; and we were almost exhausted. James was so tired he rammed the van into a post at the car park. We got back to Rock and put the pieces we'd left in the garage into a large plastic box with a lid. Then we filled it up with several large tins of aggressive paint remover that we sell for commercial use. We'd seen the warning on the tins "Do NOT splash onto your skin". For us that was a good sign. Next morning, when we looked into the box, we could see why. Huge chunks of the flesh had dissolved. It was mostly bone that was left.'

'And what happened to that?'

'This had all happened on Saturday night. The next day was Sunday – fortunately. We didn't open on Sundays. We didn't wake up till mid-morning. When we looked out of the window it was a fine, calm day. We got up and had some breakfast even though we didn't feel very hungry. Then we went out to the garage.'

Another pause. But Travers didn't need to push her any more. Elspeth was in her own world now and would continue in her own time.

'We looked in the box and saw to our relief that it was mostly bones. They would certainly sink. James very carefully poured away the paint remover – there's a drain outside the garage. "Give the sewage works something to think about", he muttered.

'Then we decided to hire a boat for the day. It was the height of the holiday season, so we rang the Rock Sailing Club to make sure they'd got one available. We took the box down to the jetty, along with various distinctive pieces of Cécile's equipment - and the power saw. We wouldn't be using that again. We hired an inflatable with an outboard motor then set sail for the middle of the Camel estuary. Where, keeping to the side of the boat away from the Stepper Point Lookout, we quietly dropped the pieces overboard one by one. We took a couple of hours over it – "no need to hurry this last stage", James remarked - but at last it was done. And we could come home and try and resume normal living.'

There was another silence: less tense now, the primary confession was over. Applegate had still not spoken. Travers had plenty more questions but he was sure he had enough already to arrest and charge the woman.

There was the question, for example, of Cécile's dog. Was it just the dream of dumping the much-hated dog into the pool which had made a frustrated James push the Environment Agency for an early water quality inspection in late July? A premeditated plan to kill the animal off, which had been super-seded by the spontaneous killing of its owner?

Or was the dog dead as well, killed after Cécile's death, still lying in the pool at the quarry waiting to be discovered?

Either possibility was a neat example, he thought, of how a murder could be spontaneous, yet have aspects which made it seem pre-planned.

Travers turned to Elspeth. 'You and I need to go to a police station.'

'Yes. James and I have both been incredibly stupid. He was sure we'd get away with it. But I was never so confident.'

She turned to the still-silent Applegate. 'If I leave my key with you, could you ask the neighbours to keep an eye on things, please? I fear I may not be back for some time.'

Travers took Elspeth Hammond downstairs and locked her in

the back of his police car. He decided that Exeter Police Station must be their next stop. With luck Marcus Chadwick would be on duty.

'Don't worry about me,' declared Applegate, 'I'll ring for a taxi to take me back to my car at Pendoggett.'

'A good morning's work, Travers,' he continued. 'Well done. I'll make sure that higher authorities are made aware of how well you've handled it.' He fished in his pocket. 'Here's the tape recording – let me have the recorder back when you've finished with it.'

'And will you take steps to lift the embargo, please? Preferably before I reach Exeter.'

Applegate smiled. 'I'll do it at once.'

He brought out his phone and chose a special number. 'Hello, Jeremy Applegate here. About that temporary embargo I asked for a couple of days ago, on Inspector Chadwick's investigation. We don't need it any more, thank you. And Sergeant Travers is on his way over to you. He has some results that you may find rather interesting.'

CHAPTER 48

Bill Gilbert's funeral took place on a beautiful late-summer day, towards the end of September. The post mortem, and the subsequent inquest that always followed a shipwreck, had delayed the event by a further week.

It appeared that Bill had no close relatives, apart from a distant nephew that George had never met and who, clearly, had never heard of her. George was grateful that someone from the PRAM committee – the Major? - had remembered she was indirectly related to Bill and would appreciate the occasion. Her firm had given her a day's compassionate leave to attend.

The memorial service was to take place in St Petroc's, starting at noon. By setting off from London before six and not worrying much about speed limits, George managed to reach Padstow with half an hour to spare. She parked at the top of the hill, slipped down the footpath through the woods and settled herself in the back of the old church. She didn't need to be in any place of prominence, it was simply enough to be there.

There was a sizeable congregation by the time the service began, of all ages. Bill was obviously a popular figure in the town. After the early formalities there was an opportunity for tributes and memories from those present.

Some words of appreciation came from representatives of Bill's generation. One of these was the Major. He spoke of Bill's many years' naval service. It was a shock for George to realize that her uncle-in-law had been in command of one of the vessels that had helped retake the Falkland Islands in 1982. He had obviously had a long and significant career in the Royal Navy – and later the Ministry of Defence.

Then a young man came forward. He was wearing a suit and dark tie but didn't look much used to formality. His blond hair was tousled and out of control.

'My name is Toby Flanders,' he began. 'As you can see, I'm young. I didn't know Bill for decades, like so many of you. But I knew him in one of his main retirement projects, which was maintaining the Doom Watch at the Stepper Point Lookout. Looking around, I can see several other volunteers here today. A couple more will be up on Stepper Point as we speak, keeping watch on behalf of us all. I was Bill's latest recruit there. And I just wanted to say how grateful I am for all the training and wisdom he was able to give me over the past couple of months.'

Toby paused to gather his thoughts. George remembered Bill had told her about Toby on her first day in Padstow: was that less than a month ago?

'You see, I had plenty of enthusiasm for the job – keeping watch over the estuary, with all the swimmers and surfers and kites and boats that make such good use of it. I know it's not always as safe as it looks. But my enthusiasm tended to overshoot. On my second day on duty at the Lookout I had two lifeboats called out to rescue what turned out to be a piece of seaweed.'

A ripple of laughter went round the church. It was good, George thought, to release the tension on such a solemn occasion.

'But Bill could see beyond my blundering enthusiasm,' Toby went on. 'He saw that deep down I wanted to be useful. He said

I had "a heart to serve". And slowly, gradually, he was helping me to achieve that. Not by being directly critical, you understand, but by helping me to be critical of myself. He knew all the tricks and in his time he'd probably made most of the mistakes. But that meant he could draw on them in his training and help me to learn from them too. I shall miss him so much. He was a great bloke. But the memory of him will inspire me more than ever to keep on with the task at the Lookout Doom watch.'

George was by no means the only one in tears by the time Toby had finished. For a few minutes she cried unashamedly. Dear, dear Uncle Bill: always wanting to do his best for others. Quietly and without any fuss. She hadn't known him well. But it had been a privilege to know him at all.

After the service the congregation was invited to share some light refreshments in the church hall next door. George wasn't sure if she should go, but was swept in by the crowd. She recognised the faces of many who worked around the harbour though she did not know their names. She could see one or two members of the PRAM committee. But she wasn't drawn to them today: she was a Padstow outsider now.

She had talked to the Major by phone after she had gone back to London. He had received her report. Her analysis of the committee's own holidays had shown that none had much heart to emulate Newquay. And George had demonstrated the difficulties of making their plans work otherwise.

But more significantly, the death of Bill Gilbert, followed by the arrest of Elspeth Hammond for manslaughter, had knocked the stuffing out of the committee. Local journalist Harriet Horsman had been at the press briefing in Exeter and her report ensured the case made a substantial impact. PRAM had been an interesting exercise, the Major said. But they were much humbler now about what could be done.

Then George saw, standing back almost as much as she was, a man with a lofty manner in an exquisitely-tailored suit. It took a few seconds to remember where she had seen him before; then she recalled the meeting in the snug at the Fourways Inn. It was the man who had been the first to arrive - Applegate.

She wondered what he was doing here. Then, thinking back to her days in Bill's cottage, she remembered that he had been the man her uncle had rung up after she had told him about the police embargo.

No-one else was talking to him. Serve him right for being so secretive. Then she realised that today was a day for all of them to be charitable. If no-one else would talk to him then she would. She sidled over to him.

'Hi, I'm George Gilbert. Bill was my uncle-in-law. I was staying with him just before . . .'

Applegate looked surprised to be approached then collected himself. For a second he seemed to be processing the information just provided and fitting it into place. Satisfied, he held out his hand. 'Very pleased to meet you, George. Bill mentioned your name.'

George noticed that he had not given his name; maybe that was all part of the need-to-know culture. Perhaps it was an Official Secret? She was tempted for a second to address him by name in a loud voice. That would shake him. But the occasion restrained her. Bill had given allegiance to this man. It was incumbent on her to give him the chance to win her over.

But she didn't want to be dismissed as inconsequential. There were questions about Bill that she would like answered that

Applegate could help with.

'Bill never told me anything about his work for you. But you can't live with someone and not pick up some of the bits and pieces of their lives. I had to take a few phone calls for him, for instance. They were always cryptic messages; they didn't give anything away. But that in itself was puzzling. And Bill warned me when I first arrived that he often had to go out at short notice – but he wouldn't ever say where he was going. I found that odd as well.'

Applegate was starting to look worried. Good, thought George, he needs to know that secrecy can't be kept completely secret.

'I was the one, you know, who spotted the tube on the wreck on the Doom Bar. Took the various pictures of it and blew them up to examine. I think Uncle Bill sent copies on to you.'

'Of course,' George went on, 'I'm not intending to do anything with them; I'm an intelligent and a responsible woman – and discreet. I don't go in for gossip. But a few words of explanation would be far more likely to keep me quiet than leaving me in frustrated ignorance.'

Applegate was a man used to dealing with face-to-face pressure and working out how best it should be handled. He looked at her hard for a moment; then a wry smile spread across his face. 'OK. In this special case I agree with you.'

He gestured around him. 'All this will go on for ages; but we can't talk properly here. Why don't you and I slip away and have a more private chat at some nearby coffee shop? I'm sure there are plenty to choose from.'

In the end they settled on lunch in the upper room at the

Shipwright Inn. The tables were busy outside, as usual. But George remembered the spiral staircase tucked away in the corner; and recalled, with sadness, that it was her Uncle Bill who had shown it to her on her first afternoon in Padstow.

'I've driven down here from London this morning,' explained George, 'and I've got to drive the whole way back again later on. If you don't mind, a good meal now will help me stay awake.'

'Fine,' replied Applegate. 'But I insist on you letting me pay. To say thank you for the wreck's tube pictures, if nothing else.' He had obviously made his decision to be selectively indiscreet and was now in a relaxed mood.

'I think the best thing for me to do is to tell you a story. You may know some of it already. I won't include all the details and I'm sure you understand that. Of course, it'll be up to you whether or not you believe it. But I'm telling it to you in confidence. If you try and publicise it any further you can be sure that I will deny this conversation ever took place. And make sure that others in authority know what we had agreed as well. Do we understand one another?'

George had never been given information on this basis before. But it was better to agree informally than to end up signing any sort of affidavit. She didn't want to be dragged into the rigours of the Official Secrets Act.

Their lunch was brought to them at this point. George took a few minutes to pour some brandy and peppercorn sauce on to her sirloin steak and chips. She didn't usually have such an expensive lunch - but it was, after all, being paid for.

'There are some high-up politicians who come on holiday around here,' Applegate began. 'And of course the State has a responsibility, first to protect them and then to safeguard their privacy. I can't tell you all the ways that that is done; but I can tell you that one extra layer of protection is provided by retired members of the Armed Forces. You can read between the lines on that if you want.'

'Help,' said George, as she knocked a small piece of steak off her plate and onto the floor.

Applegate looked surprised. He wasn't sure whether George was subtly teasing him. He was increasingly convinced that she was a resourceful woman. He shrugged his shoulders and carried on.

'This summer there have been a series of leaks from one of these key cottages. Which baffled those who are meant to be preventing them. One question was how the listening equipment had been smuggled into the cottage. A second was how anything that was heard inside was being smuggled away.'

'Mm. I think I see where this story might be going.'

'That's right. The tube you spotted on the wreck turned out to be a retractable aerial that could be raised to full height, out of the water, to pick up signals from the listening equipment. When raised it was in line of sight from the key cottage. That's why the wreck on the Doom Bar was such a good location. The aerial was on a timer; it came up at half past two every morning to pick up any new recordings. These would be stored inside the aerial until required.'

Applegate paused for another mouthful. But he could see George would not let him stop there. He continued, 'Once or twice a week, we think, one of the eavesdroppers would go out on the Coast Path towards Stepper Point at dead of night - the same time as the aerial was visible - to interrogate the mast and collect the consolidated signals.'

'I see. And how were the signals assembled in the cottage in

287

the first place? Aren't these kinds of places swept for listening device before anyone arrives? '

'You're right: they are. That was what was so cunning. It turned out that the device – a small recorder with a short-range UHF radio attached, that could pass on the latest recording to the aerial - was hidden in a polystyrene body board. They're two inches thick, you know; once they're in use no-one ever checks them carefully.'

'But how..?'

'The board with the listening device hidden inside was green: identical in every other respect with the one favoured by our politician. So it was the politician himself who took the device back in to the cottage after the family had been out surfing. The two boards were swapped by the eavesdroppers on one of his first trips to the local beach.'

'And I suppose the Security Forces would only re-sweep the cottage while the politician was out with his family; so they never had the chance to find the device in his surf board?'

'I guess that's how it happened. Not their finest hour.'

Applegate stopped talking and for a few moments both concentrated on their lunches. It was George who took up the conversation.

'Thank you very much. My curiosity is well satisfied. There's lots I don't know – and don't want to know – but that's enough to keep me quiet.'

She munched on; then decided it was worth asking the question. 'There is just one thing, though, and it relates to Bill. What will happen to this extra layer of protection now Bill is dead?'

Applegate looked pensive. 'It's always the case that some bits of security work better than others. The idea of assembling an extra layer of security-aware locals seemed good at the time; and it was some sort of response to cuts in the Security budget. But it depends on having the right people to run it. And no chain is ever stronger than its weakest link.'

George felt protective and angry. 'Are you saying that Bill was the weak link?'

'No, no, no. I'm sorry, I phrased that very badly. Bill was the lynch-pin of the whole thing; he's almost irreplaceable anyway. But there was another link that failed – failed very badly indeed. I don't think the extra layer will continue in any form in future years.'

There was not much more to be said. The two finished their meal, Applegate paid the bill and they walked back together round the harbour.

Applegate announced that he had paid his respects to Bill so was not going back to the church hall. George decided that she would look in briefly to say goodbye on her way back to her car.

It was as well she did so. The crowds had thinned out now and an official looking gentleman approached her. 'Are you, by any chance, George Gilbert? I've been on the watch-out for someone of that name all through this sad occasion. The trouble was, I was looking for a man. It was Paddy Watmough that put me right.'

'Yes, I married Bill Gilbert's nephew, Mark. But Mark died earlier this year. So I'm only a relative of Bill's by marriage. And you are . . .'

'I'm sorry, I should have introduced myself. My name is Smith; Timothy Goodall-Smith. I'm a solicitor here in Padstow and I'm the appointed executor for Mr Gilbert. He had no close family relatives, you see. That's why he chose to rely on me.'

George held out her hand. 'I'm pleased to meet you. Is there something I can help with? I should warn you, though, I haven't got long. I've got to drive back to London this afternoon.'

'A couple of things, actually. But neither will take long. As I say, Bill doesn't have any close relatives. His nearest blood relative is a nephew currently living in Australia. I've been looking at his will. It was drawn up a couple of years ago, while Mark was still alive.'

'Yes?'

'The crucial point is this. Bill directs that the bulk of his estate be split between the nephew in Australia and his other nephew - Mark. But there was a further detail. It specified that if something happened to Mark, his share of the legacy should be passed on to his wife – you. So when all the paperwork is done you should be receiving a substantial inheritance. But first of all I need an address I can write to.'

This was a complete shock. George had never considered herself as someone who should expect anything from her uncle-in-law. It had been enough that he had offered her support after Mark's death.

She looked at him carefully. But the solicitor was serious. It wasn't the sort of day for jokes. She reached in her handbag for an address card and handed it over.

'Crumbs. I hadn't expected anything like this. It never once crossed my mind. I suppose, though, if that was what Bill really wanted, then I should be grateful. And I am. Wow.' George was reeling.

'The other thing is less significant, I think. I've been going through Bill's papers since his death. And I came across this.' The solicitor reached into his jacket pocket and brought out a letter. It was addressed by hand to George.

George took it from him. 'Do you know anything about this?'

'Not much. He wrote it in the first week that you were staying with him. Told me he hoped it wouldn't be needed for many years. I've no idea what it's about.'

'Well, thank you. I won't open it here. Given it's a last letter from Uncle Bill, I'll find somewhere more private to do that. Thank you very much indeed.'

CHAPTER 49

A lthough a lot had happened that day it was still only half past two. George Gilbert computed her journey times and decided she could stay down in the Padstow area for another hour before she set off for home. The later she left the more the traffic would have died down by the time she reached London.

But she wanted to get away from Padstow. She'd had enough intensity for one day. She might not be in this area again for a while; where could she go to set her mind at rest?

At once she thought of Polzeath. There wasn't time today to walk there from Rock. But whatever happened she had to go home via Wadebridge. Checking her map, she saw it was only a five mile detour to the coast.

George resolved to take a last visit to the beach where she and Mark had enjoyed so many holidays. She would read Bill's last letter while she was there.

The tide was out when she reached the coast, so she could park on Polzeath beach itself. The weather was fine but the wind was blustery. It was too cold today to sit on the beach – even for a few minutes.

George spotted the Galleon cafe, nestling on the edge of the sands. A mug of hot chocolate would set her up for the journey home. The drink was ordered; she sat once more at the end of the cafe furthest from the door. Now was the time for Bill's letter. She reached into her pocket, pulled it out and opened the envelope.

Padstow

Sept 7th 2008

Dear George,

I hope that it will be many years before you read this. I am currently in good health and enjoying life to the full; and I'm only sixty nine – not old by today's standards. So, by the time you read this, the topic addressed may be of no consequence. Or you might have re-married and no longer care; and of course you would do so with my blessing.

But I am prompted to write because when you came to stay I realised for the first time how frustrated you were and how little you knew about Mark's death. And maybe that uncertainty is making it harder for you to "move on".

I told you I knew no more than you about Mark's death. Strictly speaking that is true. But I have some insights which may make the circumstances clearer.

I have never told you – or anyone else - that I have been involved in state security in my later years. Not the professionals, of course. They eat from some very queasy dishes and I don't have the appetite for that (or the fitness). But there is also a need for what you might call ancillaries – honourable men (and women) of impeccable credentials who carry out minor but essential tasks to help the security work properly. I have carried out such tasks; and I am helping with another, here in Padstow, even while you are staying under my roof.

I do not know if Mark performed a similar role on any of his trips abroad. Anyone doing such work is strongly advised, for their own safety, to tell no-one what they are doing. So even if he had been into security in some way, you would not have known. What I do know is that I was asked, a couple of years ago, to help vet my nephew – the checking that always comes before security involvement. I could only speak most highly of his integrity

293

and his competence. I do not know if anything happened as a result.

To me, Mark's death in the back of beyond could best be explained if he was involved in some security activity – possibly as a courier. His business role would give him perfect cover to take a top secret document, say, from one hard-to-reach Middle East country to another. So there may have been extra factors behind his death, in addition to the tragic plane accident. Of course the accident itself would be just a horrible coincidence that could have happened to anyone.

If Mark was a security ancillary, you can be very proud of him. It is an honourable role, done for the best of reasons. You will never know for sure but it may help to account for some of the oddities you mentioned. I hope so.

And I hope that taking account of this possibility helps you move on.

Your loving Uncle,

Bill

George read the letter very slowly and carefully. She would have expected any document about her late husband to make her feel sad. But, oddly, it didn't. It made her feel proud.

She would never know whether Mark had done ancillary work on security. But if he had it was for the best of motives. She had some sort of explanation; that was enough. Her job now was not to stand still, stuck in his memory, but to go forward.

'You look a bit happier today.'

She was hearing voices again. But this was, after all, the place where she had heard them before. She looked around; then saw Quentin Arnold smiling at her from his financial cage.

She smiled back. 'Yes, I am. I still think about Mark a lot. He was a wonderful man - maybe I'll never know just how wonderful. But now I know there's life beyond him for me. He wants me to claim it. And I want to make the most of every single day that I've got left.'

As she drove back towards the main road, George noted how many fond memories she had of the area. Could she use the money Bill had left her to give herself a more lasting presence here? That would be one simple memorial to the man she loved; and one, she believed, he would have approved of.

AUTHOR'S NOTES

All the characters in this story are fictional, but the places are as real as I can make them. Most have been revisited since I started writing this book.

The Doom Bar sand bank has been guarding the Camel estuary for many centuries; and it does shift over the years. I have not come across any logical reason for this so the outline model developed by George is purely conjecture. Reliable data is always needed to produce credible models.

The Stepper Point Lookout operates daily and welcomes visitors. The incident in chapter one was prompted by an event described by staff there. The Lookout has a chart showing the positions of many wrecks in the estuary, including the SS Antoinette, which set sail with a cargo of coal in 1895, foundered near Lundy Island and limped back, only to be wrecked on the Doom Bar. Her remains were spotted in 1996. In the end a bomb squad was sent out to remove them in 2010.

The now-closed Prince of Wales Quarry outside the village of Trewarmett has an Engine House on the skyline; and a quarry behind, with a pool at its base, protected by a tall fence and a mass of brambles. But I do not know if Environment Agency scientists take quality samples from its waterfall. To the casual observer the water looks pristinely pure.

At least one major politician regularly brings his family to holiday in this area. I have no idea where he stays or how his secu-

rity is organised. But I am sure it is done far more professionally than that offered by the characters and the systems in this novel.

David Burnell
July 2013

Website: www.davidburnell.info

A Cornish Conundrum

SLATE EXPECTATIONS starts as George Gilbert acquires
a holiday cottage near Trebarwith Strand.
She becomes part of an outdoor drama, based on 19th century
events in the Delabole Slate Quarry – a drama heightened when
one of the cast is found dead,
part-way through the first performance.
The combined resources of George and Police Sergeant Peter
Travers are needed to disentangle the past and find precisely
how it relates to the present.

*"Slate Expectations combines an interesting view of an often
overlooked side of Cornish history with an engaging pair of sleuths
who follow the trail from past misdeeds to present
murder." Carola Dunn, multiple crime author*

LOOE'S CONNECTIONS sees George on another project
in Cornwall, this one evaluating flood relief in Looe.
But crime once again rears its ugly head.
For a time George herself is under suspicion. Eventually she
finds a new ally to help find her way through the maze.
Even the Romans have a part to play.

"History, legend and myth mixed with a modern technical conun-
drum make this an intriguing mystery."
Carola Dunn, multiple crime author

"A super holiday read, set in a super location!"
Judith Cutler, multiple crime author

TUNNEL VISION unpacks the conundrum of a skeleton
found in an old tunnel on the North Cornwall railway.
As reporter Robbie Glendenning starts to probe, he comes
across buried secrets and family feuds.
George Gilbert, arriving late on the scene, makes
a crucial discovery.
Someone, though, is determined to keep the identity of the
skeleton hidden forever.
And as past and present collide has Robbie asked
one question too many . . .?

*"Enjoyable reading for all who love Cornwall and its dramatic
history." Ann Granger, multiple crime author.*

.

Printed in Great Britain
by Amazon

60227057R00180